PHANTOM REALM

THE HAUNTING OF MISERY MANSION

NEIL SATER

WEST KILBRIDE LLC

Book Cover by Dark-Designs.com

Library of Congress Control Number: 2023911661

ISBN: 979-8-9885508-0-8

Published by: West Kilbride LLC 6618 Morningside Dr. Cleveland OH 44141

First edition - 2023

Sign up for Neil Sater's newsletter through his website:

https://authorsater.com/

For Mary.
Sorry it isn't a comedy.

CONTENTS

.

PART ONE

JESSICA - 1990

CHAPTER 1

HALLOWEEN DARE

IT WAS SUPPOSED TO be just a silly Halloween dare. Many years would pass before Jessica Putnam understood how it altered her life.

When the big red barn with CHEW MAIL POUCH TOBAC-CO painted on its side came into view, Jessica knew they were close. After passing the landmark, she turned off the radio, and her conversation with Erin Watson turned strictly-business. "Remember, knock on the rear door first. Three times. Then pass around the opposite side of the house on your way to the front door."

Erin laughed. "And after I knock on the front door, I'll have a pissed-off ghost to deal with."

Jessica laughed too, but it felt forced. "Three knocks," she reiterated.

"Got it. And since I'm going first, I'm like ghost bait."

"Totally." Jessica grinned and nodded in the darkness, noticing her palms had started sweating where she gripped the steering wheel.

Her skin prickled as the Buick rounded the next road bend, and silence fell between them. A shadowy blot arose, crouching on the gentle slope rising above the roadway. In the twilight, Misery Mansion appeared forlorn, almost brooding.

For the first time, Jessica wondered if they should have gone trick-or-treating instead. But at sixteen years old, the best-friends-since-kindergarten had elected to replace that kiddy tradition with a more mature activity: testing the legend of Misery Mansion, otherwise known by its official name, Harmon Manor.

They were also testing themselves.

The abandoned house loomed over the countryside in Ohio's unassuming Homer County, where it was impossible to avoid the wide range of rumors and folklore associated with the mansion. But the one thing all the stories had in common? The house was haunted.

Passing the mansion's driveway, Jessica slowed the car. When she spotted a gap in the stretch of woods, she brought the vehicle to a crawl, and nosed into the weed-infested gravel drive which had once served as the gardener's entrance. She held up when the overgrowth began scratching the undercarriage.

"A little further," Erin said, craning her head and shoulders around to monitor behind them.

Jessica coaxed her father's prized Buick LeSabre onward, wincing as the weeds raked the underside of the floorboards.

"That's good," Erin said.

Jessica double-checked to confirm they were tucked safely beyond the tree line. After scouting the place during daylight a few days prior, they'd decided that parking in this spot at the edge of the property allowed them to keep the car out of sight. The downside was it meant they'd need to take a path through a tree grove to reach the mansion.

Jessica put the gearshift into park, killed the lights, and turned off the ignition. Both girls sat in the darkness for a spell without talking or moving before Erin leaned forward to collect the crucifixes from the floor console cubby.

"Whatever you do, don't drop them in the woods," Jessica said. The girls had decided, as a way to prove they made it to the doors, Erin would leave one cross at each entrance, then Jessica would retrieve them both.

Jessica pulled the Maglite out of her door pocket and handed it to Erin. "Remember, it's only for an emergency."

Erin took a deep breath, pushed open the door, and stepped out into the nighttime. "Here comes ghost bait," she said, and without waiting for a response, shut the door.

As her friend disappeared down the trail, Jessica fished her Sony Discman out from under the seat and slipped on the headphones. Pursing her lips, she skipped forward to her favorite song on *Violator*, Depeche Mode's new album, and cranked up the volume. She pushed her mind into the music, bobbing her head along with the stomping beat of "Personal Jesus."

The song ended, and she decided that even her favorite band wasn't enough to soothe her right now. She tossed the Discman onto the floor behind her, pushed in the car's lighter, then plucked out a cigarette from the pack she'd stashed under the seat. This was one of the few places she could smoke freely because her mother did it in here. Her father would never suspect his darling daughter had smoked in his car, so she wouldn't even have to deny it.

It *will* stink, though. Jessica questioned whether to crack open the window. Somehow, she felt less vulnerable alone in the darkness with them closed. She knew how ridiculous this was—as if glass could stop malevolent spirits. Still, she'd keep them all up for now.

Jessica leaned forward and looked out through the windshield, straining to catch a glimpse of Erin. But with her view obscured from inside the car, she couldn't make out much of anything in the nightscape beyond. *What's taking her so long?* It should have been a five-minute jaunt, right? *Hadn't it been that long already?* She started to check her Swatch, but stopped, realizing she hadn't noted the time when Erin had left.

The lighter popped out, causing Jessica to jump. She twizzled the cigarette back and forth between two fingers while taking in, then exhaling a calming breath. *Why did I have to go second?* she thought. A few days ago, when they'd flipped a quarter to decide who'd lead off, she felt like she'd won the coin toss. Now, she wished *she'd* gone first. Here she was, trying to act fearless, the way she imagined grown-ups always felt. Yet the longer she sat alone in the dark, the more she found herself regressing into a jittery sixteen-year-old.

She yanked out the lighter and pressed its glowing tip to her smoke, feeling the heat on her face as she drew in a couple of puffs. The nicotine head rush provided a tranquilizing effect, but the bitter taste of tobacco made her grimace. Jessica didn't really enjoy smoking, but the act had rebellion value to it. Being alone in the car, however, she realized she had nothing to prove to anyone. She rolled the window down barely an inch, took one more drag, snuffed the cigarette, and tossed it into the groundcover.

Just then, a silhouette emerged on the trail, and Jessica froze, studying the shape as it surfaced from the copse of woodland. *Is it...?* She sighed with relief when her friend materialized from the brush.

Erin Rocky-Balboaed in front of the car. A wispy vapor cloud formed with each panting breath before promptly vanishing into the chill of the night. "I did it!"

"So?" Jessica said as she pushed open the Buick's door. Her head rush intensified when she stood, and the sharpness of the October night stung her face. She nudged close to Erin. "What did you see?"

"Nada, mi amiga," Erin replied, not fluent in the slightest. The girls had just started their first full year of Spanish, but enjoyed practicing with each other. "Sin el Boogey-hombre..." Erin grinned, revealing her flawless teeth. It wasn't unusual for the attractive-enough blonde teens to be mistaken as sisters, but only one of them had naturally straight teeth. Soon they'd be equals though: Jessica's orthodontist had promised he'd remove her braces by Christmas.

Sin el Boogey-hombre... Jessica had to silently mull the words over to interpret them. *Without the Boogey-man.* She almost smiled.

"No ghost? Did you *really* do it?"

"*Yes.* To a tee."

The look in her eyes was sincere, and Jessica knew she could believe her.

"Ghost or no ghost, that house is *totally* scary...God, I'm glad that's over! It's *your* turn now."

Jessica was not so giddy. Her teeth began to chatter, but she wasn't sure if it was from the cold or the apprehension. She held out her open hand. "Flashlight?"

Erin retrieved the Maglite from her jacket pocket and pressed it into Jessica's palm. "Make sure you knock loud. Maybe the spirits just need one more visitor to wake up."

Jessica turned toward the path while Erin retreated to the passenger side of the car.

"Beware the ghosts of Misery Mansion!" Erin called out over her shoulder, followed by a taunting cackle.

⸻◆○◆⸻

The woods closed in as Jessica proceeded onto the trail. The moon blazed with the essence of a sun-bleached bone. Even the stars seemed bright, the Milky Way painted across the sky more vividly this far beyond the reach of Clarkton's light pollution. The surrounding nightscape was better illuminated than Jessica had expected, and since the ritual decreed that she couldn't use the flashlight, she was grateful. As each minute passed, her eyes further adjusted to the twilight. Before long she could easily spot the stray rogue branches encroaching into the pathway.

The crinkle of fallen leaves crunching under her L.A. Gears evoked the memory of one of her first Halloweens. She was a little blonde-haired witch, clutching her father's hand as they ventured out to collect a mountain of candy.

When Jessica emerged from the woods, the hulking contours of Harmon Manor snuffed out any pleasant childhood memories. *This* was a haunted house if ever there was one. The massive structure seemed to be crouching, waiting, allowing her to draw near enough so it could pounce.

The sound of a horse's hooves clopping arose in the distance, and Jessica recoiled into the thicket. She narrowed her eyes onto an Amish horse and buggy that appeared at the bend in the roadway, a thousand feet away, coming her way. An oil lamp, mounted to the side of the carriage, cast a feeble light, so dim it seemed to serve little purpose beyond giving the vehicle an otherworldly glow.

The Amish buggy passed by, continuing its mysterious journey without any indication the hidden occupants had spotted a person—or a Buick—cloistered in the woods. When the sound of hooves departed, Jessica swallowed hard and propelled herself ahead.

There was no way to know where fact ended and fable took its place, but the students at East Homer High School believed that if you circled Misery Mansion at night, knocking first on the rear door three times, then the front door, a ghost would emerge from within, surging with anger at the trespasser. But there were other stipulations about the ritual too: it had to be done alone, and it had to be done under a full moon, with no artificial light. On this Halloween night, Jessica and Erin would find out if the legend was true.

The footpath opened into the overgrown grass beyond the swath of woods, about forty paces from the house. Tendrils of mist drifted over the lawn, and beyond, she could make out details of the mansion under the moonlight. The first-floor windows were boarded over to deter vandals and intruders. That didn't matter, though; Jessica had no plans to go inside.

In her mind, Jessica could hear her father, who did home renovations, describe the unique features of the structure—something he had a habit of doing when a house captured his attention. *This is the Victorian Italianate style. Notice how those second-story windows are tall and narrow, drawing your eye upward to the broad projecting eaves? That's a design trick, to accentuate the height of the home—to amplify its grandeur. Those corbels are so ornate…you'll never see that level of craftsmanship nowadays. The wrought iron balustrades above them seem to reach up into the sky. This style of roof is called a mansard roof, and the patterned slate will glisten in the sun, highlighting it with texture. See the large, windowed tower at the top? That's called a belvedere. It sits four stories high, and it's intended for viewing the grounds and surrounding countryside.*

Or, as Erin had simply stated, "It kinda looks like The Addams Family's house."

With a gasp, Jessica halted, her gaze fastened on the looming tower. *Was that a shadow stirring?* She squinted, straining to prove her imagination wrong. She could see no movement in the twilit window.

Don't go mental now. She shook her head as if to clear it, then continued, quickening her pace. After traversing the lawn, Jessica closed in on the east side of the house and felt herself shrinking in its presence.

She snuck around the corner and arrived at the back porch. Her mother's silver crucifix leaned against the plywood covering the door. Drawing in a deep breath, Jessica tiptoed up the steps and across the veranda to the door, letting out a nervous laugh when she realized Erin had placed the crucifix upside down.

She picked up the cross and slipped it into her jacket pocket. While it wasn't exactly her top worry at this moment, she hoped her mother hadn't noticed it missing from its normal hanging spot, where it gathered dust on the wall of their seldom-occupied living room.

When Jessica reached out to the door, she paused. *I already have the crucifix. Erin would never know if I didn't really knock.*

Lifting her chin, she banished the temptation, and rapped her knuckles on the boarded door three times. The thuds resounded on the hollow sheet of plywood. *Even hard-of-hearing ghosts will hear that,* she thought wryly, then retreated, leaping down the stairs in a single bound.

Fallen leaves had accumulated along the west side of the house, blanketing the ground halfway to her knees. As Jessica waded through the pile along the side of the house, her ears picked up the faintest tinkle of...*music*? She stopped. *A trumpet?*

She looked out at the deserted roadway. The next closest home was probably a mile away. *Did Erin turn on the radio?* She shook her head. *Can't be that—the car's too far away.* Besides, this music sounded rough and tinny—like it was coming from an antique phonograph, the type her grandfather used to have.

Was this coming from *inside* Misery Mansion? Goose bumps washed over Jessica's arms. *Except...that's impossible! Am I imagining it?* She stood frozen in the darkness, trying to pinpoint the source of the sound, but almost as quickly as it had started, the music faded away, replaced with the whisper of leaves rustling in the breeze.

Jessica trembled, yet she withstood the impulse to flee. Her ego wasn't about to let her bail now—not when she was more than halfway done with the dare. She grasped the flashlight protruding from the jacket pocket opposite the cross, but stopped herself from switching it on. Instead, she nodded as if to reassure herself, and commanded her legs to resume marching forward.

She hurried on with a clenched jaw and a pounding pulse, taking long strides through the autumn drift.

When she turned the corner, the layer of leaves thinned where the front porch extended out from the house. She broke into a run, hopped up the steps, and spotted the second crucifix, also inverted. *Thanks again, Erin.* This one was modern: rough cut wood, a figure fashioned from wire attached with heavy hand-wrought nails. It usually sat in Erin's bedroom, propped up on the bookshelf.

As Jessica bent down to retrieve the cross, a fleeting thought passed through her mind: What if Erin *hadn't* placed them upside down? She promptly brushed the disturbing question aside. Without further delay, she banged three times on the plywood and fled, adrenaline surging inside her body as she dashed toward the trail.

Just before she reached the end of the lawn, the scratchy phonograph-like music resumed. She stopped, spun around to face the mansion, and without the sound of her footsteps, cocked her head and listened. The tune *was* coming from inside the house.

She scanned the gloomy structure but spotted no sign of movement. As she started to pivot away, however, something in the belvedere caught her attention. *Oh my God...did something move?* A silhouette formed at the window. Jessica clenched her eyelids shut in disbelief. *When I reopen them, it'll be gone.* But when she sprung her lids back open, the phantom proved undeniable. She gulped. The apparition looked feminine, her face framed by long blonde hair, glistening in the moonlight.

The music stopped abruptly, leaving only the sound of Jessica's panicked breaths over the lull of the nocturnal countryside. As she backed away, the specter became more animated. The ghostly woman waved her arms and hands frantically, her mouth contorting into a soundless scream.

Jessica wanted to turn and run, but she was rooted in place. She wanted to tear away her gaze, but the apparition held her in a penetrating stare that bored *through* the darkness.

And that's when everything became purple and silent. Jessica's vision blinked out, replaced with a solid, vibrant shade of plum, and pure quietude greeted her. It was just for a wink of time, then the world fluttered back to its natural nighttime murmur and hues.

Jessica Putnam broke free and ran faster than she ever imagined herself capable.

PART TWO

DORIS - 1931

Chapter 2

Mass Panic

"HARMON! OPEN UP!" AFTER three initial knocks on the Harmon Manor front door, a sequence of poundings followed. "We need to talk!"

Doris flinched, then whipped her head in the direction of Albert. She studied him with a furrowed brow, but asked no questions. He had taught her not to pry.

Albert gave Doris a weary glance, as if admitting he had known they'd come. He folded his newspaper and pushed himself out of the parlor's armchair. "Stay here." He took the last shot of bourbon. In the midst of Prohibition, Albert had his sources.

Three men were on the porch peering into the house through small panes of the front door's leaded glasswork, their faces obscured by the misting of their breath on the glass. Despite the distorted view, Albert recognized two of the three based merely on their size.

He pulled open the huge door and the din of crickets humming their mid-August evening chorus rose.

"Gentlemen?" Albert stepped out onto the veranda. "To what do I owe this pleasure?" The question was only a formality.

Shorty looked at the others with a raised eyebrow and a smirk before responding, "We've come to make a withdrawal, Al."

Albert closed the door behind him. "The bank's closed."

"You'll open it though, see?" Shorty reached for his hip, revealing a holstered handgun under his jacket.

Poke added, "Consider it a special service for your business colleagues. We'll be discreet. We just want what's ours before the rest of the town overruns the bank in the morning."

Albert fidgeted his hands. They were wrong: it had already started earlier in the day. The bank manager had shuffled into Albert's office around two in the afternoon, almost panting, his shirt sweat-drenched. He gently pulled the door closed behind him, and said, "Al, I think we're seeing the start of a run on the bank..."

Albert implemented a withdrawal limit of one hundred dollars per day, effective immediately. Since the stock market crash a year and a half prior, there had been a steady string of bank runs across the country. Withdrawal limits were one of the few defensive measures a banker could take to control the panic. It almost never worked.

After the bank had closed for the day, Albert made his own withdrawal, emptying his savings account, totaling over thirty thousand dollars. The bank had less than twenty thousand dollars on hand after he made his grab. The men on the porch would not be happy to hear that.

"Gentlemen, I'm sorry, there's a limit on with—"

"We don't care about your damn limits," said the third man, nicknamed Cud. He took a step closer to Albert and resumed chomping. "You're the bank President. You'll make an exception for us."

Albert caught a whiff of mint, mingled with Cud's rancid breath. Wrigley's Spearmint, as always. Albert tried to back away but bumped into the brickwork of his house.

Shorty moved in, sidling up beside Cud. "Yeah, Al." He tilted his head back, raising the rim of his hat, clearing their mutual line of sight, as if the look in his eyes would show Albert he meant business.

Poke, as wide as a carnival fat man, shifted over to fill the gap between the other two. "We'd do the same for you, if the shoe was on the other foot, see?"

"Look Poke, my bank's no different from your feed store. Business is dropping off all over."

"Yeah, but your business has my money. And I want it back. Tonight!"

Albert glanced at Shorty's car, squinting like it was something important, roughly adding up how much in deposits the three men collectively held. It was over forty thousand dollars.

"You fellas need to know there may not be enough cash in the bank," he responded in a hushed tone, suddenly conscious of the risk of Doris hearing. "But look here...there's no need to worry. Things are going to recover." His voice quivered, sounding meeker than he wanted.

"Put your shoes on," Shorty said. "I'll drive."

Albert looked at his feet. He was standing in his socks.

"Just a minute," he said, pulling the door open and stepping back inside.

A scuffle upstairs grabbed his attention. His son Danny peered down from the balustrade of the gallery above the foyer. When they made eye contact, the boy swung around and scurried away, disappearing into the bedroom hallway like a mute. Albert wondered if his son had overheard the discussion through an open window upstairs.

Danny had become strangely quiet and withdrawn as of late. But Albert had more pressing things on his mind these days, so he'd paid little attention. *Better to let Doris handle it*, he figured.

Cud pushed the door open and squeezed into the hallway. Albert acknowledged the intrusion with a grunt and sat on the bench of the hall tree to put on his shoes.

When Albert stood and reached for the large keyring hanging on one of the hooks, he spotted Doris at the back end of the hallway, watching with a puzzled expression.

"Everything's fine, Doris. I just need to run to the bank."

He realized this was a poor choice of words, but doubted she'd make that connection. She just sensed something was wrong; she didn't *know* something was wrong. At least, not yet.

"I'll be back in an hour." Albert left without waiting for a response.

Cud tipped his hat toward Doris and uttered a polite "Ma'am," then followed Albert outside.

Poke led, waddling slowly, and the other two stepped aside, motioning for Albert to fall in line.

As the cluster approached the Ford Model A parked in the driveway circle, Shorty said, "You ride shotgun, Al. The boys want to keep an eye on you."

The car turned out from the driveway, pulling onto the single-lane brick road that would take them into Clarkton. Albert's abductors each had their own enterprise based there, and all of them had served as bank trustees in the past. Albert might have even considered them friends. *No more*, he thought, seething.

Eat or be eaten.

Oh, how Albert's life had changed in the past two years. The stock market crash in October 1929 wiped out almost half of his net worth. He'd managed to recover a portion of the loss the following spring, but that relief turned out to be illusory. The bottom fell out again by the end of the year, and the market continued to drop. He'd recently relieved both the maid and gardener of their duties, when it became clear the downturn was lasting. But things had only worsened since, to the situation they were in now. Albert had never imagined himself and the bank he owned—the bank his grandfather founded—being at the epicenter of Homer County's economic collapse.

After a silent twenty-minute drive, Shorty parked the car behind the bank in the small parking lot along the alley. Without a word, the three men slid out of the car and gestured for Albert to do the same. They all gently pushed the doors closed and drifted to the back of the building where they huddled inside the rear entrance way.

Albert fumbled with the keys, then attempted to unlock the door with uncooperative hands. The others remained mum while he struggled his way through the task.

Once they were all inside, Albert asked the trio to wait in the lobby.

"That's alright, Al," said Poke, speaking slowly, of course. "Something tells me you're going to need our help to find every last dollar." They followed him as he walked behind the teller counter.

Albert pulled out the leather-bound account ledger, and the others hovered as he did some figuring. He took his time tallying numbers, grasping the fountain pen with white knuckles.

"Gentlemen..." He paused to breathe, his stare anchored on the figures. "...your accounts total over forty-one thousand dollars. Cash on hand is barely eighteen thousand."

Shorty and Cud drew closer, once again flanking Albert, then unholstered their revolvers and pointed them at the banker.

Poke said, "You forgot to check your safe deposit box. Hand over the assignment registry."

Albert groaned internally. He pulled out another leather-bound volume, and slid it over to Poke, who began to comb through it. His pudgy finger landed on the name *Albert Harmon* next to *Lockbox 88*. He nodded at Albert, then pointed at the bank vault with his uppermost chin.

Albert's hands wavered as he manipulated the enormous safe's dials. After a couple of tries, it clicked free.

Poke heaved the massive steel vault open, putting all his three-hundred-plus pounds into it. Inside, Albert keyed into box 88, and stepped back, shoulders slumped, while Poke slid it out, revealing a large stack of cash within.

"Say, look at that, fellas." Shorty grinned. "Must have forgotten about this little stash, right, Al?"

The others followed Shorty's lead, and Albert found himself surrounded by a grinning triumvirate.

By the time Albert counted out enough to make the three men whole, a pile of cash totaling seven thousand dollars remained. Unsure of what they expected him to do with it, Albert stared at it, then switched his eyes to each of the others, who were watching him intently.

"We only came for *our* money," Shorty said.

Honor among thieves, Albert thought, but said nothing.

Fuming, he ensconced the seven thousand dollars in his lockbox, and updated the general ledger to show a zero cash on-hand balance.

At full dark, the Model A pulled through the turnaround and stopped in front of Harmon Manor, its engine still purring.

"Have a good evening, Al," Shorty said, feigning politeness.

"Sweet dreams," wise-guy Poke mocked from the back seat. Cud just chewed his gum, but did so triumphantly.

Albert didn't respond. He stepped out of the car, scowling at the bastards until they drove off.

When he turned toward the house, he noticed a light left on upstairs. Danny leaned against his bedroom window, motionless, like a mannequin.

Albert ignored his son and entered the house, returning to the parlor, which Doris was tidying up as she prepared to turn in for the night. She paused when he entered the room, studying him, but asked no questions.

"Good night, Doris," he said, pouring himself a drink, speaking in that assertive sort of way so she'd understand there'd be no discussion.

Doris nodded, kissed her husband on the forehead, and left the room.

Albert plopped into his armchair and sighed. The bourbon bottle rested nearby, his companion for the night. He had no plans to sleep.

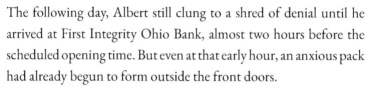

The following day, Albert still clung to a shred of denial until he arrived at First Integrity Ohio Bank, almost two hours before the scheduled opening time. But even at that early hour, an anxious pack had already begun to form outside the front doors.

Once inside, Albert phoned Pinkerton, dispatching three extra guards so four men would be on duty inside the bank. He gave instructions for two others to be sent to his home, and a third to wait beside his Duesenberg, which he had parked at the police station two blocks away.

Next, Albert opened the safe and transferred the cash from his lockbox into a canvas money bag, re-closing the massive door before anyone else arrived. He stuffed the cash bag into the inner breast pocket of his suit coat, forming a misshapen hump on his left side, just under his chest. *Maybe it's not too obvious*, he told himself.

The bank guards arrived within the hour, entering through the rear entrance around the same time as the employees, thirty minutes before the bank's opening time. But at the front entrance, the crowd swelled, pooling into the street.

Albert instructed the employees to keep the doors locked when the bank was supposed to open. As the crowd grew restless, the tellers paced the floor, each likely imagining the melee that seemed inevitable.

"Al, can we talk privately?" the manager whispered. He had the general ledger tucked under his arm.

Albert twitched his head toward his office, and they slunk inside, Albert closing the door behind them.

"What's the story with these after-hours journal entries?" the manager demanded, laying the ledger on Albert's desk, opened to the page of the last recorded transactions.

"This is my bank, and I'm President," Albert said.

"There's no cash on hand for withdrawals!"

Albert tightened his lips against his teeth and shook his head. As if by reflex, he lifted his hand and pressed it against his jacket, feeling the lump within.

The manager pulled out a handkerchief and wiped the dripping sweat from his forehead. Then he opened it and smothered his entire face for a moment, folded it, and tucked it back into his suit pocket. He drew in a deep breath, held it, then released it quickly. "I'm resigning. Effective immediately."

"No, you're fired," Albert countered.

The bank manager squinted and cocked his head. "For what?"

"Mismanagement. And insubordination."

The former manager huffed and shook his head. He navigated around Albert, pulled open the door, and trudged out of the office.

Outside, the throng of people ballooned, and another knot took root at the rear entrance. Nobody inside could leave, including the former bank manager, who withdrew to hide in what had been his office.

The church bells rang nearby, announcing the time of the opening that wasn't to be. Increasingly volatile citizens, some armed, outnumbered the security guards one hundred to one. As the minutes passed and the doors remained locked, the mass of people unified, deteriorating into a teeming herd. Members of the herd began yelling, "Let us in!" Someone pounded on the door with a brick, sending ominous echoes through the empty marble-floored bank. Before long, they began prying on the doors.

Albert slipped onto the stairway and retreated upstairs into the records room. He peeked out the front window at the angry horde, now filling the street and pulsing with rabid energy. A face glanced up and a pointing finger followed with a yell, and in a flash, the mob's countless eyes were upon him.

Albert ducked and crouched near the floor. An extraordinary cracking sound came from downstairs shortly thereafter. The doors had broken free.

A river of clamoring people poured into the bank, and Albert scrambled toward the back of the room. He peered out the window just in time to see the people who had gathered by the rear entrance realize the opposite side now offered free entry, and they dispersed toward the front, where they'd follow the crowd inside.

Albert fished his keys from his pocket and unlocked the fire escape door despite his quivering hands. In a moment, he was outside on the rusting iron platform, staring at the stairway mounted on a cantilevered hinge. A massive counterweight held it in the raised position, out of the reach of any would-be ground-level intruders.

While upright, the individual steps were not flat. He would need to walk out on the edge of the stairs far enough to overcome the counterweight's force. As the chaos inside reached a full crescendo, he pushed himself forward, grabbing both railings and telling himself not to look down. His knees wobbled while he walked out one step, then two. The stairway shuddered and the rusty joint squealed—he was approaching the point where the structure would pivot down to the ground.

"Hey! There's Harmon!"

Albert couldn't look back from his high-wire act, but he pinpointed the voice as having come from the file room. He stepped out three stairs in rapid succession and was about to take a fourth when he felt the earth rising toward him, and he realized he had gone too far, too fast—the platform was well beyond the balancing point. It was gaining speed as it dropped, and it would soon make impact with the ground. He stepped back, hoping to slow the fire escape's momentum before it hit, but his heel caught on a stair, and in a blink, he lost his sense of space and was plunging.

First, his body met the walkway, his back and head slamming into the corners of several steps. Then, the swinging fire escape collided with the pavement, toppling Albert from his precarious position. Amid his double-somersault tumble down the stairway, he caught a momentary glimpse of the oncoming concrete beyond the final step and managed to extend his arms in time to break the collision.

Pain blazed through both hands when he made impact. He rolled clear of the bouncing ironwork contraption and collapsed in a battered heap, his cheekbone and temple pressed against the gravel-covered pavement. Collecting himself, he pushed up onto his knees. Abrasions covered the base of one palm, tiny pieces of stone embedded into the deepest gouges. When he used his opposite fingers to flick the debris out, he felt bones clicking inside his hand with each movement.

"Stay there, you good-for-nothing bum!"

Albert stumbled to his feet before his mind could further assess the extent of his injuries. He was overjoyed to realize he was in good enough shape to run, but his mood soon took an about-face. As he bolted across the parking lot, he patted his torso on the outside of his jacket, and when he slipped his throbbing hand inside, Albert Harmon discovered that the bag of cash was gone.

Fact was, the events that took place on that infamous day had been at least fifteen years in the making.

Albert's grandfather—who built Harmon Manor in 1855—founded the First Integrity Ohio Bank in the heart of the rapidly growing Western Reserve settlement. Albert's father—who added the formal Victorian gardens to the estate, as fine as any in Europe—continued the bloodline's success in banking, and the institution thrived throughout the Second Industrial Revolution.

The first two generations of Harmon bankers had both adhered to conservative fiscal practices. Both understood that while these policies held back profitability in a robust economy, they provided protection when the economy turned down. During half a century of their leadership, they had brought the bank unscathed through several financial panics.

Albert considered himself smarter than his father and grandfather. Under his tenure at the bank, he established a culture of risk-taking, skirting Ohio's weak state regulation and oversight. Albert's dubious loans during the frothy Roaring Twenties saddled the bank with a loan portfolio that would eventually implode under the economic stress of what was now being called The Great Depression.

The bank's collapse was the consequence of Albert's malfeasance, with his greed and a shameful lust for self-preservation serving as its mortal blow.

Over a two-year period, several banks failed in Ohio, but none melted down in a more spectacular manner than the violent and thorough demise of the First Integrity Ohio Bank. Aside from the lucky few who'd found the cash bag below the fire escape, the rioters never touched a dollar of their savings. Farmers, store owners, mechanics, bakers, machinists, butchers, and furniture makers alike suffered the same undoing.

While financial ruin struck innumerous Homer County families and businesses that day, it was Albert Harmon who would pay the ultimate price.

———◦○◦———

Albert ran on, unable to even consider returning for the money that had somehow slipped from his pocket.

Behind him, the rusty hinge of the fire escape squealed as the counterweight lifted the contraption back into the raised position, ready to ferry down his pursuers.

"After him!"

Albert cut into the alley, legs pumping in the way a man of his age should never attempt, but certain his chasers wouldn't be far behind, he couldn't let up.

Two blocks away, the alleyway opened into Main Street, with the police station, his Duesenberg, and the waiting Pinkerton.

"Get in your car!" he yelled to the guard, who jumped behind the wheel, readying for the race.

While he made the last sprint across Main Street, Albert pulled his keys from his pants pocket with his unbroken hand, smearing blood all over his fine wool pants. He had his car started just before half a dozen men poured out from the alley.

Albert sped out of the parking lot, the Straight-8 engine roaring, tires squealing. A rock slammed into the windshield with a jarring bang, cracking the glass from top to bottom. Another man hurled a brick, hitting the front fender as he blew past the pack.

Albert tore out of town, the security guard trailing close behind. The pair made it to Harmon Manor in half the usual time, and when they arrived, the other two Pinkertons were waiting in the driveway. Albert parked in the carriage house and went about stationing one guard on the front porch, the other on the back, initiating the first shift of an around-the-clock protection detail for the mansion.

Throughout the day, a few angry ruined men clutching hunting rifles and shotguns would make the trek out to the banker's property, seeking revenge—unwilling to settle for justice. But the sentries kept themselves visible—along with their Tommy Guns, so the would-be avengers retreated without incident.

Inside the house, as a last measure of security, Albert loaded both of his shotguns, setting one in the front entrance hall and the other in his bedroom.

CHAPTER 3

---◆◯◆---

HARBINGER

Insomnia had bedeviled Danny Harmon recently. The boy was lying awake in the middle of the night when he heard a vehicle rumble along the roadway, its loud exhaust, rattling chassis, and misfiring cylinders giving it away as a jalopy.

Danny rose and stood at the window, shading his eyes. The full moon burned so bright it seemed to be *straining*...exposing the nightscape, unpeeling the confounding world in which he dwelled.

The automobile slowed near the gardener's driveway, its single working headlight blinking out as it nosed onto the gravel entrance, where it stopped, just clear of the road. A lone figure climbed out of the car. It was a visitor—*a harbinger*.

The mysterious caller moved toward the trail that cut through the swath of wood separating the drive from the mansion, then disappeared behind the trees.

Time passed. Seconds muddled into minutes; minutes blurred to hours. By and by, the solitary shadow emerged from the trailhead: a large man, carrying some type of canister, but no lantern. He snuck along the woods toward the back of the mansion.

Danny followed the man, slipping into the empty bedroom across the hall to continue his surveillance.

Taking roost at the back window, Danny watched the visitor vanish behind the garden hedgerow. Biding, he wiped the sweat from his forehead and spat the fetid saliva on his tongue.

Eventually, the figure resurfaced in the moonlight, then took cover. Perhaps the man had spotted the back porch sentry.

Before long, the shadow reappeared at the opposite corner of the gardens, slipping into the copse of trees which ran along the west side of the house. He wormed in and out of view, working toward the road.

Danny stole back to his bedroom and settled on the edge of his bed, only distantly aware of the visitor's moves, listening all the while to voices—whispers from the dark side of nowhere.

Having circled the house, the figure stepped into the front yard, stood for a moment, then receded into the brush, perhaps not yet ready for his mission, perhaps deterred by the presence of the second guard.

The visitor ran across a short stretch of lawn and ducked behind the carriage house, across the driveway.

Danny's attention drifted from the intruder to that searing moon, which blinded his vision yet warmed his skin. Like so many things Danny endured, it pained and soothed at the same time.

Flickers of orange and yellow light began to dance behind the carriage house, while the visitor crawled through the ditch along the road. Upon reaching the eastern stretch of woods, the figure climbed upright and scurried toward the automobile, which was soon careening down the roadway, disappearing into the night.

Danny reached over to the cast iron radiator mounted beside his bed. He slid his hand between two of the radiator's fins, pulling out the crucifix he had taken from the hallway wall and hidden there before bedtime.

He laid down again and pressed the comforting cross against his chest. Holding the crucifix reverently, he rubbed his thumbs over the figure of Jesus while mumbling to Him, and his glare steadily switched back and forth between the sinister orange glimmer licking the carriage house and the salving object in his clutch.

By the time the front porch sentry roused the household, the blaze had already consumed the well-aged timbers of the carriage house.

CHAPTER 4

CROWN OF THORNS

IN HINDSIGHT, DORIS HARMON could trace the escalation of her son's strange behavior to the day after the carriage house burned down. It was then she first realized something was wrong with Danny—something seriously, frighteningly wrong.

While the fire had been extinguished since mid-morning, the wreckage continued smoldering, giving off an acrid reek that permeated Harmon Manor and made Doris want to retch. She held a kitchen towel over her nose as she ascended the stairway toward Danny's bedroom.

The door was closed, as had become the norm in the past month, when Danny's habit of skulking in his bedroom began. Doris knocked.

There was no response. Danny had shown little visible reaction to the armed guards patrolling outside or the nighttime arson. Nonetheless, Doris could only imagine what was going through his head. She knocked again, harder.

"What?"

Doris felt an icy sensation in her chest from his impolite response and irritated tone. "I..." She pulled the towel from her face. "Would you like to help me bake cookies?"

"No."

She swallowed. "Chocolate chip." Her voice came out sounding frail. When there was no response, she cleared her throat and added in the cheeriest tone she could muster, "Your favorite."

"No."

She stepped away from the door, covered her nose with the towel once again, and drew in a ragged breath. In the past few weeks, no amount of cajoling could persuade Danny to engage with her. She'd attributed this uncharacteristically withdrawn manner to his transition into adolescence. *He's thirteen now. This is puberty,* she'd figured, and told herself to give him space as he adjusted.

Doris fought back tears as she headed down the stairs. She would make the cookies alone. Danny wouldn't be able to resist once he saw and smelled them. Anyway, keeping busy might help her stay calm. Her husband kept assuring her there was no cause for concern, but considering the cascade of harrowing events around her, she couldn't see a way to concur.

Albert was still outside, mulling around with a police officer and the Clarkton Fire Department Chief. Earlier, Doris hadn't been *trying* to listen in, but she had overheard fragments of the men's conversation. She almost wished she hadn't—what they said only heightened her anxiety.

She'd watched as the Fire Chief showed Albert the telltale charred can he found at the periphery of the rubble.

The policeman had shared his take. "I think we're looking at vigilantism here. You're a lucky man, Al. I'd bet they'd have burned your house down if your guards hadn't been here."

"He's probably right," the Fire Chief had said. "Although I also wonder if the front door Pinkerton might've fallen asleep, considering how much the flames spread before he alerted you."

Twenty minutes later, as she dropped the first balls of cookie dough onto the baking sheet, Doris heard Danny's voice and felt a squeeze in her chest. *Who's he talking to? Is someone in the house?* She looked out the kitchen window. The back porch sentry seemed unperturbed.

Wiping her hands on her apron, she hurried up the front hallway toward the base of the staircase. The other guard stood on the porch, beyond the door's leaded window. An intruder couldn't have entered, she told herself, but her heart continued its frantic beat. She listened.

"...Yes, Lord, I understand..."

Her brow furrowed. He was no longer behind the closed door, no longer even in his room. "Danny?"

He didn't answer her but continued speaking, most of his words inaudible.

"...the devil will be stopped. I am your servant, Jesus..."

Doris stepped under the landing of the grand staircase and called up more assertively. "Danny?"

He still didn't respond.

"...yes, Lord, I understand..."

He's praying, she thought, with a thread of relief. *Of course, the poor boy's distraught, with all that's happening,* she reasoned.

"...the evil must be stopped, and I will do it..."

A prickly sensation crept up the back of Doris's scalp. Without waiting or stopping to think, she began to climb the stairs, hoping the sound of her steps might prompt a response.

By the time she reached the top of the stairs, Danny came into view. Doris gasped. He kneeled at the end of the hallway with his head tilted back and hands steepled together, facing the crucifix hanging on the wall.

But what downright chilled Doris was the crown of thorns lodged upon his head.

Until recently, Danny Harmon had always been the remedy to his mother's loneliness.

"You're making him a mama's boy," Albert had often said to Doris. "That's how boys become sissies," he'd add.

"We're just close," she'd mutter in self-defense. But she couldn't argue about how much time she and her son spent together. They'd pass countless hours playing cards and board games or reading books to each other in the library. Doris taught Danny all the popular swing-dance moves, which they performed in the parlor to music projecting from the horn of the RCA Victrola gramophone. They picnicked in the formal gardens behind the estate, tossed a ball to one another, and sometimes played a crude form of croquet on the grassy lawn, in which they took turns just knocking the balls around since neither of them truly understood the rules.

Albert showed no interest in participating in any of this, and it saddened Doris to think that her empty marriage might have contributed to her husband's detachment from their son. Regardless, Albert could never match the love that Doris and Danny shared.

Yet everything had changed recently, particularly in the last several weeks.

When Doris saw the crown of thorns, the first notion that flashed through her mind was that Danny was getting too much religious indoctrination. Her father had been taking him to Bible study at the Clarkton Baptist Church. Doris had not objected to her father's religious influence, reasoning that it was good for Danny to learn about Christianity—and at least it was the church her father knew. After all, Homer County was a religious place even for those who weren't Amish, so if he wasn't going to this institution, classmates would pressure him to join some other church—an unfamiliar one. She had trusted her father's judgment. Bad idea.

At that moment, Doris Harmon couldn't have understood that religious influence wasn't the cause of Danny's bizarre behavior. Tragically, it never dawned on Doris just how dire the situation *really* was.

———————◆———————

Fighting through a wave of light-headedness, Doris drew in on Danny, studying the crown, struggling to sort it all out.

A sense of recognition clicked in her mind. *The hawthorn trees.* Fashioned from young hawthorn branches, twisted together, and wrapped several times around his head, sharp thorns spiked the hideous crown like barbed wire. Doris had always loved the wonderful clump of hawthorn trees growing beyond the garden hedgerow. They flowered in the spring and bore striking red berry-like fruit in the fall. Yet these favorite shrubs of hers had somehow been corrupted into a thing so loathsome, so wrong.

Driven by impulse, she reached out to pull the crown off, but Danny ducked away. He turned to her, a grimace on his face. Blood dripped down each temple, and two more red stains marked his forehead, clots matting in his hair.

"Amen," Danny said, before rising from his knees.

Doris opened her mouth, but her voice faltered. She cleared her throat, then tried again, this time managing to croak, "Danny, what's wrong?"

"Nothing's wrong with *me*." He avoided eye contact, facing neither the cross nor his mother.

"Who were you talking to?"

Danny fidgeted.

Doris reached out to wipe the blood from his head, but he pulled away from her touch.

"I was talking to Jesus." The boy glared at the floor, stepping away.

"Jesus?" Doris looked up and stared at the crucifix as if it might offer an explanation. A lump lodged in her throat, and she tried to swallow it away. "Was Jesus *talking to you*, Danny?"

Danny finally looked up at his mother, staring coldly for a spell before answering.

"Jesus *knows*, Mother."

He broke the brief period of eye contact, turning and stepping past her, heading toward the entrance hall. "That's enough for now."

Doris's eyes fluttered, and a swooning sensation filled her head. Placing a hand on the wall, she blinked several times while her body swayed. Her mind churned, feverishly working to make sense of what just happened, but it came up short, and her bewilderment only grew.

CHAPTER 5

JUDGEMENT DAY

IT WAS SUNDAY MORNING, four days after the riot, two days following Danny's donning of the crown. Since Doris simply hadn't known what to do about the incident, she'd done nothing. Unable to talk to Albert about the matter, she had told herself to disregard what had happened.

Perhaps Doris was paralyzed by the mounting layers of dread weighing on her. Worries crushed her: some untold calamity at the bank, guards protecting her home, the arson, and now, this staggering thing with Danny. On top of all that, Albert's drinking had recently worsened.

Her husband hadn't left the property since fleeing the bank, which was now closed and boarded up. Both the police and a state regulator had come by to interview him, but he had refused to answer any questions without his lawyer.

Doris was preparing pancakes when she finally heard Albert shuffling down the hallway. He had slept in late after a particularly heavy night of drinking. She knew pancakes were one of the few things that unfailingly brought her husband joy. Indeed, he mumbled favorably when he stepped into the kitchen and saw her mixing the batter.

He settled at the table, still wearing his robe over his pajamas. Doris hurried over with a cup of coffee. Albert sipped it, holding the teacup with both bandaged hands. He replaced it on the saucer, and with a faint groan, spread out the newspaper.

The comforting aroma from the first batch of pancakes caught Doris's attention, and she went back to the stove to check them. The batter sizzled, bubbling in the middle, edges forming. When she reached for the spatula, the shotgun blast went off. She jumped back, thunderstruck by the boom and the splattering of gore that appeared on the window curtains at the corner of the room.

Doris swung around to find Albert slumped in his chair, his eyes open wide, capturing his final mortal instant of astonishment. The top half of his head was gone, leaving shreds of glistening brain matter dangling over his forehead.

Posted behind his father's dead body, Danny grasped the shotgun, quivering, still pointing it at what had been his target.

The Pinkertons scrambled into the house with their Tommy Guns drawn. Danny didn't seem to notice.

One guard reached for the shotgun and the other corralled the boy. Danny did not resist. He exhibited no emotion whatsoever. All he did was mutter inaudibly with a dull look in his eyes while the guards subdued and handcuffed him.

Doris Harmon remained beside the stove, still holding the spatula, unable to move or speak.

The mood inside the Clarkton Baptist Church basement contradicted the occasion. Those members of the community who came to pay their respects appeared to do little mourning. Doris saw a few too many smiles and heard too many smatterings of laughter. Many who turned up were slipping away without goodbyes.

They said all the right things: *God works in mysterious ways. He's in heaven now. We'll be praying for you.* Indistinguishable phrases had been repeated countless times, leaving Doris with no recollection of who said what, and even worse, knowing deep down after what Albert had done, it was probably all disingenuous.

Ironically, all the condolences she'd been given were about Albert. It was like nobody knew what to say about Danny, so her boy was carefully and deliberately unmentioned. Yet the source of grief that had clamped onto her after the Sunday morning shockwave was not the loss of her husband. It was the loss of her son. She wouldn't say so to anyone else, but she could cope without Albert. Without Danny, however, she'd be ruined.

"I brought you a sandwich."

Doris felt a hand on her shoulder. The voice was familiar, but muddled, like how it might sound in a dream. It wasn't until she turned and saw Alice that she recognized who had spoken.

"You need to eat, Sis."

Doris took the plate and nodded, but immediately set it on the table.

"Albert's kids sure keep their distance," Alice whispered.

Doris looked across the room at the out-of-towners, all dressed in black. Her grown stepchildren had kept to themselves during the service. Now, as the mourners regrouped in the Clarkton Baptist Church basement after the burial, Albert's offspring assembled on one side of the room, clearly evading Doris and her friends and family.

"Just like always," Doris said. She pushed open her eyes as if letting in more light might help burn off the fog in her head. To her surprise, it did seem to make her feel more alert. "They live far away. They keep their distance. Physically and emotionally."

"I'm sure it's awkward for them," Alice responded after a moment.

Doris turned and squinted, delivering a questioning look to her sister.

Alice spelled it out for her. "It *would* be odd, having a stepmother who's younger than you, wouldn't it?"

"I suppose so," Doris conceded. This probably was a factor, but she knew it wasn't the main issue. Albert's kids had made it clear to their father that he shouldn't be marrying just a year after their mother passed away. Whether or not they knew Doris had been his mistress while their mother was on her deathbed, she couldn't be certain, but she had always suspected so. While she wasn't proud of her past, no amount of regret could change it.

"But it's not like *my* family supported the marriage either," Doris added aloud, then she immediately regretted saying it. The ache inside her head had tangled up her sensibilities. So much time had passed that it barely mattered to begin with. Now, with Albert dead, it mattered even less.

"We just wanted what's best for you," Alice said. "Albert was twice your age."

Doris said nothing. She didn't have the energy to discuss it—especially not here.

"But for Dad..." Alice didn't seem ready to drop the subject. "...it was Albert's reputation. He wasn't exactly well-thought-of around town."

Doris felt herself nodding tiredly, the temporary spell of alertness waning. She had heard all this before. Her family had pleaded with her not to marry Albert, and after she hadn't heeded their advice, they'd withdrawn. This was the primary source of her isolation and loneliness—much more so than anything involving Albert's grown kids.

Perhaps her family had been right all along. Doris never felt close to Albert, and it wasn't merely the age difference. Albert's focus was always on himself. Doris married him less out of love, but more for the kind of financial security few women were allowed access to. She convinced herself they would grow closer, but it didn't work out that way. They coexisted, and although his family's wealth provided Doris with a comfortable lifestyle, it was an empty marriage. Now, even the prosperity she had married into had evaporated, like so many of the good things in Doris's life.

"I suppose none of that matters now," she muttered.

Her sister looked at her and sighed. "I'm sorry for bringing it up."

"I just need to make it through today." Doris's voice cracked.

"You're almost done. Then we can focus on Danny," Alice said.

"Danny." When Doris repeated his name out loud, a blistering sensation spread up her throat. She felt tears welling up, but fought them back, shifting her stare to the concrete floor. She missed her son so much. Danny wasn't dead, no, but he was...taken away. Was it folly to imagine she would have him back?

Doris slid her index finger into the pocket of her jacket and rubbed the ridges of a single checkers piece. A red one, the color Danny always claimed.

There would be no more children after Danny. She didn't want any. He was her world. Her source of joy. Her purpose for living.

"Isn't one of Albert's sons a lawyer?" Alice asked, interrupting her sister's despair.

"Two of them, actually."

"Do you think they can help Danny?"

Doris winced at the idea and shook her head. His stepbrothers had never paid much attention to Danny. But now, after he murdered their father, the idea that any of them would assist the boy was ludicrous. While Albert and his kids weren't close, there was little doubt they loved their father—and they certainly weren't going to want to see his murderer go unpunished.

"I'm going to come and stay with you," Alice said. She placed her hand on Doris's arm and tried to soothe her with a kind look.

Doris merely nodded, unable to muster any words.

CHAPTER 6

---◆O◆---

DELIVERANCE

D ANNY HARMON'S LEGAL PROCEEDINGS commenced within days. Alice, knowing full well Doris was in no shape to go alone, accompanied her sister.

Alice was one of the rare women who could drive in that era, having pressed the issue with her husband until he finally relented and taught her. She dutifully ferried Doris to and from Clarkton for each of the hearings. Doris had never learned how to drive—not to mention the carriage house fire had destroyed Albert's automobile collection.

The juvenile court judge in charge of Danny's trial ordered a psychological evaluation. The results came within a week, and the head psychologist of the Homer County juvenile justice system was called to testify at the next hearing.

"Schizophrenia," the rickety old clinician reported to the magistrate.

Alice flinched when she heard the direful word. Her palms sweating, she squeezed Doris's hand, but received no response. She turned to Doris, who gazed sightlessly across the room, detached from the present, like she couldn't endure what was being discussed. At the front of the room, Danny sat in silence, his eyes darting around while his one leg bounced in a frenzied, nervous rhythm.

"Your diagnosis is schizophrenia?" the judge asked, peering over his spectacles, like he needed to make certain of what he'd heard.

The psychologist straightened his notes while nodding grimly. "This mental disorder typically nests in older victims. Late teens or adults. I'm afraid Danny Harmon has 'childhood-onset' schizophrenia. It's the first such case I've seen in my career."

"Are you certain of your diagnosis?"

"Indeed, Your Honor, there's no doubt amongst my entire staff. The signs are clear. Danny Harmon exhibits a deficit of emotional response, which is known as 'emotional blunting'. Worse yet, he's prone to suffering psychotic episodes, in which he experiences religious delusions, embodied as 'auditory command hallucinations'."

To Alice, the testimony was icy clinical jargon explaining the worst human condition imaginable. Her entire body tensed as she listened, knowing that later she'd have to decipher some version of this to her sister.

Danny's leg pistoned away, while his eyes flitted about in random movements.

The magistrate asked the psychologist for his assessment of why the defendant committed the murder. He responded professionally, but with the creaky voice of an elderly man, describing how it was not on account of any particular disdain Danny had for his father.

"Were they close?" the judge asked.

Alice felt as though the entire courtroom held its breath along with her as everyone waited for the response.

"No, Your Honor, they were not close, but this had no bearing. Danny Harmon had been fostering doubts about his father's spiritual worthiness, and eventually, the voice of Jesus Himself confirmed the man's unholiness."

"The voice of Jesus?"

The psychologist nodded. "The voice inside his head, that is."

Danny seemed to freeze for a moment. His gaze fastened on the witness stand, then he sighed and looked away, and his rhythmic leg-pumping resumed.

"What happened on the morning of the killing?"

"Albert forced Danny to miss church due to Albert's concerns over Danny's safety. This was the final straw." The psychologist snapped his fingers. "The boy's mind decreed execution of his father as the only way to eradicate the devil within him."

Silence fell as the courtroom took this in.

Eventually, the magistrate broke the hush. "Does Danny Harmon show remorse for the murder of his father?"

The witness shook his head. "No, Your Honor. He's proud of what he did. He had gone through with a necessary, purifying act, and he cannot comprehend why he's being punished."

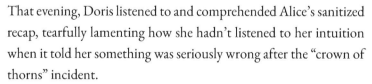

That evening, Doris listened to and comprehended Alice's sanitized recap, tearfully lamenting how she hadn't listened to her intuition when it told her something was seriously wrong after the "crown of thorns" incident.

Afterward, both sisters came to understand how when Doris had talked herself into unseeing what had transpired, she'd missed the opportunity for a psychological intervention that might have averted the ensuing turn of events.

From the perspective of the legal system, there was no disputing the facts of the crime. Danny's grandfather had taught him to use a shotgun, so the boy was adept at handling one. It was nothing more than waiting for the right moment and taking advantage of the readily accessible firearm. The magistrate noted the irony in how Albert himself had loaded the weapon, placing it in the open and practically inviting his troubled son to fire it.

With the indisputable evidence in the case, there wasn't much of a trial. The psychological report must have elicited sympathy from both the juvenile court judge and the county prosecutor, because it did not take long to reach a plea agreement, and the whole affair concluded within three months.

The court found Danny "not guilty by reason of insanity" and committed him to the juvenile ward of the lunatic asylum. He was sent to the Central Ohio Institute for the Criminally Insane, about an hour's drive from Harmon Manor.

To many of the citizens of Homer County, Danny's incarceration was a small tradeoff, furthering a higher purpose. Although nobody would have ever expected it would have come at the hands of the man's thirteen-year-old son, they felt justice had been served in Albert Harmon's death. Some even thought that perhaps it really had been a case of divine intervention.

CHAPTER 7

———◆◇◆———

DEFERMENT

WITH THE TRIAL OVER, Doris's full attention shifted to awaiting word from the State about visitation rights. The letter arrived six weeks later.

Doris tore the envelope open, unwilling to hold back long enough to retrieve the letter opener kept in the study desk. Although her legs wobbled a bit, she stood in the foyer, unable to sit, while she read:

> *Dear Mrs. Harmon:*
>
> *I am pleased to report that your son, Danny Harmon, is doing well in our custody and care.*
>
> *Danny recently underwent a special treatment, an advanced operation called a leucotomy, conducted by our Chief Neurologist. The clinical staff are encouraged by his behavioral progress since the procedure was performed, and they expect his improvement will continue during the next six weeks of recovery.*

Doris cocked her head and shot back to the beginning, scanning the words once more. She hadn't been given any say in the decision to perform this "treatment." She now saw what Danny being a custodian of the State meant. But the optimistic tone in the warden's letter gave her hope, and she latched onto the notion that the Danny she had always known and loved would be waiting for her when she finally did see him.

The paper shook in her hands as she read on:

> *The staff has granted your request for visits, starting after Danny's recovery period is completed. You will have the opportunity to visit beginning March 2, 1932, and continuing on a bi-weekly cadence thereafter, until further notice. The visiting time will be 11:00 a.m., limited to one hour in length, and will be supervised. Upon your arrival, please check in with this letter at the visitor's station.*
>
> *Sincerely,*
>
> *Thomas Miller, Juvenile Warden*

Her heartbeat quickened as the words sunk in, and she wanted to cheer but held off while she re-read the last paragraph. Doris sighed, then threw her head back and smiled, shaking her fist in both relief and anticipation.

She could see it now, in her mind's eye: her boy galloping to meet her at the gates of the asylum, needing his mother now more than ever. She would take him in her arms, embracing him like the precious thing he was—even though he had been too heavy for her to pick up for some time now.

By some benevolent quirk of the universe, Doris imagined Danny would be allowed to come home with her, and together they'd make Harmon Manor a special place, filled with happiness, just for mother and son. Truth be told, she didn't think either of them would miss Albert all that much.

Although she would still need to wait more than six weeks before she could see Danny, the Warden's letter immediately lifted Doris's spirits.

As it would be increasingly performed over the ensuing couple of decades before eventually being banished from practice as a relic of medical quackery, the leucotomy would become more commonly known as a "frontal lobotomy." Yet so little was known about the experimental procedure at that time, Doris had no basis for concern when the letter informed her of it.

Alas, Doris Harmon's desperate fantasies would soon do nothing but make her reality all the more difficult to bear.

CHAPTER 8

REUNION

C ONSTRUCTED OF SOLID LIMESTONE in the Romanesque
architectural style, the Central Ohio Institute for the Criminally Insane was an immense and intimidating building. Doris, un-
fazed, simmered with excitement as she hustled toward the entrance,
playing the joyful reunion out in her mind.

Alice took a seat in the waiting area while an overweight man
gnawing on an unlit cigar butt ushered Doris into the bowels of the
sanatorium. As she proceeded down the corridor, the smell of bleach
mingling with the stench of human waste hit her. She covered her
nose with her scarf, but her escort remained stone-faced while he
chewed.

The man stopped at a closed door with a grunt. The sign above
read VISITATION ROOM A. He removed his keyring and unlocked the deadbolt, then swung the door open and motioned Doris
in. Without uttering a word, the escort closed and relocked the door.
His footsteps receded down the hallway.

The stark room contained a single square metal table with two
chairs, all attached to the floor. Doris sat. Somewhere in the depths
of the building, someone let out a muffled yell.

Doris counted the minutes, clutching the red checker piece the guards had allowed her to take in. Eventually, footsteps came shuffling down the hall toward the room. Keys clanked as the guard unlocked the door, and Doris jumped up, preparing to give her son the biggest hug she had ever bestowed.

The door swung open, and she barely recognized the disheveled boy who stood before her. Pale and bloated, his eyes wandered aimlessly.

Doris tried to ignore the disconcerting signs, stepping forward to give him the long-anticipated hug. He was unresponsive. She patted him on the back as she squeezed him. When her hands touched a thick layer of padding at his waistline, she came to the appalling realization that her Danny was wearing a diaper.

The guard, a lanky young man with a nervous demeanor, signaled for them to sit. Danny slid into the chair opposite Doris.

"I've missed you, Danny," she said, fighting back the sting behind her eyes.

She dropped the red checker on the table with a click and slid it toward him.

Danny's gaze wandered down to the game piece, where it briefly paused before drifting onward to a spot on the table before him, his chin propped on his chest.

"Danny?" She drew in a quivering breath.

Danny lifted his head. It lolled, and he gave an unfocused stare.

Doris looked over at the fidgeting guard, but he merely checked his watch, averting her eye contact.

She turned back to Danny. Drool spilled out of his mouth, pooling on his lower lip, where it hung for a spell before breaking free and dripping into his lap. All the while, his catatonic gape persisted, without so much as an eye-blink.

Doris Harmon's befuddlement erupted into horrific recognition that the "treatment" had stolen her beloved son. Danny was gone.

CHAPTER 9

AFTERMATH

ALICE IMMEDIATELY RECOGNIZED THE sound of Doris blubbering, even before the lobby door opened and Doris stormed out, heading straight for the outside exit. The escort, still sucking on his cigar butt, popped his upper body out through the door frame long enough to watch Doris leave the building. He gave Alice an apathetic shrug before withdrawing, pulling the door shut behind him.

Stunned, Alice gathered her belongings and hurried after Doris. "Sis?" she called.

Doris, half-running, half-stumbling down the walkway, gave no reply. When she arrived at the car, she leaned against it, her body lurching with every whimper.

Alice caught up and wrapped her arm around her sister. She held her but resisted pressing for an explanation. The women stood there without speaking for a few minutes, as Doris's crying wore down into sobs.

"Let's go," Alice eventually said, and she helped Doris into the car.

They were halfway home before Alice finally asked, "What happened in there?"

Doris shook her head and stared blankly ahead. "I can't talk about it now."

Half an hour later, when Alice pulled into Harmon Manor's driveway, she said, "I'll stay here with you."

Doris, who had been sitting in silence and turned toward the window, whipped around to face Alice. "No," she said vehemently. "I'm fine now. You go home."

Regret for having left her sister alone gnawed at Alice all night, and early the next morning, she drove back to the mansion to check on her. When Doris didn't answer the door, she used her extra key to enter.

Alice called her sister's name in the foyer.

She stopped and listened, but Doris didn't respond.

A faint creak reverberated upstairs, in a distant part of the house.

She climbed the steps, hearing it again—louder this time—as she arrived at the bedroom level: *Creak.*

Alice peeked into Danny's room, where Doris had tarried for endless hours since her son's detention...yet it was empty.

"Sis?" she called into the master bedroom, but there was no response, and she grew troubled by the disquiet.

CREAK. This time she could tell the sound had come from even further upstairs. When she pulled the attic door open, a draft blew down the stairway, and she shivered. *A window is open in the attic,* her mind reasoned.

Alice ascended the steps, hearing the groan once more when she passed the landing, clearer and closer this time. The ominous sound gave her pause, and she had to goad herself to continue upward.

A few steps further and her head cleared the floor of the attic. One of the porthole windows was open, allowing a cross breeze to pass through the dreary space. The sheets covering boxes of Christmas decorations and old family heirlooms billowed in the wind, and the creak sounded yet again, beckoning her onward from the belvedere above.

As she stepped to the opening of the final stairwell, it was the stockinged, shoeless feet she saw first, dangling in the air just above her eye level. When Alice cast a glance upward, she caught a full view of her sister's lifeless body hanging from the mansion's pinnacle beam.

The tensioned rope Doris Harmon hung from creaked again as the dead woman's body swung in the breeze, while below, her sister fell to her knees and wailed.

PART THREE

JESSICA - 2003

CHAPTER 10

HOMECOMING

J ESSICA PUTNAM TURNED OFF the interstate and passed by the collection of gas stations and fast-food restaurants just beyond the exit ramp. Sensing they might finally be stopping, Arik stirred in the back seat. "Not yet, buddy," she said over her shoulder. They had been on the highway for several hours since their overnight stop on the long drive from Boston to Ohio. "Still half an hour left to go."

If it had been just herself, Jessica would've made the trip in a single day, but that would be even more unfair to the greyhound confined to the back seat of a Saab. So, they'd spent the night in that same grody motel she'd repeatedly sworn she'd never stay at again. But this time would definitely be the last.

"Recalculating..."

"Yeah, yeah." Jessica had turned off the interstate one exit sooner, and the GPS scolded her for it. Knowing the way from here, she switched it off.

State Route 880 would get them to her parents' house just the same. *It's the scenic route...*though, admittedly, it wasn't the only reason she chose this way.

She turned off the stereo next, ending Nine Inch Nails' album, *The Downward Spiral*. Instead, she'd enjoy the sunny afternoon, the rural landscape in its mid-May bloom. As if responding to the steady hum of the new roadway, Arik dropped onto the seat and settled back into his sleeping position.

Jessica felt an unexpected twinge of nostalgia seeing the countryside she had grown up nearby. Once she left for college, she didn't think she'd ever move back. But here she was, leaving behind what she'd considered her home—and her career—six months after Richard had left *her* behind.

She recalled the first time she had visited her parents with Richard a few months after they'd started dating. When she'd driven him around her childhood haunts she was so thoroughly charmed by his excitement at seeing the Amish and the rolling hills of farmland—neither of which had ever seemed very magical to her before.

Rounding a familiar bend in the road, her pulse quickened, and she instinctively scanned the terrain beyond, watching for Harmon Manor. But the FOR SALE sign stabbed into the ground beside the main driveway caught her attention first. *Geez...Misery Mansion's for sale?*

She slowed, passing the old gardener's driveway where she had parked the car with Erin Watson on Halloween night almost thirteen years prior. Remnants of the gravel pass were still visible in a slight clearing.

She coasted along further and, on a whim, turned into the main driveway. Arik, afraid he might miss something, arose behind her. His tail slapped the seat in a steady rhythm, and his head popped up beside her. She held her breath so she wouldn't have to smell his.

"Sorry, buddy." She spoke with her head turned just far enough away from his so she could avoid being licked. "We're not getting out. Just taking a quick look-see."

She let the car roll up the driveway's length until the mansion practically filled the span of her windshield, and for a moment, the rest of the world fell away. The boarding over the windows and doors had been removed, but otherwise, the old house appeared the same as she always remembered it. *As creepy as ever. Except it's creepier at night,* she remembered, nodding.

The intense fear Jessica had felt that Halloween night had dulled through the years. By now, the incident felt distant, less threatening. But as time passed and the impact of the fright subsided, an imperishable twinge of guilt from having ignored the apparition's pleas for help supplanted it. Because she had *definitely* been pleading for help. Yet Jessica had fled and refused to ever look back, and even today, a sliver of shame about her decision persisted.

As an architect specializing in historical renovations over the past five years, Jessica could now see details in an old building that would be lost on most people. From this distance, the mansion showed no indication of having fallen into disrepair. The stylized features remained intact, and even the intricately painted accents on the trim and the carved wooden corbels and balustrades remained visible.

Flipping up the visor and leaning down below her car's roofline, Jessica looked up at the top level of the house, and her heart skipped a beat as she thought of that long-ago encounter. She searched for a figure in the belvedere windows that wasn't there.

Regardless, the mere sight of it gave her a shudder, and she felt she'd seen enough. She circled the turnaround, headed down the drive, turned onto the state highway, and drove on.

The seed of an idea then lodged in Jessica Putnam's mind. She would be arriving at her parents' home soon, with lingering thoughts about Misery Mansion.

———◆O◆———

Grief turns vicious in the dead of the night.

Jessica jerked awake, the sickening thump reverberating inside her head. The nightmare had become an almost nightly routine, yet its impact never softened. She sat up, panting and trembling. It took her a moment to sort out where she was: in her childhood bed...the bed she had shared with Richard during their visits.

Jessica tried to stop herself but couldn't. She reached over and patted the other half of the mattress. It was empty. "Phantom limb syndrome," she whispered on impulse, wishing her mind had never contrived the grisly analogy.

Arik's head popped up from the floor, and he gave an inquisitive look. His ear, folded over, exposed the tattoo of his racing identification number. Jessica recalled how Richard's friends had talked him into tattooing "Jessie" on his upper arm the night of his bachelor party. No matter what she did, or how far she traveled, the memories were ceaseless. *Stop it!* Her weary plea was internal, although she wanted to scream it.

It was just after two in the morning, the first night at her parents' house. Jessica wiped the sweat from her forehead and took a long shuddering breath, then reached out and flipped Arik's ear back over. "It's okay, buddy."

Jessica sunk back into the pillow and cried.

The next day was the first chemotherapy session for Jessica's mother. The breast cancer diagnosis had been the tipping point for Jessica's decision to move back, which she had been stubbornly resisting. Because they'd detected the cancer relatively early, Nancy Putnam's prognosis was good. But the treatment routine would be grueling—every two weeks, for four to five months—and Jessica needed to be there for both her parents.

The long drive would make it even tougher. They didn't have much faith in the quality of healthcare in their rural area, so they had decided to take her to the Cleveland Clinic for treatment, a ninety-minute drive each way. Jessica was determined to accompany her mother, so her father could remain focused on his work, keeping the income coming in.

Her dad came along on this first session, but he allowed Jessica to drive. Her mom sat in the back, and on the drive home, she fell asleep soon after they entered the highway. Jessica and her father slipped into silence to avoid disturbing her. She was still sleeping when they pulled into the drive.

Leaving her father to rouse and assist her mother, Jessica headed straight through the garage to the house. She was in a hurry to get Arik out. While his racing days were over, the greyhound still enjoyed—no, he *needed*—a fast romp a couple of times each day.

Her parents' yard was too small for his needs, and it wasn't like Clarkton offered anything resembling a dog park, which were plentiful in Boston. She'd take him to the high school ball field, assuming none of the sports teams were using it for practice.

"Shit," Jessica said as she entered the family room.

Arik dropped the shoe he was chewing and tucked his tail.

"No, no, no, Arik!" Jessica scolded, and he slinked off into the kitchen.

"What did he do?" her father asked. Both parents stood inside the doorway and absorbed the sight of what remained of Nancy's leather shoe.

"It's no big deal, Jess," her mother said, either mustering sainthood or too weak to let it bother her.

"Sorry, Mom." Jessica lifted the slimy, crumbling shoe. "Not sure why he always seems to go for your stuff."

"She'll take it as a compliment," her father said, although he wasn't exactly smiling.

Jessica grabbed Arik's leash and collar, and when he heard it jingle, he pranced back into the family room, reanimated.

<hr>

It wasn't until after the third chemo treatment—six weeks later—that Jessica finally went through with placing the call. When the line started ringing, she thought, *Am I really doing this?*

"Mast Real Estate Agency, this is Bonnie speaking."

Jessica hesitated, having a notion to simply hang up.

"Ah, hello...Bonnie...I'm calling about a house you have listed."

"Absolutely! What's the address?"

Jessica read from the newspaper listing. "11360 East Main Street. Clarkton."

"Oh, yes. Harmon Manor. Incredible place, isn't it?" Bonnie spoke with that tone of candy-coated enthusiasm that all real estate agents might be required to master.

"Sure is. What kind of shape is it in?"

"Actually…" Bonnie paused as if to emphasize her point. "…and I'm not just saying this…the house is in surprisingly good condition."

Jessica listened vaguely but found herself questioning her own motivation.

"Obviously, it needs sprucing up, but its bones are solid. It's been unoccupied for many decades, so there's not much wear and tear. The Harmon family still owns it, and they've never neglected it."

"What sort of renovations have been done?"

"Well, I don't know the full history of the house, but it looks to me like it's pretty much original. I'm sorry, I didn't catch your name…"

"Jessica. Jessica Putnam."

"Oh, Jessica. I think…" As if she was flipping through a Rolodex in her mind, Bonnie paused again. "I think I know your mother. Nancy Eldridge?"

"Yes, that's right."

"Oh, she's a dear. We went to school together. She married Marty Putnam. *All* the girls liked Marty."

Jessica chuckled. "That's what he claims. I never believed him."

"Oh, you can believe him alright." Bonnie giggled. "Is he still doing renovations?"

"He is. He should be thinking about retirement, but he loves the work and business is good."

"And your mother? I haven't seen her in years. How is she?"

Jessica scrabbled for a response. "Actually, not too well. She's dealing with some health issues."

"Oh, I'm so sorry to hear that, Jessica. Please tell her Bonnie Adams gives her best wishes. Mast was my maiden name…my father started the agency. But she should know me either way: Bonnie Mast, or Bonnie Adams."

"I'll do that." Jessica felt relieved Bonnie didn't pry, and she did sound sincere. That was the kind of Homer County neighborliness Jessica appreciated.

"Are you still living in the area?"

"No. Well, yes—sort of. I left for college, then moved to Boston. I recently came back to help my parents."

"Wait...are you thinking of the house for yourself?"

Jessica recognized this as one of those occasions when having kept her maiden name allowed her to dodge uncomfortable explanations. "Yeah, just me. Me and my dog, that is."

She had been living with her parents for over a month now, and the idea of changing living arrangements had some appeal. But was Harmon Manor really a viable answer? She had turned this question over in her mind repeatedly, and at times, the answer was clear: it was crazy. But she could also see practical benefits to this house, like the vast expanse of open property around the mansion would be *perfect* for Arik. She could clean up the home, perform some modern upgrades, live there for a while, then sell it for a nice profit when she was ready to move on.

"I've always been intrigued by that home. I'm an architect, specializing in historic renovation. Mostly commercial, but some residential, too."

"Then you'd be in awe if you saw inside *this* house. I could show it to you, but I need to screen out curiosity seekers, so I'd have to see proof of funds first."

"That wouldn't be a problem," Jessica said, although it occurred to her that just because she could prove she had the funds, doesn't mean curiosity isn't at play for her.

"Wonderful. You would see what I mean then. The craftsmanship is extraordinary." Bonnie was shifting into full-pressure-sales-mode.

Jessica closed her eyes and pursed her lips while the gears in her mind began turning. A weak inner voice pleaded with her to just end the call and forget about Misery Mansion.

"You *really* should take a look at it. I'm *sure* you'll be astounded."

The question spilled out of Jessica's mouth before she could think twice: "When can I see it?"

━━━━◄●►━━━━

When she settled into her bedroom that night, Jessica searched the bookshelf for a certain book she hadn't seen in years. She was on the verge of concluding it was gone when she discovered it tucked between high school yearbooks. A ripple of nostalgia passed over her as she studied the cover:

OHIO GHOSTLY ROAD TRIP
The Most Haunted Houses in Every County

Knowing how much she loved ghost stories, Jessica's parents had given her the book for her twelfth birthday. As an adolescent, she had immersed herself in its pages, feeding her fascination with the supernatural. Each entry had a full-color photograph of the property, a brief description of its history, and a synopsis of the strange happenings purportedly associated with it. It wasn't too hard to cajole her father into driving her past some of the surrounding counties' houses featured in the book—seven of them, to be exact.

When she was a few years older, Jessica came to realize how the book leaned more toward a picture book of sensationalized stories than a serious in-depth review of paranormal reports, and it had been permanently retired to the bookshelf ever since.

She opened it, thumbing through to the particularly well-worn dual entries for Homer County: The Gould homestead (commonly known as "Ghoul House"), an isolated and now-collapsing farmhouse in the county's southwest corner (which, through a bizarre turn of events, had been recently thrust into the populace's attention), and Harmon Manor.

Jessica read the text under the photograph of Harmon Manor:

Popularly referred to as "Misery Mansion," this frightful Victorian-era manor certainly looks the part of a haunted house. It sits alone off a seldom-traveled state highway in the eastern end of Homer County.

The macabre history of this unoccupied home began during the Great Depression, with the execution-style killing of the man of the house, a prominent banker, at the hands of his teenage son, who was subsequently condemned to an insane asylum. The deranged, murderous teen's commitment prompted his mother to hang herself in the tower atop the mansion.

Decades later, an heir of the only family who has ever owned the estate died of a drug overdose in the house, and her young son simultaneously disappeared, never to be found again. Although never proven, it has been widely speculated this woman may have killed her son and disposed of his body before staging her suicide as an accidental overdose. If indeed that's what happened, could it be she'd been possessed by the spirit of the suicidal mother who had preceded her?

There are an untold number of legends surrounding the house, including reports of workers finding bones hidden inside a wall during renovation work in the 1960s, and investigators who claimed to feel an evil presence when near or inside the mansion. The home was rumored to have been the meeting place for a secretive group that conducted seances during the post-war era. It is said that the ghost of a woman can sometimes be seen looking out the windows atop the imposing and fearsome-looking house of horrors.

Beware of Misery Mansion!

Jessica pored over the text twice more, studying every word as if she might glean something new from them, but…nothing.

She slid the book back onto the bookshelf and climbed into bed.

Jessica found herself increasingly enthusiastic about the prospect of seeing inside Misery Mansion. It had been a long time since she had felt excitement toward anything, so she relished the pleasing emotion.

As the days passed while she'd been staying with her parents, her existence had drifted into tedium. Her routine involved helping around the house, making the long drive to the Cleveland Clinic, and taking Arik out for his runs. She found herself feeling guilty for resenting having taken on the role of a house-nanny, always on hyperalert, to keep Arik from becoming a nuisance. While she appreciated the time with her parents, that couldn't offset the loss of her husband, her career, and now, her independence. While she had no idea what would come of the showing, she wondered why she had taken so long to make the call.

"Buenos noches, Señor Arik," she said before turning off the light. The dog seemed to understand. He sighed his response, and his eyelids rolled down over his eyes. Jessica followed suit, and for the first time in six months, she fell asleep eager for tomorrow.

———◦———

After Jessica fell asleep, those pleasant feelings soured into the imperishable nightmare. Only the dream wasn't merely dark imagining. Like a perverse compulsion rooted in the depths of her consciousness, reliving that cold November day tormented her.

The extensive project on Boston College's Chestnut Hill Campus was almost finished, but the inspector had flagged an issue with the roof flashing. A dispute ensued over whether the problem was a result of the design, the construction specs, or the installation. As the construction manager on the project, Richard's only hope of finding a resolution was through a joint field visit, on-site with both the general contractor and the roofer. All had agreed to meet at 7:30 in the morning. Because Richard and Jessica worked at the same firm and commuted together, they would stop on their way to the office.

Jessica dropped off Richard, parked the Saab in a nearby garage, then took shelter from the frigid drizzle at the coffee shop across the street from the new building. Twenty minutes later, Richard called.

Jessica flipped open her phone. "Wrapping up?"

"Yup. We have a plan."

"I'll meet you outside."

"Don't forget my coffee."

"I drank it," she teased before ending the call, smiling as she picked up both cups.

But for the first time, Jessica consciously realized that a trace of worry had been swirling in her gut all morning. Sometimes she had spells of déjà vu, and this was one of those occasions, wasn't it? When she stepped out of the café, that vague semblance of concern bloomed into panic. She *knew* the men were not using the personal fall arrest system (PFAS). She craned her neck upward to face the top of the building. Richard gathered with the others at the edge. Desperate to avert the tragedy she somehow foresaw, she yelled—but Richard was beyond earshot.

She watched in utter helplessness as her husband stepped from the roof to the scaffolding, slipped, grabbed at the railing that eluded his grasp, and fell four stories, landing on the walkway just a hundred feet from where she stood.

THUMP.

Jessica jolted awake at the sickening sound. She battered at the intolerable memory hanging in her mind, attempting to smash it away: Richard's contorted body crumpled on the pavement, two nearby students screaming with the shock of what they'd witnessed. Richard had been a tall, robust man, but now he was just another pile of tangled construction debris. The man she loved, suddenly like roadkill, flung into a mangled heap beside the expressway.

She pushed herself upright and a glob of vomit erupted into her mouth. She gulped it back down, and as she tried to collect herself, the question she'd asked a thousand times rattled in her brain: *Why didn't I remind him to use the PFAS?*

Jessica Putnam reached out and touched the mattress beside her...there was no one there.

CHAPTER 11

THE SHOWING

STANDING IN HER PARENTS' driveway, Jessica faced the darkening western horizon. A whopper of a thunderstorm was heading her way. As the wind blew, whipping her hair around, she questioned whether to reschedule. She checked her phone. No missed calls from Bonnie. If the real estate agent was willing to brave the weather, so was she.

She backed out of the drive and headed east out of Clarkton. Just past the outer edge of the Clarkton business district, the storm overran her. The black clouds ruptured, dumping a flood of heavy raindrops, pummeling the car's roof and windshield. She turned the wipers on, and before long, rolled the switch onto high speed, but even that couldn't keep up.

Jessica white-knuckled the steering wheel at ten and two, leaning forward to catch each fleeting glimpse of the road while the wipers labored away. Twice each second, their sweep would reveal a snapshot of the roadway, as if she was watching a low frame rate stop motion movie.

When she rounded a bend, a truck suddenly appeared out of nowhere, filling the road, barreling toward her. As the deluge blurred the image away, she yanked the wheel to the right and hit the brakes. Her Saab hydroplaned, and she could do nothing but brace herself and pray while the car shimmied out of control. The next momentary view was the truck's tsunami wake, breaking above her before crashing into the car. But—*by some miracle*—there was no impact between the passing vehicles.

The truck plowed on, and the Saab's tires soon regained their grip on the asphalt. Jessica slowed, edging over to the roadside to pull herself together. She sighed and said aloud in a wavering voice, "Well, Richard, I almost moved into your neighborhood, darling."

Despite the numbness spreading through her arms and legs, she didn't loiter in what would be a very bad place to park. When she resumed driving, she crawled along at a fraction of her previous speed; what should have been a ten-minute drive to her destination turned out to take more than twice that long.

She eventually arrived at Harmon Manor, relieved to have survived the pilgrimage, but surprised Bonnie's car wasn't there yet. She nosed into the driveway and navigated to the turnaround in front of the house, where she parked, facing the mansion.

Remaining in the car while waiting for the real estate agent to arrive, Jessica leaned back and attempted to recuperate from the harrowing near-miss. She alternately watched the downpour and studied what little she could see of the home's architecture. The rain hadn't let up—so it wasn't very much.

She had spent the morning weeding the landscape beds at her parents' home. Her mother must have felt guilty about having neglected the gardening, because she kept insisting that she would help. But Jessica pushed back hard. Arik was her only work companion, sleeping in the grass nearby. They made a good team and completed the chore by lunchtime.

When Jessica came out after her shower, she found her mother fast asleep on the family room couch, with Arik conked out on the floor beside her as though the long outdoor nap had exhausted him.

Before Jessica had slipped out on her adventure, she scrawled a note on the kitchen whiteboard: *Went to the garden center to pick up mulch.*

She had debated whether to tell her parents about the showing. On the one hand, her father's advice would be beneficial, on account of his forty years performing home renovations.

Jessica had seen how knowledgeable her father was, having worked with him for five summers while in high school and early college, until landing her internship at the firm she ultimately hired into full time. The construction skills she had learned from her dad helped her architecture career, even though what he'd taught her was just a fraction of the expertise he possessed.

But on the other hand, she worried her parents would try to talk her out of looking at Harmon Manor, and since there was a good chance that nothing would come from the showing, what was the harm? She anticipated coming across some major flaw in this initial showing that would be an obvious deal-breaker, and if so, she would simply walk away, at least having had the opportunity to see inside the legendary mansion.

In the end, she decided not to inform them. If it turned out she determined the home was a viable consideration after this first look, *then* she would tell them, and include her father, for a closer inspection.

A gust of wind rocked the car, and lightning flashed, followed by a bellowing thunderclap a second or two later.

Jessica dug her cell phone out of her purse and discovered she'd missed two calls from Bonnie, with the sound of the ringtone drowned out by the storm. She was preparing to call her back when the agent rang again.

"Hi, Bonnie," she answered.

"Hi Jessica, are you there?" The agent spoke fast, sounding harried.

"Yes. This is quite a storm."

"You can say that again. Listen, a tree came down in the road. I'm taking a grand detour to come in on 880 from the east. I'll be half an hour longer, at least."

"Do you want to reschedule?" Jessica asked, secretly hoping Bonnie would decline.

"I have another idea. I'm not supposed to do this, but I could give you the lockbox code and you can let yourself in. It would be safer inside than sitting in your car."

"I'd be okay with that." Having pulled through the hair-raising close call, Jessica wasn't as concerned about safety as she was eager to start exploring.

"Okay, the code is two, zero—"

Jessica guessed where this was going, but let it play out.

Bonnie carried on, "—zero, three."

A smirk formed on Jessica's face, but before she had the chance to rib Bonnie for using such an obvious code, the call dropped. She stared at her phone for a beat before flipping it closed.

Jessica took one more look at the mansion, which shifted and wavered as the water running over the windshield distorted its image. She scanned the structure, side to side, bottom to top, then nodded, ready for a self-guided tour.

In a futile attempt to stay dry, she opened her umbrella with her door cracked ajar, and scurried underneath it as she rushed to the front porch. She arrived on the veranda half soaking wet, and with a laugh, shook the worthless shield.

Rain overwhelmed the gutters and downspouts, creating a curtain of water down each of the open sides of the porch. Jessica fought against the wind to collapse the umbrella before laying it along the base of the brick wall.

She wiped her face and looked around, examining the millwork of the house and the veranda's trim, all of it intact and quite well preserved. Then, an uneasy feeling took hold in her mind as she suddenly became hyperconscious of where she was. She now stood in front of the spot where Erin had left the inverted crucifix in their door-knock-ritual dare.

When they were young, the ominous imagery in Jessica's father's copy of the Black Sabbath debut album had infatuated Jessica and Erin. On the cover, a woman in a black cloak—a witch, perhaps—stood amongst the trees in front of an old house, clutching what the young girls believed was a black cat.

Inside, the album hid the graphic of an inverted cross. This dark iconography had mesmerized them. Several years later, while in their early teens, they rented VHS tapes of old horror movies, including *Rosemary's Baby* and *The Omen*, which only cemented the unholy implications of the image.

However, during one of their Parish School of Religion classes, the instructor, Mrs. Weber, had explained how an inverted cross (which she called the "Cross of Saint Peter") didn't have anything to do with Satan. It was a "symbol of Christian humility" the teacher had contended, taking great delight in debunking pop culture's association of the symbol with evil. Mrs. Weber acted like good had triumphed that day, and she deserved credit for the assist.

After class, the girls laughed about how all of a sudden that frightening Black Sabbath album art seemed a little less so. Jessica always knew Erin had placed the crucifixes upside-down not to scare her, but as an inside joke between them, and as a mischievous jab at the holier-than-thou Mrs. Weber.

A blast of wind sprayed water onto the porch, obliterating the memory. Jessica's drenched clothes clung to her skin, returning her thoughts to the one task that mattered: getting inside.

Crouching to the lockbox attached to the door handle, she rolled the dials and pushed the latch release. The lockbox popped open, exposing a brass key inside.

Jessica plucked it out as a thunderous lightning clap exploded nearby.

Jessica edged into Harmon Manor's entry hall.

The storm-darkened skies left the interior dim, filled with dusty shadows. She clicked the light switch, and when the bronze and crystal chandelier hanging above her illuminated, she released the breath she'd been holding onto.

Jessica swung the door closed, instantly muting the sound of the rain when it latched. With brick and plaster walls and a roof composed of slate and copper, the shell of the house formed a dense barrier from the outside.

The stale scent of abandonment pervaded the air. She sniffed, noting how the odor was merely musty, but not dank, meaning there was no mildew or rot...at least not in this part of the house.

The wind howled. Two or more fireplaces mourned a chimney wail, and a chill slithered down Jessica's spine. Standing inside the house that had been a source of fear while growing up, she found herself charged with apprehension. Yet she also felt excited to see the interior of such an amazing mansion. It was as if the teenage part of her mind and the architect part were facing off in a wrestling match, and it wasn't yet clear who would be the victor.

With no furniture or décor in sight, the architectural details were on prominent display. She examined the abundant black walnut woodwork. Judging by the style and patina of the wainscoting, crown and baseboard moldings, and the door and window trim, the finish carpentry was original to the house, and still in good shape, considering its age.

Bonnie had said it well: this house was even more impressive on the inside than on the outside. While the mansion's condition was not pristine, it had never been allowed to fall into disrepair, despite being unoccupied for so long.

A library was situated off the grand entrance, beyond the staircase. She stepped inside and mouthed a whistle. Ornamental book shelving fitted the wall opposite the windows, while burled walnut paneling adorned the others. The library was the front portion of a large L-shaped room, transitioning into another living area stretching along the west side of the house, with a beautiful fireplace at the junction.

Jessica found herself wishing Richard were here to see what she was observing.

She returned to the foyer and saw she had left a small puddle on the parqueted floor, where she had entered. She would have to look for a towel in the kitchen.

Heading down the hallway connecting to the back of the house, her footsteps on the wooden floors echoed through the empty corridor, and she came to a halt. *I'm in the core of Misery Mansion,* she thought. Was anyone—*anything*—present? Watching her? Listening? Will Halloween Ghost Lady appear? Or had her spirit since moved on, having found someone else to help her? *Since I hadn't,* Jessica thought in an accusatory way. *But maybe I can redeem myself if she reappears.* With a shudder, Jessica shut the thoughts down and shifted her concentration back to examining the home.

An expansive dining room was on the right side of the hall. A carved marble fireplace centered the wall opposite the room's entryway. Stained-glass windows flanked the mantle, each one unique, both depicting medieval hunting scenes. The window on the left portrayed a man on a horse, poised to thrust his spear into a stag. In the other, two dogs were chasing a stag toward the horse-mounted hunter, who awaited his game with his lance.

Just then, a brilliant flash of lightning burst through the colored glass, followed by an explosion of thunder so jarring it seemed like the antique windows would shatter. Jessica jumped back. She retreated from the windows and headed toward the rear of the house.

Across the hall, an open door revealed a stairway that descended into the darkness of the cellar. She leaned away from the opening as she passed.

The hall ended at the kitchen and its pantry, which filled one corner of the house. A paper towel roll sat beside the sink, which she made a vain attempt to wipe herself dry with before giving up and pocketing a few for the puddle.

Jessica made a quick pass through the room. The fixtures, cabinets, and counters were very dated, some perhaps even original. She resisted the temptation to lose herself in the kitchen, and moved on, keeping focused on the overall layout of the mansion so she could establish a clear picture of the floor plan in her head.

Another corridor ran along the back of the house. *So many rooms!* Jessica turned on the lights for each one, briefly examined their details, then returned them to gloom. Varying patterns of floral-print cloth wallpaper, old-fashioned and aged, yet still intact, covered the walls.

The parlor featured a barrel-vaulted ceiling spanning its entire width and length. A third fireplace accented the back wall, with an oversized beveled mirror mounted above the mantel.

A back entrance hall that opened to another veranda separated the parlor and the kitchen. The corridor running along the rear of the house led to a spacious half bathroom, which would have been an extraordinary luxury in the period when the house had been constructed.

Jessica made her way back to the front foyer and peered out the narrow window beside the door, checking whether Bonnie might have arrived yet. Nope. She pulled out her phone. No service. *Wonderful*, she thought and slipped the device back into her jacket, then went about wiping up the floor.

She thought about how fun it was going to be telling Erin about how she went inside Misery Mansion. Although the frequency of their communication had fallen since they both graduated college and moved away, the childhood friends remained in touch. Now married, Erin lived in Cincinnati, with a two-year-old daughter and another baby due in January. *No Way!* Jessica imagined Erin would say, to which she'd respond *Way!* All these years later, the friends still put to good use the language borrowed from their beloved *Wayne's World* skits on *Saturday Night Live*.

Jessica decided to explore upstairs.

The grand entry staircase was constructed with a half-turn landing separating two parallel flights. After climbing the steps, she held up at the gallery balustrade and glanced down, imagining the foyer as it appeared in the home's heyday, furnished, with residents bustling about.

She wandered into the bedroom wing. Each of the bedrooms seemed larger than the last. Three of them had fireplaces, situated above the three downstairs, so they could share a double-flue chimney. The master bedroom was the size of a ballroom, with a stretch of extra floor space functioning as a dressing area, plus a vast adjoining bathroom beyond. Jessica stared at it, envisioning it as her own.

She left the master bedroom and returned to the hall. On the opposite side, one shut door filled the space between two bedrooms. Jessica cracked it open and peered in. A dusty stairway led up to another level. Finished with bare maple wood and lacking the rich trim used in the rest of the house, this stairwell was clearly not intended to be part of the day-to-day living space. *The attic,* she deduced, then, with a wince, ...*and the belvedere is above that. Is the ghost hiding up there, where I once saw her?*

Jessica pulled open the attic door and started the ascent toward a landing, in which the stairs turned back into another stretch, forming a U-shaped layout. She mounted the second flight. When she reached the cavernous attic, she paused. Small windows opened through the mansard roof, which served as the attic's inward-slanted walls. Raindrops pattered above and around her, as heavy as ever.

One last stairway led to the apex of the house, the tower. Jessica looked up and discovered the hatch at the top propped open, inviting her to continue her climb. A wrought-iron balustrade encircled the entrance opening, and the trap, which appeared to be another full-size door, held latched against one side of the railing.

Jessica almost lost her resolve, but after a moment she pushed herself forward, ascending the steps while holding her breath, watching...but when her eye level crested the floor, she found the room empty. Jessica turned right. As she stepped up to the windows at the front of the house, her eyebrows sprung up. Although the rain spraying on the windows obscured her view, the belvedere offered a sweeping panorama, extending far beyond the limits of the property.

Outside, the winds blew fiercely, rattling the panes of glass in their frames, and she stiffened when she felt the chill of a draft passing over her damp clothes. Jessica granted herself early release. Circling the room, she glanced out at each of the other sides—concluding with the east-facing window. She felt a rush of cold ripple through her when she saw the trail she had fled on, realizing she stood where the apparition had appeared.

She resolved to not linger and was soon hastening down the sequence of stairways. The instant she stepped into the bedroom wing hallway, lightning struck somewhere nearby, and when the house clattered with the monstrous peal of thunder that followed, she felt relieved she wasn't still at the tippy-top.

When she returned to the foyer, Jessica looked out the front door window again. Bonnie *still* hadn't arrived.

She walked back to the entrance of the cellar and peered at the murk below. Skimming her hand along the wall, she found the light switch, and when she flipped it on, bright light bathed the passageway.

When most people look at a house, they ignore an unfinished basement, her dad had explained on many occasions. *But that's where you can see the guts of the home—its foundation, framing, ducting, plumbing, wiring...*

Jessica summoned her courage and proceeded down the steep steps, grasping both handrails as an extra precaution. As she approached the bottom, she could see little beyond the floor immediately in front of her. She gulped in a breath of air as that fleeting surge of bravery she had gathered at the top waned.

She toggled the switch at the foot of the stairs, flooding the cellar with light, then she exhaled. Ceramic light fixtures, mounted every six feet, generously illuminated every corner of the expansive cellar. With reassurance of sight, she began her inspection.

Her inner architect was soon astonished. Steel posts holding a framework of I-beams, interconnected with gusset plates, formed the mansion's skeletal superstructure. "Incredible," she whispered. This build technique would have been a radical innovation in the period the house was constructed. It became commonplace in commercial architecture over the ensuing decades, enabling the design of ever-taller buildings, some eventually reaching heights so high they would become popularly referred to by the new word "skyscraper." The steel beams appeared to be completely solid, showing little more than occasional surface rust.

Mortared hand-chiseled sandstone blocks, the likes of which belonged in a castle, formed the foundation walls. The floor was concrete, which also would have been unheard of in those days before ready-mix, when leaving a dirt surface was common practice.

Jessica studied the carpentry and the exposed infrastructure above her head. The oak floor joists were precisely cut, the extensive bracing tightly joined. "Nice work," she complimented the long-departed tradesmen.

She found remnants of knob and tube wiring, but noted the electrical lines had been replaced with modern wiring at some point, including the important ground wire.

Gleaming copper pipes showed the plumbing had been recently overhauled, with modern PVC installed as sewer lines.

A cast iron oil furnace anchored the corner, a beast so bulky and antiquated-looking Jessica envisioned it as an apparatus in Frankenstein's laboratory. As ancient as it was, Jessica knew older units were simple and well made, so they tend to hold up for eternity. A tag hung on the fuel line, confirming the system had been serviced just last month.

As she studied the furnace, something touched her back.

A scream formed, but froze within her throat, and her body went taut. Then, just as quickly as she felt it, the sensation was gone. She swiveled around, but nothing was there.

Before she could further contemplate exactly what she had felt, lightning flashed from the stairwell. A split second later, a bone-rattling thunder crack followed, then the lights dimmed and fizzled out.

With no windows in the cellar, blackness immersed Jessica, stranding her in its most distant corner. Her legs went watery, and in her blindness, she felt herself tottering. Certain she could hear her own heart thumping, she urged herself to keep it together.

She pulled out her cell phone and flipped it open, then held it with the screen facing the floor. The faint glow materialized little more than a silhouette of her feet on the concrete. She shuffled in the direction of the stairs, reaching a quivering hand out, feeling for anything she might bump into. *There was nothing there*, she reminded herself.

Then the backlight timed out. She groped around for a button, and when she found one, pushed it to reactivate the screen. As she crept toward the steps, dim light flowing from the top portion of the staircase became her beacon.

Footsteps scrabbled above, in the direction of the foyer. Jessica froze, and her mind snapped back to the apparition she'd seen in the window so long ago. *Or was it Bonnie?* The latter explanation comforted her, so she went with it. She felt for the banister and started climbing, the light increasing as she made her way toward the top.

"Bonnie?" Jessica tiptoed slowly, listening.

More footsteps, but no response.

Jessica arrived at the top of the stairs and held still, head cocked.

Silence.

She withdrew from the stairwell and turned into the hallway, dusky, but nothing like the pitched-black far reach of the cellar. "Bonnie?"

Just then she saw movement through the leaded glass window of the front door. But had the footsteps she'd heard been *outside* the house?

A figure leaned into the leaded glass window and peered through, and Bonnie was instantly recognizable from her photo in the real estate ads. When she spotted Jessica, her face lit up, and Jessica felt a surge of relief.

The handle turned, and the door swung open. "Mercy, what a storm!" Bonnie declared as she shook herself off. She collapsed her bright yellow umbrella and propped it against the brick beside Jessica's, then stepped in.

Jessica gathered her wits as she followed the corridor and crossed the entry hall, extending her arm to offer a handshake. "Nice to meet you. I'm Jessica."

"So nice to meet you, Jessica," Bonnie said a trifle too sweetly. Somehow the thunderstorm hadn't blemished her painted face or coifed hair, but the moisture seemed to have enhanced her perfume.

They shook hands, and the real estate agent held her grip. Another thunder report bellowed, but it was one of those slow rollers, off in the distance. The rain was slackening off too.

"Oh, you're wet," Bonnie said, looking over Jessica's clothes.

Jessica scoffed, then grinned. "Not as wet as I was half an hour ago."

"Well, I'm so sorry to keep you waiting." Bonnie finally released the extended handshake and looked around. "Quite a place, isn't it?" She panned across the foyer with genuine admiration.

Before Jessica had a chance to respond, Bonnie reached for the light switch and asked, "Can we turn some lights on?"

"The power went out."

"Oh, my…" Bonnie said, clicking the switches repeatedly, without effect. "After all this effort for us to get here? You really need to see this one-of-a-kind property to appreciate it."

"Actually, I took a pretty good look around before the lights went out." She felt ready to leave. "But let's plan on another showing when the power's back on."

Bonnie smiled over her frustration. "Shall we call it a *raincheck*?"

Jessica chuckled at the lame quip, and chose her words carefully, trying not to signal strong interest. "I'll have fresh eyes. I'd like to bring my father, too."

———◆○◆———

Jessica watched her dad, eagerly awaiting any indication of his reaction.

"Are you thinking of major renovations?" Marty Putnam looked up from the crude sketches he had been studying, peering at her over his reading glasses. Jessica had drawn out Harmon Manor's floor plan after her visit, to help her remember the layout of the rooms.

"The kitchen and bathrooms need a complete overhaul. Other than that, nothing major. If the home is as solid as I think it is, it would be a shame not to keep it original."

"I was thinking the same thing," Marty said. "Besides, with those sprawling rooms, it's not like you'd need to find ways to make the space more efficient."

"Jess, are you sure you can afford this?" Nancy Putnam asked from the opposite end of the couch from her husband. Arik, belly up between his grandparents, lifted his head off Nancy's lap and looked across the family room at Jessica like he had the same question.

"No worries, Mom. Heck, if I'd known how much Richard's parents had left him in their Trust, I'd have married him a lot sooner." She mustered a feeble smile.

Her tactless attempt at lightheartedness fell flat. Both her parents responded with an uncomfortable simper and left it at that.

They hadn't asked the question Jessica had expected to field: *why would you buy* this *house?* It's a good thing since she'd been interrogating herself with this stumper and hadn't yet hit upon a serviceable answer. She couldn't exactly say, "Good question…somehow, I feel *drawn* to it." Perhaps her parents were avoiding the question simply because they didn't want to disrupt her sprouting interest toward something—toward anything.

Jessica broke the awkward silence she'd induced. "Anyway, I'm pretty confident I'd make good money on it when I do sell."

"I'd say so, based on how aggressively they priced it," Marty said. "Remember, with your historic renovation experience, nobody's better equipped to take on that project than you are. Even a modest makeover on this house would be daunting for anyone else."

"Thanks, Dad." Jessica took the compliment, although she wished she were half as capable as her proud father assumed her to be. "But I won't be able to do it without your help. Are you game?"

"Of course," her father said. "It'll be so much fun working together on this." He smiled, swinging his head between Jessica and her mother.

Jessica's heart melted a little, and she returned the smile. She had half expected her parents to push back on this crazy notion, tell her all the reasons it didn't make sense. Not only had they not pushed back, but they even seemed to be excited about the idea—despite the home's history.

Although they didn't say so, Jessica suspected her parents believed restoring the mansion would be a good way for their daughter to stay occupied and avoid being smothered in her grief. Then again, perhaps that was simply what *she* thought, and she was projecting her logic onto them.

"When do you two want to see it? Bonnie said she's available this weekend."

"Take your dad to look. I'd just get in the way," her mother said, like she was acknowledging this was a father-daughter thing.

But Jessica saw through the ruse, and she felt the smile fade from her lips. Her dad's smile wilted, too. Her mom looked so tired when she spoke. While she hadn't lost her hair from the radiation (at least not yet), the treatments were taking a toll, and she looked increasingly fragile.

———◆◇◆———

"That place is built like a brick shithouse!" Marty Putnam announced to Jessica as they walked away from Harmon Manor, out of earshot of Bonnie, who was still inside turning off lights.

"It's like a fortress," Jessica agreed. "To be honest, Dad, I was half hoping you'd spot some deal-breaker flaw in the house."

Marty turned to take in the mansion one last time. "Why's that?"

"It would have made it easy to walk away." Jessica went to work removing the stake that fixed Arik's leash in the middle of the driveway turnaround.

Bonnie came out, and while she locked the door, called to them, "I have to ask…" She kept them waiting for her question until she stepped off the porch on her way to her car. "You keep your dog on such a short leash, like it was made for a dachshund. Don't you want to give him more room to move?"

"Can't do that with a greyhound," Marty answered. "This breed can launch from a dead stop to 45 miles per hour in just three steps. A short leash avoids the risk of him breaking his neck when he gives chase."

Impressed her father remembered the facts, Jessica felt glad she didn't have to explain them to yet another uninformed observer.

"Oh, that's a horrible thought," Bonnie said as she opened her car door. "I wish I hadn't asked!"

Jessica and Marty gave one another sideways glances, then climbed into Marty's work truck with Arik.

"Anyway, if there *is* a fatal flaw in the house, I missed it. The craftsmanship…" He shook his head in disbelief while starting the pickup. "I had high expectations based on what you'd told me, but they were exceeded."

"So, do you think it would be crazy to make an offer?"

"Hell yeah, it's crazy…" He paused and snickered. "It was crazy to build that house in the first place! But you only live once, right?"

Jessica nodded while she bit her lower lip. "That's what they say."

"Damn…can you imagine living in that mansion?" Marty said this aloud, but didn't seem to be asking her so much as pondering the concept himself.

"Who knows? Maybe someday you and Mom will move in with me."

"That would be cool, but you know how much your mother loves her house."

The unintendedly loaded comment hung in the cab like a noxious odor. Neither of them went there.

When the truck turned onto the roadway, Jessica took one last look at the house from a distance, and she caught herself eyeing the windows of the tower. There was nothing there, of course.

"One of my roofers does a lot of work with slate and copper," Marty said. "If you decide to make an offer, we'd want to have him do a thorough inspection."

"Definitely," Jessica said. "There's something else I'm toying with, though. You know, with that steel framework, I don't think any of the walls are load bearing."

"None of them?" Marty asked incredulously.

"I think they're all curtain walls. The superstructure carries the load."

"Wow. If that's true, you could move—or remove—any of them."

"Exactly. I think it would be awesome to combine the parlor and kitchen by removing the hallway in between. Make that one big main living area."

"Nice. Buyers want open rooms these days," Marty said. "I know a structural engineer who can verify your theory. Anything else you're thinking of?"

"A total gut of the kitchen and bathrooms."

"Makes sense. Even people who like old houses want those rooms to be modern."

"I'd want to add central air."

"I can get one of my HVAC guys out too...make sure that's an easy enough change."

"Eventually I'd want to add a garage," Jessica added, "but that can wait until next year. It would have to be detached. I wouldn't want to ruin the aesthetics of the house."

"It's surprising there isn't one," he said.

"There used to be. Bonnie told me the carriage house burned down a long time ago. I found the foundation stones hiding in the grass."

Their conversation trailed off for a few minutes while they made their way back toward Clarkton.

"Jess?" Marty eventually interrupted the quiet. "Are you worried about the history of the home?"

Arik popped up between them like he needed to hear the response.

She shook her head and stared at the passing countryside, turning away from Arik so his smelly tongue couldn't make contact with her cheek. "Nah, you know me. I like that sort of stuff."

Marty chuckled. "No kidding! I remember how many times you watched *Poltergeist*! But they've been saying Harmon Manor's haunted as long as I can remember."

"Well, remember what Mom says..." Jessica reached back and scratched Arik under his chin.

Marty nodded and smiled. "I'm more afraid of the living than I am of the dead."

CHAPTER 12

ACCESSION

J ESSICA WAS ALREADY PUNCHING the phone buttons before she had fully slipped out of the room.

It only took one ring before her childhood friend picked up, "Asphinctersayswhat?"

Jessica laughed, but didn't fall for it. "Never gets old, dude. But you're *not* going to believe what I just did..."

"I'm *intrigued*. Do tell."

"I...bought...Misery Mansion!"

Erin fell silent.

Jessica let the words sink in. She looked back at the title company's conference room. The geeky (and overdressed) lawyer representing the Harmon family and the closing agent were making small talk while gathering their paperwork. Bonnie stood near Jessica's mom and dad, all three hovering over the large sheets spread out over the table. After the signing, the lawyer presented Jessica with an oversized rigid folder containing the original blueprints of the mansion, as well as the design prints for the formal gardens that had once surrounded the mansion. Jessica couldn't wait to explore this unexpected goldmine.

"I'm not shitting you," she said, preempting Erin's imminent question.

"That...must've escalated quickly. I didn't even know you were house hunting."

"I'm sorry. I've been dying to tell you, but waited until it was official."

"So, you bought it...like...to live there?"

"Sure did. For a while, at least. And you're going to visit me?"

"Of course, I will," Erin said a bit too quickly, suggesting she didn't want Jessica to think she might have qualms about the concept. "I just can't believe it, Jess! Have you been planning this for a while?"

"No, not long. But my dad and I did our homework. We had a bunch of inspections done, and they checked out. I made an offer ten percent under the asking price, and they took it without even countering." She didn't specify, but she'd paid a mere $360,000 for the mansion, which included the 68 acres of land it sat on.

Jessica's mother shot her a questioning look from the conference room.

Jessica responded with the "one moment" index finger wag. Her parents had accompanied her to the roundtable closing not to offer any advice, but because this was such a momentous event, they couldn't possibly miss it.

"I'd better get going now. I can't wait to show you."

"I can't wait to see it!" Erin responded. "We'll be coming home for Thanksgiving—if I don't pop first."

"I'll have it ready for a tour by then."

"I'll be sure to knock three times!"

When she returned to the conference room, the blended mood of relief and elation was palpable. But Jessica's excitement was dampened by the longing she had for another life in which she and Richard might have been taking on a project like this together.

The next day, Arik accompanied Jessica to her new home, licking her ear throughout the drive.

It dawned on her that she wasn't sure what to call her newly acquired house. Since it no longer belonged to the Harmon family, should she still refer to it as Harmon Manor? Or was it better to keep the name as an homage to the family who built it 150 years earlier? *Except...* Who was she kidding? *It will always be known as Misery Mansion.*

She parked her Saab at the end of the driveway and staked Arik's dachshund-leash in the grassy center of the turnaround. Lying in the grass on a sunny day was always a special treat for him.

"Be a good boy, Arik." Jessica stroked his head before setting off for the house.

Arik had become a bit of a nuisance to her parents. They liked him well enough, but he had already made chew toys out of the fourth pair of her mother's shoes. To give her parents a break, until she could move in full-time, Jessica would make every effort to bring Arik along for as many errands as possible.

When she called the moving company that morning, they'd established a delivery date for her belongings (they'd been in long-term storage) six weeks out. She didn't expect to be sleeping in the house during the initial renovation, knowing what a mess the construction work would make.

At the foot of the porch steps, she paused to soak it all in. She regarded the mansion and the property surrounding it, finding it so hard to believe she now owned it.

Jessica turned to face Arik. Lying on his side in the grass, he looked her way, and his tail started flopping like a fish on the ground. Not wanting to give him false hope, she turned away to smile while rummaging in her jacket pocket for the keyring.

Her new set of house keys were already mounted on the old key chain Richard had made from the handle of an antique silver spoon. He had fabricated the decoration in ninth-grade metal shop class and had proudly carried it until the day he died. Jessica had considered it to be a bit tacky and had teased him about it. After Richard's death, she claimed it as her own.

She combed through the keys to find the newest member of the set while approaching the entrance. The lock box was gone, reinforcing the point that the house had been sold. Jessica finagled the sturdy bronze lock while marveling at the door, four feet wide, crafted from thick black walnut.

When the bolt released, she took a moment to run her fingers along the beveled glass leaded window in the door and nodded approvingly. She had learned in one of her first architecture classes how the entry of a building serves as the focal point and should have an appropriate level of attention dedicated to its design and construction. Clearly, the mansion's architect had applied this logic.

When she swung the door open, a bottle of red wine and a card sat on the floor just beyond the threshold. She picked up the envelope and pried it open with her thumb.

Welcome to your new home!
Sincerely, Bonnie

It was a nice gesture, but Jessica would need to re-gift the wine. She was proud of the strength she had shown by quitting drinking shortly after Richard's death, having seen how alcohol amplified rather than dulled her sorrow. Ironically, it was cigarette cravings that she struggled with most after his passing, despite having given up smoking seven years prior.

As she set the bottle and card aside on the stairs, Arik started barking. *That's weird*, Jessica thought. He was one of those very placid dogs that rarely barked, extreme even by the standard of the breed.

She stepped out onto the porch. Arik pulled against his leash toward the house, yapping at something in that direction. "Hush, Arik!" she commanded, but this yielded just a momentary pause. She headed his way. *What's he barking at?* she wondered, glancing over her shoulder and ducking her head for a better angle around the porch.

Suddenly, the unmistakable sensation of being watched enveloped Jessica, and her skin crawled when she realized the dog anchored his gaze above and behind her—in the direction of the belvedere. Time decelerated. When she began to twist her head around to look, her tightened neck tendons grated in protest. As she tilted her head back and lifted her eyes, the feeling of being watched snapped away. She scanned the windows and exhaled when she saw nothing—or no one—there.

Could have been a squirrel on the roof, she told herself. Greyhounds are sight hounds, capable of spotting a rabbit half a mile away. He could've seen something she missed.

After taking the measurements she needed inside the house, Jessica locked the front door and returned to Arik, who had remained quiet since his earlier barking episode. "Good boy," she told him, patting him on the side. "Want to go for a walk?"

Hearing this set Arik off in a frenzied dance while she detached his leash from the stake. Jessica led the way in the direction of the side yard, where, as a teenager, she had followed the pathway through the woods.

She felt excited about the work she planned. The kitchen area would undergo the biggest renovation, a complete gut and re-build. Her plans entailed joining the kitchen and parlor into one large open space, which would serve as the home's main living area. She was particularly tickled she'd been able to work out a way to keep the parlor's impressive barrel-vaulted ceiling in the integrated room. In addition, all the bathrooms would be stripped and rebuilt, and ducted HVAC would be added. The rest of the house would retain its original configuration and finish. Harmon Manor would be restored true to its historic splendor but appointed with select modern upgrades. She'd hold off on building a garage until the following year.

Jessica examined the terrain as they passed the mansion and considered how it had been landscaped in its prime. The elaborate gardens that had once been maintained had since been indiscriminately cleared, probably many decades ago. Now, nothing but poorly tended grass surrounded the home, mown with a tractor four times a year, by a neighboring farmer.

All that remained was a single overgrown arborvitae crowding the east side of the front veranda, stretching up almost as high as the roof. The evergreen obscured the front view of the house, detracting from the home's aesthetics—and even if it didn't, Jessica had adopted her dad's fierce disdain for this type of tree. *Devil bushes*, he called them. When left unchecked, they grow into structures, tearing up siding, gutters, and roof shingles. At least this one grew far enough from the house, so it didn't appear to have done any such damage. Regardless, this devil bush would be gone soon.

When she rounded the corner of the home, the pathway into the woods appeared. Arik took the lead and headed precisely in that direction, pulling Jessica along. As she neared the trailhead, an impulse overcame her; she stopped and looked over her shoulder...but the windows of the house were all vacant. A surreal feeling passed over her, and she blinked, fighting back an impending gush of tears. The pervasive, crushing longing for Richard swelled in her mind, somehow triggered by her sojourn into this location. She slipped her hand into her pocket, grasped the spoon-handle keychain, and went to work habitually burnishing the silver with her thumb.

So, this is where I'll spend the prime of my life—not in Boston with my soulmate, but alone at Misery Mansion. She weakly smiled to herself. *Fitting. Maybe someday I'll fall in love with an Amish man and I'll try to convince him to join me on the dark side.*

She swept aside her self-pity musings with a shake of her head. If Richard's death had taught her anything, it's that life is fleeting, so she should appreciate spending time with her aging parents—she was now so keenly aware the opportunity wouldn't always be there.

Arik tugged the leash, and they moved on, following the trail into the thicket until it ended at the old gardening access drive.

Jessica scanned the area she remembered vaguely from her adolescence. With summer fading, the vegetation surrounding her was languishing, relenting to the looming threat of winter. On the ground, stretches of gravel remained visible amongst the encroaching groundcover, a waning relic of the driveway that had once been located here a century ago. The patches traced tire track ruts, hinting at bygone days when the formal gardens behind the house were professionally tended.

Everything withers away. The gardens were nothing but a historical legend now. This driveway was a mere vestige of what once was, as was her own adolescent memory of this place, both dulling and receding. Richard had departed, and inevitably, she feared her remembrances of him would steadily slip away from the grasp of her consciousness. Eventually, all becomes lost to time.

Yet that spirit she had seen in the house...it *endures*.

A truck rumbled by out on the roadway, interrupting Jessica's introspection.

"C'mon, buddy," she said, setting off along the remnants of the driveway. They wandered deeper into the property, and when they arrived at a clearing, Jessica released Arik from his leash. He bolted out across the open grass stretching along the back flank of the plat.

Jessica strolled along the edge of the woods forming the border of her lot, switching her attention between Arik as he'd dash past, and the rear elevation of the mansion.

At the end of the field, she reached the western hem of her new lot, where she turned back to cross the grassy tract toward the house. Arik trotted up, panting, and she reattached the leash. "Had enough?"

He began to lead the way to the car, indicating that indeed, he had.

A few minutes later, they piled into the Saab. "I feel better now, don't you?"

Arik popped his head into the front seat and wagged his tail, slapping the seat in a steady rhythm as she turned the ignition.

Her eyes began to sting, but this time, Jessica permitted herself to cry. "For you, Richard," she whispered, and she smiled when Arik licked the tears from her cheek.

CHAPTER 13

REVIVAL

J ESSICA RAISED THE SLEDGEHAMMER over her head.

"Watch how she does it, boys," Marty Putnam said to the two men on his crew. "This kid's a master with sledgehammers and pry bars."

Jessica paused to chuckle. Her father had been declaring her "a master" at demolition since she'd worked on his crew during summers in high school and early college. It's true that Jessica loved the adrenaline surge that came with wreckage duty, and always found the act cathartic—removing something that needs to go, making room for something better.

She pulled back her arms, inhaling with the wind-up, then exhaled as she swung the hammer forward, crashing its head through the plaster of the hallway wall.

"Yay!" all three men cheered at the maiden smash.

The two members of Marty's crew immediately stepped forward with their own sledgehammers, and her solo act became a trio. After a few minutes she let the two laborers—one sporting a mullet, the other bearded—take over, and she withdrew to the kitchen to go over the prints with her dad.

"Hey, check it out!" one of the men called.

Jessica and her father wandered over to see what had him so excited. The bearded man, who had light brown hair on his head but a distinctly red beard, carried something out from the dust cloud, and all of them huddled up at the end of the hall.

"I think it's an old beer bottle." He held up a brown stoneware vessel. "I found it on the wall sill, buried behind the plasterwork."

The other crew member, who wore his prematurely graying hair in a shoulder-length mullet and always smelled like an ashtray, reached for it. "Too bad it's empty!" He grinned, exposing a missing lower tooth. "It's marked FOREST CITY BREWERY." He handed the ancient find back to Beard-man.

"It must have been from a brewery in Cleveland," Marty said. "They used to call Cleveland 'Forest City'."

"Some dude building the house probably drank it here, then buried the bottle inside the wall." Beard-man handed it to Jessica. "Might be worth something."

She took the vessel and ran her thumb over its clay finish, feeling the imprinted inscription. Having been protected from the elements inside the wall, the bottle appeared brand new.

She held it out to Beard-man. "Finders keepers, if you want it."

He shook his head and leaned away. "No way—I ain't taking the Misery Mansion curse home with me!"

Mullet responded with a phlegmy snicker.

Beard-man started to join him in laughter, but when he saw the scowl forming on Marty's face, he backtracked. "I'm just kidding. But it belongs here. It's yours."

Indeed, this was a Harmon Manor artifact that really should stay with the house, Jessica admitted to herself, relieved the laborer had declined her offer.

Later that evening, before locking up and leaving, she set the stoneware beer bottle on one of the bookshelves in the library, then stepped back to ponder it. Almost a hundred and fifty years ago, someone left this inside the wall. How ironic that this insignificant item was most likely all that remained of his life. As she turned away, Jessica reached into her pocket and drew out her keys. She walked toward the door, clasping Richard's keychain and rubbing her thumb against its smooth silver finish.

⸻◄◦►⸻

Two weeks later, Jessica barely recognized the kitchen. The crew was now gutting the last portion, salvaging the wonderful original cast iron sink and the stove, to be reused in her new design. Gone were the old cupboards and the walk-in pantry, soon to be replaced with handcrafted cherry wood cabinets made by a local Amish furniture maker. A new refrigerator, dishwasher, and microwave would be installed, as well as granite countertops. The main part of the kitchen floor would be marble tile, transitioning into salvaged walnut floorboards. The rear hallway was history, removed to combine the parlor and the kitchen into one large space, just as Jessica had envisioned.

In the meantime, plumbing and electrical subcontractors toiled in the bathrooms. The tradesmen initially refused to work at the same time as one another—each preferring to have free range of the worksite. However, Marty cajoled them into agreeing on a co-ordinated schedule so they could progress in parallel, allowing the project to be completed sooner.

Portions of the master bedroom and its bathroom sat directly above the kitchen. With the extensive plumbing work underway, Marty decided to open the ceiling, providing easier access for the rerouting of pipes. The large gaping hole into the master bath and bedroom was unsightly, but thankfully temporary, to be re-patched when the brand-new flooring above was installed.

"Jess, can you help me pull out the stove?" Marty asked.

"Gladly." Jessica was happy to extract herself from the tight squeeze under the sink, where she'd been struggling to disconnect corroded piping. She was ready to delegate this job to the plumber, anyway.

"This thing is solid as a rock," Marty said as he attempted to shimmy the appliance away from the wall.

"That's why I'm keeping it," Jessica said, taking her position beside him. "It's a classic Jenn-Air downdraft model. It was either never used, or barely used."

Once they had a gap between the stove and the wall, they were able to get a grip on the back, and the classic rock slid out with minimal effort. When the appliance cleared the cabinet, a poster flopped into the void.

"What's this?" Marty asked, reaching over to retrieve it. "Oh, man, Janis Joplin! Your mother was a huge Joplin fan."

Marty laid the psychedelic concert placard on the worktable and began brushing it off with a dust rag. The two laborers took a break from their upper cabinet removal duty, and all four gathered around the find.

"Where was it?" the worker with a red beard asked.

"Propped in that little gap between the stove and the cupboard," Jessica said. "There's no year...it just says, 'August 29'."

"I bet that hippy woman stuck it there," said the laborer with the mullet, and Jessica caught a whiff of his ashtray breath.

The comment dangled over them for a moment before Beard-man broke the silence. "Who?"

"Dude, the woman I told you about," Mullet said. "...went crazy...killed her son...then herself?" He turned his attention to Jessica and Marty, and went on to explain, "They never found her son's body. His bones are probably hiding in the walls."

"Right..." Marty shook his head. "Let's get back to work."

"I know what Mom's getting for her birthday," Jessica said, carefully lifting what she figured was probably a collectible poster. "Until then, I'll keep it in the library."

She laid the placard on the shelf below where she had recently placed the antique beer bottle. Jessica stepped back and stared at it without pause. A sweep of goose pimples ran down her arms. Who knew what dark secrets of Misery Mansion this newly discovered artifact might hold?

<hr>

The following week, the kitchen cabinets were delivered and installed, which, through a stroke of unlucky timing, turned out to be the same day the movers arrived with Jessica's belongings. It made for a chaotic scene, with the crews having to maneuver around one another, none of them pleased about the circumstances. Jessica's father tried to placate the cabinet installers while she worked on the movers. She played traffic cop in the front hallway for a couple of hours in the morning. Later, she drove out to Clarkton to load up on enough pizza and pop to feed everyone at lunch, which did wonders to ease the tension.

By mid-afternoon, the cabinetmakers were cleaning up and gathering their tools. The movers had finished and departed, and Marty headed to another jobsite to check on the progress of his laborers' demolition work.

Meanwhile, with Jessica unpacking in the library, a commotion came from the back of the house, voices raised in a heated discussion. She walked toward the kitchen where one worker—an Amish teenager, no more than fifteen—stood, leaning on a newly installed cupboard, pallid, and visibly shaking.

"I'm certain...I saw someone!" Rather than using his first language, Pennsylvania Dutch, Jess inferred the teenager wanted her to understand him, since he spoke in English.

Leon, the business owner, turned and looked at Jessica, as did the rest of the crew, like they were counting on her to referee.

"My grandson Jonas insists he saw someone in here," Leon said to Jessica as though she might be able to explain.

"Standing right there," Jonas said, pointing his quivering finger at the corner of the kitchen. "Looking up into the bedroom, through the hole." He then pointed at the opening above, into the master bedroom and its adjoining bathroom, which hadn't yet been dry-walled because the plumbing wasn't finished.

Their driver went back to picking up the worksite, like he figured it was better to let the others sort out what had or had not happened. He was English, which is what the Amish call *everyone* who isn't Amish, hired specifically for transporting them around (obviously Leon belonged to one of the more liberal Amish churches which allowed business owners to hire an English driver, a loophole circumventing the Amish rules against driving).

At a loss for words, Jessica glanced up into what would soon become her bedroom, beyond the floor joists and the newly installed plumbing. "You sure?"

"Yes ma'am," Jonas answered, leaning forward, his eyebrows raised.

"A woman?" Jessica asked.

Jonas began opening his mouth.

"...long, blond hair?" Jessica added.

"No, ma'am." His eyebrows dropped, and he cocked his head. "It was a boy."

A boy? Jessica considered this but came up with nothing.

"I went out on the porch to go...." His head slumped and his gaze drifted down to the floor for a moment. "...for a break. When I looked in the window, I saw the boy."

Jessica's mind did a double take and got hung up on Jonas seemingly having peed out back rather than using the bathroom at the end of the back hallway, as Marty had instructed them to do. She started to wonder if other workers were doing the same thing, but decided now was not the time to dwell on this irritating facet of the conversation.

"When I came back in, he was gone," Jonas said, his gaze reeled back off the floor, eyebrows arched high once again.

Jessica looked at Leon and then at Jonas's father, but they both shrugged.

"Well," she said, replying with her own shrug. "I don't have a boy living here."

"Could be one of the ghosts," said the driver, matter-of-factly. "They say this place is crawling with them."

"Well, that could be it, Jonas," Leon said, shrugging one more time. "Maybe you saw a ghost." He then went back to collecting tools, which let everyone know they'd wasted enough time already and it was time to drop the matter.

Jonas sighed and shook his head, and the crew went back to their clean-up duties.

Jessica returned to the library, where she absently unboxed electronic equipment while contemplating what had transpired. She was holding up the DVD player, examining the connection points on the back when the driver stopped in the foyer. "Hey, sorry about that comment."

"Sorry? No need." Jessica gave a dismissive wave.

"I know they say this is a haunted house, but *I* didn't see a boy," he assured her. "And I was *right there*."

"Well, I don't know anything about a boy ghost," Jessica said, wondering if he'd think it odd that she'd specified the gender.

"Maybe just being here spooked Jonas," he suggested with the "who knows?" open-upward-palms gesture. "The Amish are superstitious people. Sometimes their imagination goes wild."

"Yeah. Could be that," Jessica said. "But let me ask…you said this place is 'crawling with ghosts'…"

"Well, that's what they claim," he said, like he already knew what she was going to ask. "I don't have any first-hand knowledge or anything. Just heard the stories, you know?"

Jessica nodded slowly.

The driver turned, hesitated, then headed back to the kitchen.

Within minutes, the crew had loaded themselves into the box truck. With room for only four tightly squeezed in the cab, Jonas climbed into the back and sat in a corner. *That can't be safe*, Jessica thought, monitoring them through the library window.

She watched the truck off, then went back into the kitchen and stared at the hole in the ceiling.

CHAPTER 14

HABITATION

WITHIN A WEEK, JESSICA approached a milestone event: she would spend her first night in Harmon Manor.

By this point, it was mid-October. The fall colors were peaking, the days shortening, and the nights were chilly. She made her bed with flannel sheets and the winter comforter, holding back the electric blanket in her arsenal until after Thanksgiving when frigid weather *really* arrived.

Marty had loaned her electric heaters until the new HVAC was operational. She set one up at the foot of her bed, turned on with the fan running continuously so it wouldn't disturb her by cycling off and on. The hum of the fan created low-level white noise, lulling Jessica into slumber.

But her sleep was soon interrupted by a vague awareness of something strange. As she clawed her way back to wakefulness, she gradually began to realize she heard music.

She bolted upright. Her hazy mind fumbled for a few panicked breaths, then settled on the memory of that long-ago Halloween night when she heard a Victrola playing inside the house. Indeed, this sounded much the same: the scratchy tune playing on an antique gramophone, the notes inexplicably floating in the air, barely audible beyond the humming space heater. Jessica immediately became that same frightened teenager.

Straining to clear her head, she glared across the room. Plastic hung from the ceiling at the passageway into the construction zone of the master bathroom, serving as a meager barrier against the dust and cold. Was the music coming up through the hole in the floor beyond? She couldn't tell, but something about that corner of the room and the underworld beneath it made her want to look away.

She pushed the blankets aside. The tags on Arik's dog collar jingled as he stirred. He lifted his head from his bed on the floor and looked up inquisitively, ears perked. *Does he hear it too?*

Jessica crawled over the mattress, reached down, and switched off the heater. She crept back to her pillow and wormed her way under the bedcovers. As the fan spun down to a stop, so did the tune. An unsettling hush doused her surroundings, leaving her pounding heartbeat the only sound that lingered.

Her body tensed up while her brain crunched away, working to make meaning of the situation. Had she really heard music? Perhaps in her slumber something had poked at that hibernating memory, awakening it, dredging it up from the depths of her head, warping it into a fresh pseudo-experience.

Except...what if she hadn't imagined it? *Should I look around downstairs?* She recoiled at this notion, and lay still, searching for justification to stay put.

Then there was that hole in the bathroom floor. She felt like she should peek around the plastic barrier, down the chasm, into the kitchen. But this idea horrified her. As long as it remained quiet, she told herself, she could stay in her bed. She patted the mattress, and

Arik promptly jumped up from his bed, then flumped down and curled up beside her. "Don't get used to it," she told him.

Blessedly, the night remained still. Her body eventually slackened, and a feeling of composure gradually took root. Arik laid his head down, and a few moments later, closed his eyes. Jessica felt reassured the dog wasn't perturbed by sounds. She followed Arik's lead and closed her eyes too, consciously striving to relax. She attempted to think about the renovation work as a way of blocking the questions swirling in her head.

But alone with her thoughts, her mind kept reverting to what she surmised was a Victrola playing. For the first time, Jessica Putnam started to wonder if she could handle what she'd gotten herself into.

The disturbing essence of Misery Mansion went fallow with the arrival of daylight. The new day fostered in Jessica a flush of determination to discover the truth of the house. She called Erin before anyone arrived—Erin had always been an early riser.

"Jess, I'm going to be frank…" Erin answered.

Jessica didn't miss a beat. "Okay, can I still be Jess?"

The women laughed in unison. Jessica leaned out from the corner of the porch, seeking to catch the strongest possible cell signal. She'd given up on getting her cell phone to work inside the house, and she figured out that none of the other service providers fared any better.

"This is *definitely* a haunted house, Frank," Jessica said in a serious tone. The crisp air numbed her throat and lungs, and she tightened her winter coat around herself. Arik sprinted by, lost in some chimerical race.

"I thought we already knew that," Erin responded.

"True enough," Jessica said. "I did see Halloween Ghost Lady with my own two eyes."

Erin had coined the name "Halloween Ghost Lady" for the apparition. Jessica never liked it, because it sounded like Erin might have created it in jest. Anyhow, the name stuck.

Jessica told Erin about the unexplainable incidents at the mansion. First, feeling what she thought might have been a hand on her back while in the cellar. Then, Arik barking at something in the house (something he saw in the upper floor windows?). Next, the Amish teen who claimed he saw a boy in the kitchen. And now, a phantom Victrola playing in the middle of the night.

Erin responded with an occasional "uh-huh" or "hmmm," just to make it clear she was still listening.

When Jessica finally finished, Erin asked, "But no sign of Halloween Ghost Lady?"

"Not directly, at least. Who knows if she has something to do with these other things?"

"Are you worried?" Erin asked.

"That might be the oddest part," Jessica said. "Not really. I mean, none of this seems very threatening, does it?"

"Plus, you like creepy things," Erin added. "The creep factor was part of the home's allure, right?"

Jessica chuckled and took it as a compliment. "Guilty as charged. I guess I don't mind having ghosts around. How many people can say they live in a haunted house? But if there *is* a presence here, I wish it would just come out and show itself."

"Careful. You might regret saying that."

A black pickup truck appeared on the roadway.

"I need to let you go, Frank. My dad's almost here. I'm not telling my parents about this stuff. They'd just worry themselves sick."

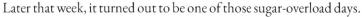

Later that week, it turned out to be one of those sugar-overload days.

Jessica had taken her mom in for her final scheduled chemo treatment. Nancy Putnam was gaunt and now wearing a wig, but otherwise holding up okay, considering what her body had been subjected to. Consuming calories—even sweets—was good, so after the concluding treatment, mother and daughter celebrated with a stop at the donut shop. They would have to wait another week for the oncologist's appointment when they would find out where things stood, but at least they could hope she was done with chemo.

After dropping her mom off at home, Jessica followed the *really* back roads and discovered a Mennonite family's apple farm. The family pressed their own cider, which tasted exceptional. They'd explained how they used only the sweetest apples and didn't taint the blend with bitter-tasting preservatives, or subject it to the pasteurization process. She also bought homemade sweetbread for a second celebration of the day, this time in honor of being able to watch her favorite show, in her new home.

Jessica turned on the TV and nestled onto the couch with a slice of pumpkin bread and a glass of apple cider. She was in the library, her temporary main living room, since the construction in the back part of the house was not yet completed.

Cable service had been established over the past two days, which involved pulling coax more than a mile to reach the mansion's remote location. It had appalled Jessica to learn it would cost over eight hundred dollars for the installation, yet she had little choice but to proceed with the order. These days, internet connectivity was a necessity, as was cable phone service, when your cell phone won't work inside the house. And of course, so was *CSI: Crime Scene Investigation.*

Richard had bought a state-of-the-art 32-inch flat-screen plasma television just a couple of months before he passed away. Jessica made sure to set it up by Thursday, in time for her show.

The *CSI* episode was "Feeling the Heat," about a multitude of corpses that turn up in Las Vegas, ostensibly related to a week-long heat wave. She was already used to watching alone, as Richard had never shared his wife's appreciation for the program. The graphic images that the series was notorious for didn't bother her, but Richard was more squeamish. Jessica winced, recalling how she had vaguely resented his jokes about her passion for the show. Now she'd give anything for Richard's teasing.

She unfolded the blanket on the back of the couch and spread it over her legs. The heating and cooling contractor promised the new central heating system would be running by winter, but the days were getting nippier, and the space heaters in the library and foyer barely managed to keep the chill out.

Arik clambered up and wandered into the front entry hall. He turned back and gave Jessica the earnest "you know what I need" look.

"Just a minute, buddy," she told him. "We'll have a commercial soon."

As if the dog understood, he sat in the foyer and waited.

———— ◆◯◆ ————

Arik scampered off into the darkness as soon as Jessica opened the front door. She bundled the blanket above her shoulders and wrapped it over her arms, then ventured out into the autumn night.

The sole light above her didn't illuminate much beyond the front porch. She moved to the steps, descended, and followed the walkway in near blindness, feeling her way with her feet to its end at the driveway. She shivered while she waited, billowing clouds of vapor with every breath.

"C'mon, buddy," she called to Arik. His collar jingled in response, somewhere in the distance. She heard him darting across the lawn, then his shadow flashed by. *Better let him burn off some energy*, she reasoned, and gave him another minute, allowing the dog to run back and forth a couple of times.

"Arik, let's go in," Jessica called as the bitterly cold air pierced through to her core.

The dog obediently appeared from the darkness, panting, tail wagging. "Good boy," she said and patted him. As she turned toward the house, Arik let out a growl. Jessica followed the line of his eyes, and when she glanced at the front door, a jolt clobbered her. She froze, then blinked, like doing so might clear her vision and set it straight. But when she reopened her eyes, the staggering sight remained. A small figure stood on the other side of the leaded glass window, a pair of eyes staring through a narrow pane of beveled glass. Her gaze met the stranger's gaze for a moment before the shadow pulled away from the door and dissolved from view.

Jessica's jaw hung open. She was not only unsure of what to do, but unable to even bring herself to move.

First, she questioned if she had seen what she thought she had. But it was Arik who first tipped her off, right? Jessica flashed back to the Amish teenager who had insisted he had seen a boy in the kitchen, and her doubts abated swiftly. *I guess he was right,* she thought, nodding with astonishment.

Next, she asked herself if she should go inside or stay outside. Then, the absurdity of this question struck her. She felt strangely violated, standing *outside* her own home, with someone—something—*inside*, and suddenly her fight-or-flight response swung from the latter to the former. Without further delay, she sprang into action, scurrying toward the door, Arik trotting alongside.

Inside the entry hall, she found it empty. She flipped on the lights in the front hallway and foyer…also empty. The library, the length of the hall toward the back of the house, and the balustrade gallery over the foyer were all deserted.

"Hello?" she called. "I saw you! Where are you?"

Arik stood still, leaning against her leg. Jessica felt his body tremble. The cold forgotten, she pulled the blanket off her shoulders and dropped it in a bundle on the floor.

"See anyone?" She whispered the question, but Arik simply pressed harder, his head twitching with agitation as he sniffed at tendrils of air.

After pushing the front door closed, Jessica turned the deadbolt and cocked her head. The TV murmured to one side, while the nearby space heater hummed nearly inaudibly on the other. With nothing covering the tall window next to the front door, she grew keenly aware she was like a fish in a fishbowl to anyone who might be outside. She made a mental note to install sheers the next day.

At the end of the front hallway, a plastic sheet hung from the ceiling, serving as a barrier to reduce the migration of construction dust into other parts of the house. It would be impossible to see anyone—anything—that might have slipped beyond the curtain.

"Sorry, buddy, we've got to look around."

She stepped forward, tiptoeing down the hallway with Arik ambling reluctantly beside her. She turned on the lights in the dining room, where she saw nothing unusual. The cellar stairway was next. It, too, was clear.

Jessica continued down the corridor, stopping at the plastic sheet hanging between the front and rear hallways. There were no lights on beyond, and as bad luck would have it, the switches were on the dark side of the barrier. She stood within arm's length of the shroud and hesitated. Arik nestled his quaking torso against her thigh. An unnatural quietude had settled into the house, as if it was merely feigning stillness, and Jessica's curiosity gave way to fear.

She took a long, slow breath, then held it while reaching out for the plastic. In one quick movement, she pushed it aside with one hand, and with the other, groped for the light switches, toggling them on when she found them.

Jessica scanned the large open room but spotted no boy. She exhaled and a faint vapor ghost formed around her breath, then quickly dispersed, the air extra chilly behind the plastic.

She wriggled past the curtain. The smell of sawdust and drywall mud permeated the area. Arik squeezed through the gap, following Jessica as she moved toward the back entry. She found the door deadbolted, as she had left it. When she turned on the rear exterior lights, she saw nothing in the vicinity.

Jessica returned to the kitchen and glanced at where the hole in the ceiling had been, now cloaked with fresh drywall. Rummaging through the tools, she found a flashlight. She also grabbed a claw hammer, figuring the possibility of a human intruder couldn't be ruled out. "Doubt this will do me much good," she told Arik, "but just in case."

Forcing herself to look through the rest of the house, she started with the bathroom at the end of the rear hallway, then the cellar, and finally, the bedroom level. She scanned each room with the flashlight, but there was no sign of anyone. Arik tagged along in close proximity. Whether he was protecting her or unwilling to be alone, Jessica couldn't be certain.

She held up in the bedroom wing, knowing full well she hadn't checked the upper levels. *Do I really need to?* She tried but couldn't come up with a good reason not to look there as well. While she loathed the idea of venturing up into those isolated rooms, with nothing in them, they would be easy enough to search quickly. *It will only take a minute,* she assured herself.

Opening the door to the attic stairs, she turned the lights on while a wave of cold air poured from above, adding to the uninviting aura of the floors aloft.

Arik lingered as she stepped into the stairway, letting her know he shared her lack of interest in attending this part of the tour. "C'mon, buddy," she whispered. As she began to scale the stairs, her feet felt heavy, anchored by trepidation. Arik followed reluctantly, his nails clicking on the soft, unfinished maple wood of the steps, his pace closer to that of a turtle than the fastest breed of dog.

It was a very long ascent to the next floor. At the end of the second flight, where the stairs opened into the attic, the darkness seemed to tarry. Jessica flicked on the switch and immediately felt better with the advent of light. Her eyes darted about the room, dusty, but empty.

The two of them moved to the mouth of the final flight of stairs, those leading up to the last remaining place in the house: the belvedere. The hatch door at the top was propped open, creating a gaping hole into solid blackness. Blackness, preparing to pounce.

She pushed onward, feeling that if she didn't begin climbing right away, she might never start at all. Arik trailed behind, plodding up one step at a time, whimpering in protest along the way. Jessica gripped the hammer tightly in one hand, the flashlight in the other. The beam from the flashlight quivered. She commanded her hand to be still, hoping to broadcast calm through the rest of her body.

When her head cleared the floor level, she swept the light shaft across the room, carving the inkiness up there apart. The railing around the opening cast long, shifting shadows as the rays passed over.

Two steps later, she toggled the light switch, then scanned the illuminated room once again, using the flashlight like a pointing device. The beam danced haphazardly around the alcove as it reflected off the windows, confounding Arik.

But there was nothing there.

<hr />

Jessica couldn't decide whether to be relieved or dismayed. Regardless, she called off the search and settled back on the couch.

It was too late to phone Erin, so she tried to watch the tail end of *CSI*, but barely absorbed any of it. After it ended, she went upstairs for the night, placing the hammer and flashlight on the nightstand.

Arik began snoring, but Jessica could not subdue the thoughts fermenting in her head. She tossed around, unable to find a relaxing position.

Perhaps it was the loneliness of the night, but the more she thought about it, the more convinced she became: the boy *had* to be a ghost. Jonas, the Amish teenager, described how the boy he'd seen simply vanished, and tonight, the boy she'd seen dissipated just the same. Who was he? What was his connection with Halloween Ghost Lady? Is *she* still here? Could there be other ghosts here?

Ironically, Jessica didn't feel particularly frightened by the idea she'd seen the specter of a boy. Bewildered? Yes. Troubled? Of course. But not exactly frightened. The ghost of a child didn't feel so menacing. Ghosts of children make you feel...sad...not scared, right?

Considering the prospect of phantoms in the house, Jessica wondered if Richard could be one of them.

For the first time, she questioned whether this might have been a subconscious motivation behind her decision to buy a house widely believed to be haunted. *This would be the perfect house for Richard to haunt*, Jessica concluded as she eventually slipped toward sleep, finding a sliver of solace in the notion.

CHAPTER 15

TEMPEST

THE NEXT DAY A supercell thunderstorm hit Homer County.

While Marty and his crew were working elsewhere, the countertops were being placed in the kitchen and bathrooms of Harmon Manor. The granite installers arrived early, and the job was half finished by the time the tempest broke.

Jessica monitored the sky through the library's windows. It had already darkened forebodingly, and now the wind, which had started as a remote roar off in the distance, kicked up savagely, whipping fallen leaves past the house. Distant thunder rumbled, causing Arik to skitter off and cower down in the cellar, where the cannon-like sounds were more muffled.

When they were living in Boston, Arik would always retreat to the guest room bathroom, jumping into the tub, where he would take shelter until the storm passed. Richard would say, "Arik's taking a bath."

The wind gusted while rain and hail took turns pelting the house. Jessica's anxiety mushroomed as the storm mounted in intensity. Then, after one especially close lightning strike, the house lost power. *Not again!* As she made her way back to the kitchen, she wondered if she should invest in a generator.

The supervisor declared they couldn't work without light, and the crew sat idle, waiting to see if the power would be restored. Jessica offered her flashlight, but the men laughed, knowing it wasn't going to make enough difference. Fifteen minutes later, the supervisor gave up. They would return the next day—assuming the power was back on by then.

The two other installers were delighted about the shortening of their workday. As they walked down the hallway to leave, Jessica overheard one of them say, "I survived Misery Mansion." The other snorted through his nose.

The supervisor tailed them to the truck, and Jessica watched as they drove off through the ferocious storm.

Arik whined from the cellar. "It's okay, buddy!" Jessica called to him. She headed his way to offer the comfort of her presence, understanding from almost three years of living with him it would do little good.

After retrieving the flashlight from the kitchen, she descended the cellar stairway. Arik stood, quaking, about ten feet from the bottom of the stairs.

"Poor baby."

Consternation bloomed in his eyes; his ears pinned back to his head.

Jessica gave him long, soothing strokes with her free hand. "Buddy, it's just thunder."

Not a moment later, something touched her back. She stiffened in response, jerking away from Arik. What felt like a blood bubble dislodged from her chest and gurgled upward into her throat, where it stuck. Her mind swerved to the memory of feeling a touch—the same way, also in the cellar—a couple of months prior.

Then, in rapid succession, a sizzling noise arose, along with rustling seeming to come from all directions, but outside the house. A faint hiss followed, and static lifted her hair while a couple of clicks sounded. An explosive *CRACK* rang out, coinciding with a surge of brilliant light that lit up the entire cellar from the sole entrance point at the top of the stairs.

For just a wink of time, a solid bloom of purpleness engulfed Jessica, while a stifling hush smothered her. Then her senses flashed back to normal.

The entire house shook and rattled. She flinched, and the flashlight slipped from her grasp, its spinning beam sweeping across a stretch of the floor until it clattered on the concrete, extinguished.

The flashlight rolled to its resting place, somewhere in the darkness, and blackness immersed Jessica. Her ears rang and her eyeballs throbbed in their sockets.

She realized with dread that something still pressed against her. She peeled away and straightened up to collect herself while echoes of rumbles and booms steadily diminished.

"Lightning."

Jessica jumped at the utterance. She almost cried out, but her throat clenched her voice.

She turned, trying to adapt her eyes to the darkness. Soon, a small figure took shape, within arm's reach. She gasped and shrank back.

"The house was struck by lightning."

Jessica recognized a child's voice, holding a tone of reassurance.

She edged deeper into the cellar. "What...what are you doing here?" she stuttered, hardly recognizing her own embrittled voice.

"This is where I live."

"You...live here?" She felt like she coughed the words out.

"Yeah...sort of," the kid responded, but strangely, left it at that.

Positioned between her and the steps, the child blocked her exit. The idea of fleeing was absurd anyway, as she had little confidence her jellying legs would cooperate.

With her eyes beginning to acclimate to the darkness, she could now see it was a boy. He had straight longish hair, parted on the side, and wore a simple striped shirt.

"I'm not going to hurt you," he said.

"Can I leave?" She heard how stupefied she sounded, but couldn't help it.

"Well...we can go upstairs," he offered like this meant something.

Then it hit Jessica: Arik was gone. "Where's my dog?"

"He's not with us," the boy said, "but he's okay."

He's not with us. Jessica turned the words over, trying to understand their meaning.

The boy swung around and started toward the stairs. He moved as silently as a spider.

Rather than stay in the dark cellar alone, she drew forward and felt like she walked on a layer of air just above the surface of the floor. She tried to ignore the unsettling sensation as she fell in behind the boy.

As she ascended the steps, it dawned on Jessica the sound of rainfall had ceased. It was as though the lightning strike had shut off the downpour.

There was also bright light in the hallway at the top of the stairs–not electric light, but daylight. Jessica stepped into the hallway beside the boy, aghast. Sunlight radiated through the windows of the surrounding rooms. Wool carpet runners covered the floors, and there was no dust, none of the odors associated with construction.

The plastic blocking the end of the hallway was gone, providing an unobstructed view of a furnished kitchen. The hallway wall she'd removed was back. Diagonally opposite the cellar doorway, a table and chairs filled the dining room. Jackets, hats, and umbrellas hung on a showy hall tree in the foyer. Handsome-looking curtains or sheers adorned each of the windows.

Jessica swooned, but she fought the woozy sensation off. Desperate to escape the house, she slipped past the boy and bee-lined toward the entrance hall, disregarding the strange feeling of walking on air with muted footsteps.

She reached for the door handle and her hand melted right through it. She tried her other hand, with the same result, like it was merely a mirage.

Jessica leaned her face into the door's leaded glass window. Her car was not outside. She vanquished the urge to shriek, certain that doing so would give voice to the panic she struggled to suppress.

Formal and well-tended gardens lined the porch, walkway, and driveway, which was gravel rather than asphalt. A large carriage house stood between the mansion and the road, connected off the side of the drive, in the very spot where she had found the old foundation stones.

She opened her mouth and turned to the boy. He nodded, acknowledging her bewilderment, but didn't address it.

If she couldn't touch the door, did that mean the door wasn't really there? If not, she could simply step out—walk *through* the doorway. She spun back to the door and tried but couldn't pass through it. It wasn't as though she bumped into the door, but rather like she was being held from behind. She tried again, pushing even harder, but the counteracting force holding her back strengthened.

Jessica pivoted around, choking up, as hysteria overtook her.

The boy waited until she stopped and their eyes met. "That's the weirdest part...we're stuck."

PART FOUR

DENNIS - 1969

CHAPTER 16

RELOCATION

Patricia Harmon woke up to the smell of an out-of-place odor.

She rolled over and reached for her watch on the bedside table: 6:40 a.m. But she hadn't changed the time yet, so that was Chicago time. *Earlier or later?* She had to think about it, but then she nodded. *It's 7:40 here in Ohio.*

It took her another moment to pinpoint the odor. Pot smoke?

She looked over at her open windows. The smoke *must* be wafting in from outside, right?

Patricia swung her legs out of bed, slid into her slippers, and shrugged her bathrobe over her pajamas. After descending the stairway in the grand entrance hall of Harmon Manor, she peeked through the leaded glass window of the front door. A gray van was parked in the driveway, with *Richardson Electric* painted on the side, and while the rear doors were wide open, there was nobody in sight.

She walked to the back of the house and looked out the kitchen window. On the rear veranda, a long-haired man leaned against one of the porch columns with his back toward her. A thin wisp of smoke drifted from his hand, a joint pinched between his thumb and index finger.

Patricia went around to the rear entry hall, unlocked the deadbolt, and pulled open the door. The morning warmth flowed over her face.

Startled, the man turned around and looked her way, hiding the contraband behind his cupped hand, at his hip. *Ooh,* she thought. *A hunk!* Looking impossibly cool—like he walked off the cover of a record album—he appeared to be in his mid-twenties, about the same age as her. He wore his light brown hair parted in the middle, tucked behind his ears, flaunting extended sideburns...but thankfully, no other facial hair. Patricia saw no reason for a mustache or a beard on a man this good-looking. *Why cover it up?*

Smoke wafted up his side and into his face, prompting him to give up his lame concealment attempt. "Sorry," he said, eyeing what was left of the joint. "Just killing a few minutes waiting for eight o'clock to arrive." He looked up with glassy eyes and smiled at her.

"It's groovy," Patricia said, becoming self-conscious for not having dressed before coming downstairs. She started straightening her hair with her fingers.

"I'm Keith Richardson," he said, giving a dramatic bow. He straightened, sticking up his pointer finger for emphasis. "Not Keith Richards's *son*. Keith *Richardson*." He smiled slyly, making it clear this was a well-rehearsed way of introducing himself.

Patricia felt herself beaming in response to his corny charm. "I'm Patricia. Patricia Harmon."

"Pleased to meet you, Patricia. Want a hit?" He took a drag on the joint.

She scoffed. "I quit all that two years ago."

"That's cool," he said, exhaling the smoke. "Do you prefer I not light up?"

Patricia hesitated. She'd be better off without the temptation around, but she was disinclined to say so. "No...mellow-out, man." She paused for a spell. "You're the electrician?"

Keith nodded as he took another toke, which he held in while stubbing the roach on the heel of his work boot. He then released a steady billowing exhale, forming a perfect cone of smoke, in the direction of the lawn. "It's my father's business. But this hairy project is all mine. I've got to totally rewire this huge house."

Patricia nodded like she cared what he was saying, but mostly she just gaped at him.

"It has ancient knob and tube wiring, probably added around the turn of the century. But it all needs to be replaced. It's a monster of a job."

Patricia continued to smile and watch.

"I'm three weeks in, and my dad only budgeted for eight. I'm going to need ten...or more." Keith suddenly shut up, like he had caught himself rambling. He looked around at the porch. "This place is unreal, man."

"Yeah, it's a trip alright," Patricia said, and she too made a show of looking around.

"The workmanship...it's *so* far out."

"It's been in my family for six generations. But nobody's lived here for almost forty years. My parents are fixing it up to retire here."

Keith nodded. "So, you moved in over the weekend?"

"Yeah—came in from Chicago Saturday night. My father and brothers drove a moving van. They split yesterday."

"And you're staying in this huge pad all by yourself?"

"Dennis is with me."

Keith's face lit up with confusion, which Patricia figured he would have hidden better if it hadn't been for that joint.

"He's my son."

His look of confusion shifted to surprise.

Patricia was used to this reaction. "He's ten. I had him when I was young. I've always been a single mom."

She didn't mention how her deeply Catholic parents had almost disowned her for becoming pregnant when she was fifteen years old. Her older boyfriend hadn't split the scene *because* she was pregnant...he was gone well before she even found out.

By the time Dennis was a toddler, she was consistently shirking the motherly duties she had never wanted in the first place, and her son was mostly being raised by his grandparents while she snuck off to party.

But she had been out of rehab and clean for two years now, making every effort to dedicate her time and attention to the son she'd neglected.

"He's still asleep, for some reason. Might be the time difference."

"And you're living in this mansion all by yourselves." Keith's eyes turned up and scanned the back of the house, as though he was trying to absorb the idea.

Patricia shook her head. "Just for the summer, while Dennis is out of school. My dad wanted someone here to help oversee the work."

Her parents had started to trust her, and reasoned her living independently would be the next step in her recovery. For Patricia, putting some distance between herself and her family was a welcome change. She had convinced herself she was ready for this freedom, even if a small part of her wasn't so sure.

"Bummer," Keith said, staring at his watch. "Eight o'clock. Better get to work."

"Peace." She flashed up two fingers.

"Right on, man." Keith held up his own deuce and smiled.

Patricia reluctantly pulled herself away.

Patricia cracked her son's door open. That radiant sunlight of early June streamed in through the uncovered windows, crowding his sparsely furnished bedroom with a sparkling swirl of dust motes. "Honey, are you awake?"

Dennis stirred and rolled over, blinking. "Hi."

"You sure slept in late! Did you rest well in our new pad?"

"Yeah..." The boy paused. "But who was playing music?"

Patricia pushed open the door and shot him a confused look. "Music?"

"Yeah." He sat up in bed. "Old music. Downstairs." He rubbed his eyes.

Patricia wandered in and sat on the edge of his bed. "I didn't hear music, honey. Maybe you were dreaming."

"I *wasn't* dreaming," he said, then studied her for a moment. "You're all decked out?"

Patricia shook her head. "No. No...I'm not decked out." But she felt her cheeks getting warm, so she stood and turned away.

Her son had called her out, though—the reality was she *had* done some grooming. She needed to make sure Keith knew what a fox she was.

"C'mon down and let's get breakfast. You can meet the electrician."

———◆○◆———

"Want a pop?" Patricia held out a bottle of grape-ish-flavored O-So, the glass clouded by condensation.

Keith peered down from the ladder set up in the cellar.

"*That* would be groovy," he responded, licking his lips. "Cotton-mouth sucks."

He ducked his head to stay clear of the floor joists and wiped the sweat from his brow. It was an especially hot day, and even the cellar was warming up.

She stepped forward as he dismounted the ladder.

"Wow!" He waggled his eyebrows.

Patricia gave a proud smile in return. They held each other's gazes while he took the bottle of pop.

"You're welcome to come upstairs if you want a break."

"Sure. Thanks. I need to grab some more wire from my van anyway." Keith's glassy eyes wandered downward, hovering in line with her chest, then crept southward from there.

He could at least be subtle about it, Patricia considered, even though she'd made a point of putting on these particular curve-hugging jeans for a reason. He was probably still high anyway, so what could she expect?

"My son's up now," she said after a moment of awkward silence and turned to head upstairs.

"Cool." He said it cheerily, like he knew he had to say *something*, but this was the best he could come up with. Without another word, he followed her.

The boy, sitting at the kitchen table, stopped eating his cornflakes and wiped his mouth with the back of his hand when she introduced them. "Dennis, meet Keith. Keith, meet Dennis."

"Give me some skin," Keith said, holding out his hand to Dennis.

Dennis rose and vigorously shook the electrician's hand. "How do you do?"

Keith cracked a smile. "Pleased to meet you, man."

Patricia found the exchange entertaining. Her father had taught his grandson the proper way to greet someone, but the boy didn't seem to realize there was a counterculture demographic who didn't adhere to the same social niceties as his grandpa, while Keith wasn't used to children addressing him so formally.

"Want something to eat?" Patricia asked.

"Nah... No, thank you."

Based on how he hesitated before answering, she could tell he was conflicted on the matter. But she let it go.

"What do you think of your new pad?" Keith asked Dennis.

"It's cool," Dennis said, without much enthusiasm. "But it's pretty creepy, too. It's like The Addams Family's house."

Keith laughed. "Well, they say *this* house is haunted, too."

"He loved *The Addams Family*," Patricia said, steering away from such talk. She didn't want to have to deal with the fallout if it kept her son up at night.

"Not as much as *The Munsters*, though," Dennis clarified.

"Yeah, he was pretty sore when they canceled *The Munsters*."

"*Batman* replaced it. I like *Batman* too."

Ever so slightly, Patricia winced. Her parents had told her how the boy had watched *Batman* begrudgingly at first, yet it quickly grew on him (which they partly attributed to the show being broadcast in color). This had transpired during the five months she had been away at the finest in-patient rehab program Chicagoland had to offer.

Keith pivoted back to his campfire story act. "They say some woman named Doris is the ghost." He raised his eyebrows at Dennis.

Patricia snapped back to the present. "Yeah, we've heard stories," she said in a dismissive tone. This was one of those rare moments where she really felt her mothering instinct—either Keith had *not* picked up on her cue to drop the haunted house talk, or he was ignoring her.

"Doris?" Dennis prompted Keith, eager to hear more.

"She lived here back in the days of the depression," Keith continued, speaking grimly.

"We've heard all about Doris," Patricia interjected. "She was my great-grandfather's second wife."

"Oh..." Keith said like it was just now sinking in that this was a relative they were talking about. "...sorry."

"It's okay," Patricia said. "We never knew her." Doris was the only relative in her family's recent history who had generated as much gossip as Patricia herself did, but she'd rather not have anyone talking about the poor woman's demise. Her mind rifled around for a graceful way to change the subject, but soon ran out of time.

Exculpated, Keith turned back to Dennis. "Doris hung herself. *In this house.*"

"I guess she'd be your great-great step-granny." Patricia nodded at Dennis and smiled, striving to take back the conversation and relieve the macabre topic's tension.

"They say you can sometimes see the ghost of Doris looking out the windows of the belvedere," Keith continued. "That's where she hung herself."

"What's a belva-deer?" Dennis was rapt.

"It's the big room on the top of the mansion." He pointed up and in the direction of the center of the house. "It has lots of windows for viewing the surrounding countryside."

"Isn't it called a cupola?" Patricia interrupted, making a lame attempt to lead the conversation away from the tale of Doris.

"Some people call it that, but actually, a cupola is 'ornamental'," Keith said, scrunching his fingers into air quotes. "And smaller. A belvedere is a full-blown room. I can take you up there if you want to see it."

"Can we, Mom?" Dennis pleaded.

"Yeah, Honey. Later. Just as long as it's not at night!" She smiled nervously at Keith, hoping he hadn't picked up on her passing disapproval of him, and when his eyes met hers, she knew he hadn't.

"Anyway," Keith said, finally ready to let it go, "I've been here for three weeks, and *I* haven't seen anything supernatural."

Patricia exchanged prolonged eye contact with Keith, and he returned her smile.

When she eventually switched her eyes back to her son, Patricia found him studying her with a discernible furrow in his brow.

Chapter 17

Exploration

Dennis was raring to explore the mysterious room at the top of the house.

"You're *not* going up there without *me*," Patricia had told him repeatedly, "...and *I'm* not going up there without Keith."

Late in the afternoon on the following day, he would finally get his wish.

A doorway across the hall from their bedrooms concealed the stairwell to the attic. Keith swung the door open and waited, but Patricia leaned back, and Dennis made a point not to budge.

"Okay." Keith shrugged. "I'll go first." He started climbing the steep and narrow steps.

Dennis followed him, and Patricia brought up the rear. The temperature rose as they climbed, and the air became stagnant and musty. They reached a landing and took another flight that opened into the attic.

"I already rewired up here." Keith gestured to the empty, dust-coated room as Dennis and his mom moved beside him. "It's easy because the walls and joists are all open. Always start with the straightforward part, my dad taught me—like he needed to tell *me* to do that!" He guffawed.

Keith led the way to the opening of the final flight of steps, and they all gazed up the single linear stairway.

At the top of the passage, a full-sized door, mounted horizontally and flush to the attic ceiling, served as a portal through the underbelly of the top-level room. "Wow!" Dennis said.

"Unreal," Patricia said. "Look, it has the same glass doorknob as the rest of the house."

"Yeah, pretty strange, huh?" Keith said. "And they say this is where Doris hung herself."

Patricia shuddered and turned away.

Dennis drew forward for a better look, and he strained to imagine it.

"Here, Dennis, take this." Keith lifted the top wire milk crate off a stack at the foot of the stairs and handed it to the boy. "So you can see out the windows."

Keith then climbed up half of the steps and reached for the door handle, turned it, and swung the hatch open, attaching it to a latch above. A squall of dust snowed down.

"Gross," Patricia said, wiping her face and adding a weak cough as a dramatic flourish.

When they set foot in the hot, stale air of the belvedere, Dennis was half disappointed but half relieved there was no step-granny-ghost waiting for them.

He walked across the unfinished wood floor to the front-facing windows, placed the improvised booster step under the middle pane, then mounted it. "Cool!"

Being four stories above ground level provided a sweeping view of not only Harmon Manor's property, but a wide swath of the

surrounding landscape as well. The two-lane state highway stretched
to the bend in the road in both directions. Even the water in the creek
running along the opposite side of the roadway was visible from this
height, and he had the idea this was something he'd need to explore.

"When I started this job, some of the windows were cracked, and
two were broken and boarded over," Keith said. "A stern old Amish
dude replaced them during my first week here. It was a trip—he
brought the glass on a buggy and carried it up all those stairs by
himself."

"My dad started having work done a while ago," Patricia said.
"The slate and copper roofs and the copper gutters were replaced
before you even started."

"Don't forget the new driveway, Mom," Dennis reminded her.

"Oh yeah. They put the asphalt driveway in last fall. The old one
was gravel."

A tractor pulling some type of farm equipment emerged from
the eastern curve in the road. Dennis watched it for a moment, then
turned back to discover Keith and his mom standing unusually close
to one another as they looked out the adjacent window. They both
pitched far enough inward that their shoulders were touching. He
frowned, but kept his thoughts to himself. It took close to a minute
before the tractor rumbled past the mansion, and another minute
before it rounded the western bend.

"Come check this out, Dennis," Keith said, motioning him over.

Dennis carried the milk crate and placed it on the floor beside
Keith, opposite his mother, then climbed atop it.

Keith pointed in the distance. "See that hill?"

A grassy mound protruded up from the horizon, way beyond the
much closer hills and treetops. "Yeah?"

"That's Kassel's Hill. Tallest point in the county. Pretty cool how we can see it from here. It's about five miles away, as the crow flies."

"As the crow flies?" Dennis asked.

Keith laughed. "That means if you measure a straight line from here to there, it would be five miles. But there's no direct road between the two points, so it's probably a twenty-mile drive to get there. Dig it?"

Dennis nodded, eyeing the distant peak.

"I used to hike up that hill when I was a kid. If you go up at night, you see a complete view of the sky. It's a totally groovy way to look at the stars."

"That sounds cool," Patricia said.

"Oh, man, it's out of this world!" Keith turned back to Dennis and added, "If you want, I'll take you and your mom up there one night."

"Maybe." Though intrigued by this idea, Dennis knew not to become attached to the men in his mother's life.

Dennis found a promising-looking rock—flat, about eight inches wide. He crouched and lifted it gently out of the water, with minimal disruption. He waited for the current to clear the creek's turbidity, and there it was: a big fat crayfish, just standing there, stunned, wondering where its shelter had gone.

He closed in on it slowly from behind, his fingers positioned like a little cage. Suddenly the crustacean scooted away, but backward, and right into the boy's waiting hand-trap. He scooped in with his other hand and repositioned his fingers, softly pinching the fat part of its shell so it couldn't use its claws as a weapon. He held it up for inspection, looking into its tiny black eyes, then dropped it into the bucket.

At first, Dennis had thought that crayfish were impossible to catch. Finding them was easy. Half the rocks he checked had crayfish underneath. The hard part was corralling the creatures. But now that he knew the trick, discovered through a lot of trial and error, he could capture almost every one he found.

Catching frogs was a different story altogether. After a couple of weeks of searching in vain for the right technique, the boy could still only nab one frog for every half dozen attempts.

Dennis watched the five crayfish maneuvering at the bottom of the bucket, each one warily backing away from the others. Above them, the bullfrog floated on the surface, sprawled out with arms and legs extended.

A vehicle approached on the road, and when its brakes squealed, Dennis hopscotched across half a dozen rocks, climbed the bank, and peered through a gap in the trees. A white truck stopped in the apron for a moment before proceeding up Harmon Manor's drive. Bright red lettering on the side spelled out:

C&C APPLIANCE
Serving Homer County since 1946

Clueless as to why the truck was there, Dennis hopscotched back, being careful to avoid stepping into the sand patch he feared might be quicksand. Unsure what quicksand looked like, he'd seen enough TV programs to understand its peril. He dumped the bucket, freeing his afternoon haul before heading across the street to investigate.

The vehicle nudged up into the space beside Keith's van. By the time Dennis reached the top of the drive, his mother had stepped out onto the front porch. The driver slid out sluggishly, then paused to shift a ratty John Deere cap around on his mop of gray hair. The passenger, wiry and sporting a bright red bandana headband, bounded out next.

"Good afternoon. Mrs. Harmon?" John Deere called.

"Patricia," she answered, stepping off the porch.

He tipped his green hat to her while Bandana hopped onto the tailgate and unlatched the truck's rolling doorway. "We'll bring the television in first."

Dennis's head whipped around to his mother, who walked toward him, smiling and nodding.

"Killer!" He grinned, and after a moment, he tried putting on a poker face but couldn't.

"I know how much you've missed your shows, honey."

He nodded, still grinning. "They're repeats during the summer, but I don't mind."

The men went to work unloading the delivery. They followed Patricia into the house with the TV while she specified where to set it up.

Dennis followed them in and took a position in the parlor entranceway to witness the momentous unveiling of a state-of-the-art console set.

"Grandpa bought the TV," Patricia said as she sidled up to Dennis. "He wanted it here for when he visits this weekend." Grandpa would be arriving tonight for the upcoming Fourth of July weekend. It wasn't a social visit—that would be out of character for the man—he was coming to check on the electrical work, and to finalize the plumbing contracts. Nonetheless, Dennis looked forward to a change from what had become a pretty dull routine in the three weeks he'd been living in the mansion.

"But we get to use it after he leaves, right, Mom?"

She winked like it would be their little secret. "We're also getting a new refrigerator and stove."

When Mr. Deere turned on the TV, he was impressed by how the set picked up all the network stations. "First time I've seen that in these parts."

"It's the antenna," Keith said, making his appearance at the watch party. "I'd bet it's the tallest one in the county. I attached a space-age behemoth to the very top of the house. Fished the cable down here through three levels."

The men nodded their approval as they went on admiring the clarity of the long string of commercials that were airing.

Patricia busted up the affair unceremoniously by walking over and turning off the television. "Let's get the old appliances out now."

Dennis moved from the parlor to the library, where he could observe the loading and unloading of the truck.

When they maneuvered the new fridge into the front entry, the men paused for a breather. "I guess we ain't seeing where Doris hangs out," Bandana said with a grin. "No pun intended."

Mr. Deere nodded, wearing a somber expression as he looked up at the foyer gallery above. He examined their surroundings like he might be able to spot some evidence of the home's dark history, all the while patting sweat from beneath the bill of his green name badge, using a threadbare handkerchief.

Next came the stove, but Dennis lost interest. Anxious to make use of the TV, he slipped back into the parlor. Unfortunately, rotating the dial through the channels confirmed what he feared, considering this time of day: nothing but crummy soap operas. He turned the television off.

From the other room, his mother was telling Keith how the stove was a "Jenn-Air downdraft range," but this didn't seem to impress the electrician much. He seemed more intent on explaining to the delivery men how he'd rewired the outlets for the stove and fridge. But in turn, they did not seem to want to hear about the wiring.

As they headed to their truck, Mr. Deere said to Bandana, "It's about time we got out of here. This place gives me the willies."

<hr>

The parlor had only a single armchair, so Keith offered to donate his parents' old couch since they had recently upgraded their living room furniture. An hour later, he returned with a pal to drop it off.

When the van arrived, Dennis followed his mother out to the driveway.

Keith's friend grumbled a curt "Hi," and then wandered down the driveway. He turned back to scrutinize the mansion with a wary eye while waiting to be called upon to help carry the furniture.

"The sofa just fit—once I removed my tools," Keith said as he swung open the rear doors to reveal the delivery. "Snug as a bug in a rug."

He hopped into the van and patted the arm of the couch. "This makes a pretty groovy mobile love pad, Baby." He oscillated his eyebrows at Patricia.

"Yeah. Who needs a kitchen or a bathroom?" she asked sarcastically while inspecting the delivery. "It's a pretty groovy sofa though, don't you think, Dennis?"

"I guess so." Dennis knew as much about furniture as most ten-year-old boys, but what wasn't lost on him was the value of pairing it up with the new TV.

"My dad thinks my mom is crazy for buying a new couch," Keith said, shaking his head. "The way she keeps updating furniture, you'd never dream she was raised Amish."

After the two of them moved the sofa into the parlor, Keith took his unsociable buddy home. He returned later, alone, bearing pizza and pop, and the trio dined on the new old couch while watching *The Flying Nun*.

Patricia's father was expected by nine o'clock, so Keith departed by eight.

CHAPTER 18

INDEPENDENCE DAY

D ENNIS HESITATED BEFORE SLIDING into the car, then decided to ask one last time. "Are you sure you don't want to come, Grandpa?" Then he waited. Only his mother wasn't waiting—she closed her door and started the car.

"Heck no. I need to recover from that long drive," his grandpa yelled back from the veranda. "It's a TV night for me. Enjoy!" He gave one of those get-out-of-here waves and disappeared into the house.

Dennis shook his head in disbelief. To him, the Fourth of July fireworks were the highlight of each summer, so he couldn't understand how anyone would choose to miss them.

When they turned onto the road, Patricia announced, "We're meeting Keith for the fireworks."

Dennis nodded. He had little doubt this had been his mom's plan all along, and she waited to tell him until after they left because she didn't want to risk having her father find out. Keith seemed nice enough, so Dennis had nothing against him. But why did his mother need to sneak around?

"Just so you know," Patricia said as they made their way toward town, "I'm taking you to the fireworks for your entertainment. It's not that I'm celebrating Independence Day."

"Okay," Dennis said.

"My anti-war feelings are universal," she continued. "Not just the Vietnam War. All wars—including the Revolutionary War."

Dennis nodded again. Although he didn't understand how even the current war had any direct impact on his mom, he didn't question her. Politics wasn't exactly a topic he knew much about, and the war confused him thoroughly. Everyone seemed to have such strong feelings on the matter, including his mother—or at least she felt she should, and telling him whose side she was on seemed to make her feel better.

The Independence Day celebration was arguably the biggest event of the year in the strongly patriotic Homer County, so naturally, the town square swarmed with people. The smell of deep-fried elephant ears greeted them as they approached.

"Mom, do you think they have cotton candy?"

She laughed. "I bet they do. Maybe that'll be your dessert."

A band in the gazebo played "The Stars and Stripes Forever." Dennis sang along, using the parody lyrics he'd learned in the Cub Scouts: "Be kind to your web-footed friends... For a duck may be somebody's mother..." He trailed off, unable to remember any more.

Patricia giggled like she'd never heard that version.

As the car navigated around the crowded town center, Dennis watched the throng through his opened window and realized he was seeing kids for the first time since his arrival in Ohio almost a month prior. He gawked at the people as they passed, wondering if he might be able to meet new friends his own age this evening. But before long, he dismissed the fanciful thought as just that. An outsider here, he knew how unlikely it was he'd find the opportunity to make new acquaintances in such a foreign land. Friendships would probably have to wait until the summer ended, and he returned to Illinois. They'd be back in Barrington before the end of August, so his stay in Ohio was already almost half over.

"We're meeting Keith in the county courthouse parking lot," his mother said as she crossed the town square. "If you see a sign, let me know."

"There it is!" Dennis pointed at the "Homer County Courthouse" sign, proud of himself for having spotted it with such ease. They pulled into the alleyway and drove past a long row of Amish buggies, parked along one side of the square that had been configured with hitching posts. A mass of Amish youths congregated in a nearby corner of the block, and Dennis couldn't help but stare at the isolated bunch of teenage boys and girls who were all dressed alike.

The gray *Richardson Electric* van stood out in the sea of vehicles. Keith guarded a nearby parking space, waving off a blue-haired couple cruising their fire-engine red 1950s Cadillac convertible, who wanted to lay claim to the space. The driver yelled, "Get a haircut, you damn hippie!" and punched the gas, peeling out, just as Patricia rolled up.

Keith smiled and stepped aside, giving a dramatic "you may enter" gesture with his sweeping arm. Patricia wedged the Chevelle in.

"Man, I thought the townspeople were going to tar and feather me." He chuckled and opened Patricia's car door. "That geezer was one of the more genial ones."

"Poor baby," Patricia said, stepping out and wrapping her arms around her new boyfriend.

"Hey, good lookin'," he said, burying his face in her hair and rocking her against his body.

Dennis shook his head and looked away, trying not to let their display of affection bother him. It took a minute before the lovebirds remembered they weren't alone.

"We have a choice," Keith said, coming back in the moment. "We could either watch the fireworks here, with all these people, or alone, from the top of Kassel's Hill."

"Kassel's Hill sounds interesting," Patricia said.

"It'd be a special treat, guaranteed."

"What do you think, Honey?" She asked.

They both looked at Dennis as if it were he who could make the call. Only he didn't feel like he had much choice in the matter.

"Okay," he answered, and any lingering thoughts he had about making friends that evening ceased once and for all.

Before leaving Clarkton, the three of them meandered through the crowded midway of fair food trailers. Keith bought three corn dogs at one stand, three lemonades at another, and at the last stop, cotton candy for Dennis.

"We'll eat while we drive," Patricia announced, and she led the way to the parking lot.

"We have to take your car," Keith said with a laugh. "There's only two seats in my work van."

Dennis thought it strange when his mother slid into the middle of the bench seat of their '66 Chevelle Malibu and signaled for him to sit beside her on the passenger side. Keith settled in behind the wheel, like he was playing stepdad or something.

The corn dogs and lemonade were all gone by the time the Chevelle was cruising the country roads south of Clarkton. Patricia leaned into Keith, who put his arm around her, steering with his left hand only. It occurred to Dennis the road might have been too winding to be using just one hand, but he kept quiet.

As much as he tried to be neat, it wasn't long before Dennis had pink stickiness smeared over his fingers and much of his face. He didn't have nearly enough napkins for the mess he'd made, and anyway, they were those useless waxy types that absorb nothing and tear apart so easily. Fortunately, neither his mom nor Keith seemed bothered.

She soon returned to the topic of war. "You know, Dennis, Keith stayed out of Vietnam by becoming a conscientious objector."

Using the last remaining napkin, Dennis was attempting to wipe out the goop between his fingers. But he felt his mother waiting, so he was obliged to ask, "What's that?"

"People who object to war based on religious beliefs," Keith explained. "Would you believe I'm Amish?" He turned to Dennis and flashed a goofy grin.

Dennis studied him, trying to sort it out. "No."

"Don't blow my cover, man. The U.S. military believed it. My mom was raised Amish, but she left the community. So, I've got some Amish relatives. They're pacifists, so they were happy to help with my ruse, all in the name of keeping someone else out of the war. Uncle Sam granted me a conscientious objector deferment. Shows what a bunch of *dipshits* they are!"

Dennis did not really get it, but he did appreciate how Keith was willing to use adult language with him.

Pleased with his cleverness, Patricia snickered and leaned into her draft-dodger beau, nuzzling him.

"Hey Jude" by The Beatles came on the radio, and she promptly turned up the volume and sang along. Before long, Keith made it a duet.

Dennis, more of a television lover than a music lover, had recently started to pay attention to rock music, and he certainly knew—and liked—"Hey Jude." By the middle of the tune, Dennis joined in, and the three of them repeatedly belted out the chorus in unison.

After following State Route 83 south for close to half an hour, they turned off onto a single-lane gravel road that disappeared into dense woodlands. Dennis spotted a rusty sign reading TOWNSHIP RD 258, and Keith piloted through the forest for half a mile, kicking up a big cloud of dust behind them.

"We're parking nearby, on the adjoining property," Keith said over the sound of crunching gravel. "A family friend owns it. I spent a lot of time here growing up."

The woods opened to a clearing around a tiny red cabin. Keith pulled the car into the tall grass. "We're here!"

Dennis stared at his surroundings in astonishment. Having grown up in the Chicago suburbs, he'd never seen anything as remote and undeveloped as this natural countryside. When he turned to his mother, she was gawking wide-eyed out the windshield, and he could tell she was thinking the same thing.

Keith removed the contents of the box he had put in the trunk: a flashlight, a blanket, and a can of Off! bug repellent, which they generously applied before setting out on their trek to the hill.

They followed a trail behind the cabin, which led to a pond. Dennis crouched at the water's edge to wash the sugary stickiness off his face and hands before they continued into the woods. Keith pointed out poison ivy patches along the path, and he claimed that the stand of pine trees they crossed had always bristled with rattlesnakes. Dennis couldn't tell if he was serious or just trying to scare him (or maybe his mom...or both of them), but he carried a solid stick and stayed vigilant, just in case.

They arrived at a barbed wire fence, which Keith helped them climb over, one at a time. He was extra grabby with Patricia, who giggled and playfully swatted his hands with feigned indignation. Neither of them noticed Dennis rolling his eyes.

The pasture began on the other side of the barbed wire fence. Countless cow patties checkered the field, some so fresh they were teeming with flies, and others so dry they might be considered a wildfire hazard. Cows clustered some distance away, on the opposite side of a creek, but Keith assured them they needn't fret about venturing into their territory. "Bulls would be a different story," he said with a grimace.

Mostly covered in grass, with an occasional tree jutting from the slope, Kassel's Hill was a near-perfectly shaped dome. Climbing it was difficult, as dusk dew dampened the groundcover, and their feet often slipped on the incline. Dennis discovered it was much easier to ascend if he used his hands to grab hold of grass tufts on the hillside. By the time they reached the summit, all of them were out of breath.

"Far out, don't you think?" Keith held his hands out wide, tracing the horizon.

Patricia raised her eyebrows. "Right on."

A cow mooed in the distance like it concurred, and all of them laughed.

Dennis smiled and nodded as he scanned the skyline. He had to agree how cool it was to be able to see the horizon in all directions, just as Keith had described. It wasn't dark yet, but the brightest stars in the Milky Way were already enkindled, stretching from one end of the heavens to the other.

Patricia extended her arms and slowly spun around, singing what Dennis recognized as the opening song to *The Sound of Music*, having recently seen the movie at the theater with her and his grandma.

When she finished what little she knew of the song, Patricia spread out the blanket, and they each picked their spot. Dennis took one corner and his mother sat beside him, but Keith settled in right next to Patricia and promptly wrapped his arm around her.

The sun dropped below the skyline, and while the eastern horizon had darkened, the western side still glowed, as if an enormous shade was being slowly drawn across the sky, from east to west. They would need to wait more than half an hour for complete darkness, though, when the fireworks would begin.

"Just think, man..." Keith said, surveying the hills in the east, where the sky had started to darken, "...somewhere out there is your house. We'd see the top, at least."

All three of them looked in that general direction.

"Five miles, as the crow flies," Dennis said, staring at the endless panorama of the countryside and trying to gauge how far that would be.

Patricia chuckled. "Good memory!"

"But good luck finding it." Keith emphasized his point with a shrug. "Like a *tadpole in Lake Erie*!" And with that, he gave up searching and lay down.

When the pyrotechnics started, it was something to behold. They were off some way in the distance, but the entire performance was visible from where they sat. The colors lit up the surrounding hills, and while the booms were muted, they could still be heard clearly, albeit completely out of sync with the flashes, due to the long distance.

After watching the display for a while, Keith pulled out a strangely shaped cigarette and lit the pointy end. He smoked it himself for a few minutes before Patricia reached for it.

"You sure?" Keith asked her in a whisper.

She nodded. "Just one hit."

The cotton candy in Dennis's gut suddenly wasn't sitting so well. He looked away, in the direction of the fireworks, but the magic in them was gone.

CHAPTER 19

⎯⎯⎯◄◊►⎯⎯⎯

DILEMMA

K EITH EXPERIENCED A TWINGE of guilt when he handed the newspaper cutout to Patricia.

MUSICARNIVAL
COMING SUNDAY JULY 20, 7 PM!
LED ZEPPELIN

"What do you think?" he asked.

"I don't know," Patricia answered slowly, studying the ad. "That's this Sunday."

In the depths of his consciousness, Keith felt bad, having a sense it wouldn't take much to coerce his girlfriend into relenting. Yet he pressed on. "Do you dig The Yardbirds?"

Patricia affirmed by breaking out in song, singing "For Your Love." She dropped the ad on the kitchen counter and danced up to Keith, lifting her arms above her head, exposing her midriff.

"Yeah, baby," he said with a smile. He found her rhythm and synchronized his hips to it. While he danced, his hands slid across her tummy before settling in a grope of her waist. "Anyway, Jimmy

Page, The Yardbirds guitarist? Now he's with this new band: Led Zeppelin."

"Crazy name...Lead Zeppelin? Sounds more hazardous than The Hindenburg." Patricia snickered, then peeled away, stopped dancing, and looked down the hall in the direction of Dennis, who had ventured out to catch frogs in the creek across the road. "I just don't think it's cool to leave him alone."

"He's ten years old, man. He'll be fine."

She stared down the corridor for a spell before turning back, her lips scrunched to one side. "What time would we get back?"

"Hmmm. It's on the east side of Cleveland. The drive back is much faster now since Interstate 77 opened. Maybe midnight?" Keith bit his lower lip while he considered it further. "One in the morning, at the latest."

"Well..." Patricia sighed and gave a tiny shrug. "Let me think about it."

CHAPTER 20

MAN ON THE MOON

DENNIS FOUGHT BACK TEARS.

"Tonight?" His voice squeaked through his tightening throat. "You're not going to watch the moon landing with me?"

"Sorry, honey. I didn't know it would happen on the night of the concert."

"But I even marked the day." He pointed across the kitchen at the calendar on the refrigerator. "I can see the big red letters from here: MOON LANDING."

Patricia looked in that direction, as though it might make a difference, then turned back to him. "But *you* can still watch it."

"You said we'd watch it together."

She put her hand on his shoulder, which only accentuated his disappointment.

"If you want, I'll skip the concert."

Dennis knew his mother well enough to see through that offer. "It's alright." He shrugged his shoulder away and tromped toward the hall, leaving her alone in the kitchen.

Despite an unremitting mosquito assault, Dennis remained at the creek, determined to wait it out until his mom and Keith left for the concert.

After an hour that felt like two, the horn beeped. The van waited at the driveway apron until Dennis crawled up the bank and poked his head through the brush.

Keith waved.

Patricia leaned out the window and yelled, "Have fun, honey!"

When Dennis raised his hand in half-hearted acknowledgment, the van pulled out onto the road and went on its way. Released from his self-imposed exile, he dumped his catch and headed back to the house.

Around three o'clock, Dennis settled into the couch and glued his attention to the TV screen, tuned to CBS, Walter Cronkite narrating the historic event. He watched the entire lunar landing, mesmerized. It was unfathomable that a spaceship had rocketed away and landed on that alien world. He was becoming a fan of Star Trek, but that was just a show. *This* was real.

Well after the astronauts reported to Mission Control "The eagle has landed," Dennis broke his transfixed stare at the television, and wandered out the back door and into the nighttime lawn. While a galaxy of lightning bugs blinked in the darkness all around him, he gazed with wonder at the moon, amazed that human beings would soon be stepping onto its alien surface.

It was maddening that he couldn't share this experience with anyone else. But then he had an idea: call Grandpa. Surely, he'd be watching this, equally fascinated. Mom said he could only use the phone in an emergency, but this was a big deal. How much could long-distance calling really cost, anyway?

He went back into the house and stepped over to the wall phone in the kitchen, then lifted the receiver off the switch hook, nodding when he heard the dial tone. He knew he had to include the area code, so he started with "312" before appending his home number.

Three obnoxiously loud rising tones blasted into his ear. A recorded woman's voice declared, "We're sorry; we are unable to complete your call as dialed. Please check the number and dial again." He did just that, twice, but got the same result, unaware he needed to add a one before the area code. He gave up in exasperation and went back to the parlor, resigned to watching the events alone.

At almost 11 p.m., Neil Armstrong took his first step onto the moon, while Dennis buzzed with excitement. About ten minutes after that "giant leap for mankind," he felt the strange sensation of his hair lifting, as though he had rubbed his head against the static-charged face of the television tube. Only he hadn't, of course—he hadn't even moved. He turned, and that's when he spotted a woman sitting in the armchair, about six feet from him. She swung her head to face his way and smiled at him for but an instant, then vanished. The staticky sensation immediately abated, and his hair resettled on his head.

Maybe because he was witnessing such a mind-blowing event on TV, or perhaps it was because she seemed so friendly... Either way, though it had startled him, the woman's appearance didn't exactly *frighten* Dennis. It passed so quickly; she dissolved away before he even had a chance to react.

Dennis sat alone once again, contemplating what had just happened. Was what he saw just his imagination? Had he fallen asleep? Had he seen a shadow wrong? Light from the TV cast in a funny way? Maybe his brain just went haywire for a moment. After all, it was late, and he must be tired.

Except...this house...it's supposedly haunted...

Was that Doris? he asked himself. *My step-granny?*

CHAPTER 21

THE TRIP

AFTER A SLOPPY MEAL of burgers and fries at the Canton, Ohio Howard Johnson's restaurant, Keith sprung his surprise on Patricia.

"I've been saving two hits of acid for a special occasion," he said as they walked toward the van.

"What special occasion?" she asked.

"Seeing Led Zeppelin qualifies, don't you think?" He raised his eyebrows with the question.

"Sounds like a blast!"

Keith had expected she'd at least hesitate, but there was none of that.

Inside the van, he pulled a little envelope out of the glove box. He teased out two small tabs of colorful paper, which they placed under their tongues before continuing their journey to the venue.

He was already feeling the effects when he left the interstate and started following city roads to the Musicarnival's location. Before long, he lost track of where he was on the map, and the surrounding traffic seemed to be flowing haphazardly, like all the driving rules had been canceled. Despite his impairment, he somehow got them there.

They waited half an hour in a line of cars to enter the grassy field parking lot. By the time they were walking into the Musicarnival tent theater, everything around him blossomed into technicolor wonder.

The opening act, a local band called James Gang, featured an accomplished guitarist named Joe Walsh. Keith began noticing little corkscrewing runes that looked like something from a comic book, drilling down toward the band from the tent ceiling.

By the time Led Zeppelin took the stage with a raucous rendition of an old blues song Keith swore he recognized, both he and Patricia were having a hard time talking—so they just laughed uncontrollably.

The lights seemed to pulse with the beat, and Keith's heartbeat seemed to synchronize with both. He felt completely immersed, like he'd become one with the music.

When the concert ended and the lights came on, the audience swarmed toward the tent's exits. Keith's ears were ringing so loud he felt he could still hear the band playing under the buzz.

"I'm still peaking," he said to Patricia, his voice hoarse. "I can't drive yet."

She just stared at him with wild giant pupils, yet he was certain she understood completely.

"How does a quickie in my van sound?"

She nodded, with her big black saucer-eyes fixed on him. He was sure they were communicating through brain waves.

He lit the inside of the van with a flashlight and rolled out the two sleeping bags, one on top of the other, for a little extra cushion. They crawled over the floor to the middle of the makeshift bed.

Before long, it became clear Keith's lower half wasn't going to cooperate, so they abandoned the idea and started cuddling. He forgot where his body started and where Patricia's began. When their metaphysical voyage stopped, it had only been 45 minutes, but for all Keith knew, they had spent eons in the back of the stuffy vehicle.

They left the sleeping bags laid out and climbed back into the seats. Keith surveyed the dashboard and blinked hard. *It's so complicated.* He knew the expedition back to Homer County would be practically impossible. "I still don't think I can drive," he said.

"Driving," Patricia responded, and her eyes narrowed like she was contemplating the notion. Then she laughed.

At least she's talking now, Keith thought, before joining her in laughter.

The giggle fit was so intense it hurt, and then even this became funny.

When their laughing spell eventually petered out, Keith asked, "Should we just crash here tonight?"

She pursed her lips, then crinkled her nose. "Can we?"

"Good question. I'd better check," and that got him giggling all over again. He slid out of the van. On his way to the shack-like structure serving as the venue's office, he heard Patricia's door open, and he turned back to see her leaving the van.

"Don't leave me here all alone!" She trotted toward him, but halfway there, her pants, having never been re-buttoned, fell to her ankles. Keith laughed so hard he was soon doubled over on his knees.

Once Keith and Patricia's pants were back up, the couple headed toward the small building. The grass parking lot was almost empty of cars by now, but an asteroid belt of empty beer cans and bottles had been left behind. They sidestepped the debris on their way toward the shack.

A bearded man popped out when they approached. Keith asked, "Is it cool if we park here overnight?"

"As long as you clear out by eight in the morning. The cleaning crew arrives then."

"What's going on in there?" Keith pointed with his chin at the small crowd that had collected inside the structure.

"They're getting ready to walk on the moon, man! It's a trip...want to watch, too?"

Keith looked at Patricia, and she nodded.

It turned out the four Led Zeppelin band members were part of the twenty or so people gathered around a small television.

"More Yanks," Jimmy Page, the guitarist, announced as the tripping newcomers arrived.

Everyone laughed.

Patricia promptly shucked Keith, and ambled over to Robert Plant, the vocalist.

"I'm Patricia," she said.

He smiled at the new female arrival. "You're just in time, man. They're about to step onto the moon."

"Groovy. It's like I'm watching it with my son."

A few people looked at her funny.

"I mean, we're both watching the same thing."

"I dig it," Robert Plant said, but then he turned his eyes to Keith, then back, and asked, "He's at home though, right?"

Patricia nodded. "It's his first night alone," she said proudly.

"Alone, if you don't count the ghosts," Keith added, and then it was his turn to receive a few funny looks.

CHAPTER 22

---◆◇◆---

ALONE

BY 1:30 A.M., THE energetic thrum had drained from Dennis. The television events were long past their climax, the astronauts having reentered the lunar module, and at this late hour, he felt quite spent.

He had practically convinced himself the woman had been a product of his imagination. Besides, he had other things on his mind now. It was half an hour past the time his mom had promised she'd be home. Dennis told himself he shouldn't be surprised.

He also told himself not to think about the ghost he might have seen in the parlor. His mother would be back eventually, the sun would be shining again, and everything would be okay. By this point, he felt too exhausted to be dubious about any of these assertions.

As Dennis climbed onto his bed, something caught his eye, nestled between the fins of the cast iron radiator. He fished the object out: a silver crucifix with a brass figure of Jesus mounted to it.

He gasped when he saw it, and an uneasy feeling washed over him. Raised Catholic, crosses were a familiar sight to Dennis, but who had left it there? And when? A distant relative must have left it behind, many years prior. Stranger yet, it was ensconced in a gap barely wide and deep enough for the item, so it couldn't have simply fallen in. Someone had intentionally inserted it there. Why? The thought gave him goosebumps.

He laid it on top of the radiator, then settled into his bed.

As he bobbed on the surface of slumber, Dennis heard a *creak.* He roused himself, sat up, and cocked his head. Maybe a minute later he heard it once more, a lonely and ominous sound, flaring in volume, then dying into stillness. After a while longer, he heard it yet again.

Was it the floorboards? His mother walking downstairs? That can't be it—she'd be taking too long between steps.

The boy's pulse quickened, and he burrowed under the bedsheets, tried to breathe and think of nothing.

He counted seconds, listening with apprehension, hoping *not* to hear it.

CREAK.

No, can't be floorboards, he knew it. It was too heavy—too solid—to be floorboards. The noise sounded faint and distant, yet somehow still perfectly clear, as if it resonated *through* the ancient walls, the mansion almost shivering with each groan.

CREAK.

What is it?

The house is settling, his mother would always say, her go-to explanation for any unusual sounds he complained of hearing. Could it be that? *Except—if it's just the house settling, how come I haven't heard this sound before?*

CREAK.

Settling, settling, settling, the boy's mind reassured him, over, over, and over again. Wishing his mom would return home, he strained to ignore the groan as it continued into the night, periodically disrupting the forlorn silence smothering the mansion.

Dennis Harmon was grateful when sleep eventually overcame him, and his disturbed thoughts slid away and were soon forgotten.

Patricia studied the crucifix with a puzzled look on her face.

"Crazy, man," she said, placing it on the kitchen counter and sliding it toward Keith, who picked it up and looked at it with curiosity.

They had arrived home just after nine the next morning, and Dennis greeted them with his discovery.

"It was in the radiator?" Keith asked, turning it over and examining it from all sides.

"Yeah," Dennis answered. "I found it last night. Tucked inside, like someone hid it there."

"Do you want to keep it?" his mother asked him.

The boy recoiled slightly, then shook his head. Of course, he thought it cool to have unearthed an artifact from the faraway past in the otherwise empty house. Simultaneously, though, he felt a peculiar aversion toward the object, in large part because it had seemingly been secreted away. *What's the story there?* he kept questioning.

Furthermore, Dennis always found images of the crucifixion to be a little too gory for his taste. He never understood why church people seemed to feel the need to put gloomy images on display. Most of the statues in their Catholic church were downright frightening when you stopped to look at them—and if there's one thing a boy sitting in Sunday mass has, it's an abundance of idle time available to scrutinize every crying, bleeding, or dying one of them.

"My mother would totally dig it," Keith said. "She's guilty about leaving the Amish. This seems like the kind of thing that might help her feel better. For a couple of days, at least." He chuckled.

"It's hers then," Patricia said without hesitation, almost *too* quickly. "We're glad to be rid of it."

A few days later, when the phone rang, Dennis ran to the kitchen, eager to talk to someone. Since they had been staying in the house, only a handful of calls had come in.

"Hello?"

"Hi, it's Grandpa."

As if Dennis wouldn't recognize the voice. "Hi, Grandpa."

"Are you enjoying the summer?"

The boy pondered how to answer. What he initially hoped would be an exciting adventure had instead turned out to be a dull and lonely existence. But he couldn't say so. "It's okay."

Over six weeks in, homesickness had stricken him. He missed riding his bike on the endless stretches of sidewalk throughout his neighborhood. There were no sidewalks here. No friends either. In this isolated rural setting, he never even *saw* kids his own age. At least he had a nice color TV to keep him company.

"I bet you miss playing little league," Grandpa said, almost asserting it.

Quite the contrary. Getting out of having to play baseball was the one thread of consolation to his summer relocation. His grandfather insisted he play, yet he never even showed up to watch.

Dennis wasn't particularly athletic, so the coach always placed him in the outfield, where there was little action. He would bake under the scorching sun, waiting endlessly for someone to smack one out there. When it finally did happen, he'd panic, hoping he wouldn't make a fool of himself by misplaying the ball. Most of the time he did alright, but not always. He couldn't help but feel disadvantaged by not having a father to teach him sports, although his uncles had filled in a bit of the paternal void in their bastard nephew's life.

"Yeah, I miss baseball," Dennis said, giving Grandpa what he needed to hear. "Is Grandma there?"

"Oh, she's busy with something. You know how she is."

Indeed, Grandma was always busy with something or other. Dennis just figured she didn't like children. Which was strange, given how many she had.

"This is long distance, so it's costing me a fortune. Can I speak with your mother?"

Dennis flailed around for what to say. "She's...not here."

"Not there?"

"She had a...special thing to go to." He wasn't at all prepared for this and knew he was flubbing it. She had left an hour earlier with Keith, and offered no explanation of where they were heading.

"On a weeknight?"

"Mm-hmm." He hoped the line of questioning would end there.

"Did she say when she'd be home?"

"Ummm..." Dennis bought himself some time by blowing out through his lips. "Not that I remember." He couldn't exactly say she might not come home until the morning, and anyway, he hoped it wouldn't come to that. Although spending the evening alone had become almost routine, he wasn't growing any more comfortable with the circumstances.

"Have her call me please," Grandpa said. "I'll be making the trip down in a couple of weeks, so I'll see you soon."

After hanging up, hunger germinated in his gut, and that's when Dennis realized his mother had forgotten about dinner.

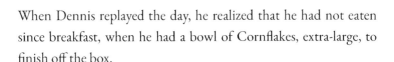

When Dennis replayed the day, he realized that he had not eaten since breakfast, when he had a bowl of Cornflakes, extra-large, to finish off the box.

Foraging through the pantry, everything he found required some sort of preparation. He'd never cooked on his own before...but a box of macaroni and cheese should be easy to make, right? He pulled open the cupboard and crouched to peer in. "Crap!" The shelf was bare.

Heating a can of soup would be simple. He pulled open the next cabinet over, but it was empty, too. Standing up, he blew a raspberry and said, "There's nothing to eat here!"

Quit it, Dennis reminded himself. For reasons he didn't understand, he'd developed the bad habit of talking out loud to himself, which was weird—like something an old person might do.

He wondered if he could skip the meal altogether—simply *ignore* the hunger pangs, but he knew his appetite would only intensify with time. He needed to find *something* to eat.

He lifted the milk bottle out of the fridge, revealing a slab of sliced bacon in the meat drawer beneath it. "Mmmm," he said aloud. "Sure wish I knew how to fry up bacon."

He scrounged up an apple, a glass of milk, and the crumbs at the bottom of a tin of Dan Dee potato chips his mom and Keith had been scarfing down before they left. After licking the salty, oily chip residue from his fingers, he treated himself to a few sips of maple syrup—another of his beloved foods, straight out of the can.

Dennis would never have swigged the syrup directly if he was still living with his grandparents. Once, his grandma had caught him doing this, and she gave him holy hell over it. But he was alone now. He could have as much as he pleased. His mother would never notice. She wasn't a fan of pure maple syrup anyway, preferring Log Cabin, Aunt Jemima, or Mrs. Butterworth's, all of which contained no trace of actual maple syrup, and none of which Dennis could stand.

He returned to the parlor and watched *Tarzan*. The episode was a rerun he had already seen, which he didn't mind, but the program couldn't distract his underfed, growling stomach. He attempted to disregard it, hoping it might somehow stop on its own.

About the time *Tarzan* ended, he suddenly smelled...*bacon? Couldn't be.* While there was no logical explanation for it, that's exactly what he smelled—and it sure smelled delicious.

He wandered into the hall, where the glorious scent grew stronger.

Stopping at the entrance to the kitchen, he blinked, then his jaw dropped open. A plate layered with pancakes sat on the table. A pat of butter melted on top, with four slices of fried bacon arranged neatly on one side. The same can of maple syrup he had sipped from earlier sat beside the utensils, opened and ready to pour. The food smelled incredible and looked every bit as good as the flawless stacks featured on Bisquick commercials.

Dennis gulped. His heart raced as he struggled to sort out the scene. No doubt the ingredients had all been in the house, but who could have cooked this wonderful meal?

"Mom?"

He waited for a beat, then went looking for her. He went down the rear hallway and peered out the back door onto the porch and into the lawn beyond, but there was nobody there.

He returned to the kitchen. "Hello?"

Only silence came back.

He searched cautiously through the surrounding section of the house, meandering through the rooms, half expecting his mother might pop out to surprise him. He found solace in the prospect of this outcome, but she never appeared.

The snapshot of the woman he'd seen in the parlor kept flashing in his mind's eye, pestering him. *Is she here?*

Dennis returned to the kitchen and stared at the surprise feast. His mouth watered. While he couldn't deny the mysterious offering was tempting, it also wasn't hard to imagine perilous outcomes if he ate it. *Might be poisoned...*like in that Vincent Price movie he'd seen recently: *Twice Told Tales.* He chewed the inside of his cheek. *But still...* His belly grumbled once again, louder yet, as if cajoling his brain to forge ahead with what it was considering.

Shrugging to himself, he reasoned that while it was a baffling affair, so too was the fact his mother had managed to forget about providing dinner for her child.

He tried to brush aside the nagging sensation that someone—or something—was in the house, hidden from view. Indeed, when he peered under the table, it was vacant. He moved the place setting to the back side so he could sit against the wall, providing him with a full view of the kitchen. His eyes flicked sideways, and he tuned his ears for the slightest of sounds.

Using his fork, he poked at the pancakes, tearing them open to examine the insides, but they looked normal. He took just a nibble first, but the taste was delectable, so he promptly followed it with a larger bite.

Unable to shake the disturbing feeling he was not alone, he ate slowly, keeping on high alert. But nobody appeared. Overlooking the admittedly questionable wisdom of his decision, he felt grateful for the meal's inexplicable creation.

After finishing off the food and licking the last of the maple syrup off the plate, he remained on edge while he cleared the table, then he returned to the TV in time to catch the beginning of *The Beverly Hillbillies*. The full feeling in his stomach calmed him, but not enough to make him willing to venture out beyond the parlor. *Green Acres* followed, which he watched distractedly, still trying to sort out what had happened.

Hawaii Five-O was on next, one of those programs that mostly went over Dennis's head. The lonely boy's mind felt worn out, and with the help of a show that was lost on him, it wasn't long before he fell fast asleep on the couch.

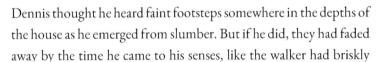

Dennis thought he heard faint footsteps somewhere in the depths of the house as he emerged from slumber. But if he did, they had faded away by the time he came to his senses, like the walker had briskly stridden off, out of earshot.

Then he realized he was in his bed. *Didn't I fall asleep on the couch?* He had no recollection of turning off the TV or going to his bedroom. *Did I sleepwalk?* No way—he had never done that before. Perhaps his mother had carried him up.

Dennis sat up and examined his surroundings. Two nightlights spilled dim incandescence from opposite walls, and shadows lurked about the room. The clock showed almost three in the morning.

He laid back down but remembered he hadn't brushed his teeth. Most ten-year-old boys probably wouldn't have given this a second thought, but the very concept of a dentist's drill made Dennis's skin crawl. He inspected the sticky film coating his teeth by rubbing over them with his tongue. *All that maple syrup!* He was *sure* cavities had already started forming.

He hurried across the room, then peeked out into the dark hallway.

Flipping on the switch to the wall sconces, he stepped down the hall, passing beyond the closed door to the stairs leading to the upper levels. His mother's bedroom door jutted open, but he couldn't see her bed. He leaned forward, stepped into the doorway, and scanned the charcoal silhouettes of the dusky room, finding it empty.

He walked timidly to the other end of the hall and glanced over the railing into the cavernous foyer. The twilit lower level of the house remained quiet. Although he didn't *hear* anything down there, he *felt* something, like static, charging the surrounding air. *You're just scaring yourself,* he contended, but the undercurrent of fear swelled in his gut.

He crept back from the balustrade and into the empty front bedroom across from his own, peering out the window into the night. Keith's van remained parked in the driveway, but his mother's Chevelle—which the couple had taken—wasn't in sight.

If Mom didn't carry me up to bed, how did I get there?

Utterly distressed by this mystery and the eerie hush of the house, he scurried into the bathroom and quickly brushed his teeth, then retreated to his bedroom. Shutting the door behind him, Dennis pulled the sheet over his head, hid underneath, and melted in terror.

When he awakened in the morning, Dennis found his mother still wasn't home.

After he dressed, he searched again through the almost bare pantry and refrigerator, and, unsurprisingly, found nothing new to eat. He thought about the pancakes and bacon but didn't go as far as to wish more would materialize. His breakfast would consist of another apple and the last of the milk.

Killing time in anticipation of his mom's arrival, he took advantage of the perfect summer morning and headed outside. He was soon cruising on his bicycle up and down the long driveway. His new bike was a Schwinn Stingray with a banana seat and long butterfly handlebars, which his uncles had given him for his tenth birthday. This model would no doubt raise Dennis's cool factor among his peers...if he actually knew any kids to show it off to.

He'd accelerate around the fresh blacktop driveway circle before turning onto the linear stretch, building more speed as he headed down the gentle slope toward the roadway. If he leaned a certain way and applied a hard brake at just the right moment, he found he could fishtail on the crushed gravel at the apron of the drive. He soon became quite skilled at performing this sideways skid trick. Before long, he imagined himself as Evel Knievel—although the aspiring daredevil was careful to cut his skids well short of the road.

The Stingray's rear tire sprayed gravel into the road, and when the stones came to rest, a clopping sound emerged in the distance. A horse and buggy appeared from around the bend. Dennis flintstoned his bike to the edge of the road for a closer look. A lone Amishman wearing a long gray beard and a tattered straw hat helmed the buggy. The man raised his hand stoically at Dennis, who waved back while straddling the Schwinn, staring at the spectacle until it passed.

Within a minute, the Chevelle came rumbling home and turned into the driveway. Dennis pulled into the grass to let it by and followed it up the drive where it parked next to the van.

Keith climbed out of the driver's side. "Hey, man," he said to Dennis as he swung open the rear doors of his van and began rummaging through his tools, not looking for a response.

Patricia stepped slowly out of the passenger side. Pale, her hair unkempt, she seemed to be hiding behind her sunglasses.

"Hi, Honey," she said softly to Dennis as he pulled up beside the car. "Sorry I didn't make it home. We decided to crash at the barn party."

Dennis had hoped his mother might provide a legitimate explanation for why she'd stayed away all night, but this was all she offered before setting off on a ginger walk toward the house.

"Mom?" He squinted in the bright morning sunshine. "Did you come home during the night?"

She stopped and turned around, rubbing the back of her neck. "Huh? No. Why?"

"Oh, nothing. I just thought I might have heard you." He dismounted his bike and dropped the kickstand. "Grandpa called. He wants you to call him."

"Ugh." Patricia shook her head. She turned away again and continued her shamble toward the front door, saying over her shoulder, "Is there anything to eat here?"

CHAPTER 23

MISGIVINGS

IN THAT SUMMER OF '69, Keith Richardson pursued sex, drugs, and rock & roll with gusto, all in the name of peace and love. But unlike Patricia, his pursuit of those interests fell short of reckless abandon.

Keith would never really advance beyond a recreational drug user; his usage was mostly an act of rebellion against the strict parenting he had grown up under. Just a few years later, he would find himself becoming one of the vast majority of hippies who would slide into the social norms and lifestyle they had so vocally eschewed as advocates of the counter-culture movement in their younger years.

So, in the last week of July, as he was wrapping up Harmon Manor's electrical work, Keith realized he was struggling to keep up with his girlfriend in the alcohol and drug consumption race. He wanted to trust her ability to control herself, but he had a troubling feeling he couldn't.

"Babe, maybe you should cut back on the partying a bit," he finally suggested late in the afternoon, after she had pressed him hard on what the party plans were for the evening.

The theme music to *The Little Rascals* played on the television in the other room. Keith went back to peeling an orange, hoping a casual demeanor might keep the mood light.

Patricia stared oddly at him from across the kitchen table, with an almost confused look, but since she didn't immediately respond, he misread her reaction as her being open to his opinion.

Before he even had a chance to stop himself, the other thing that had been on his mind spilled from his mouth: "...and maybe you shouldn't be leaving Dennis alone so often."

She glared at him. "What the hell do *you* know about parenting?"

His mind started to formulate the best way to answer, but then he realized she wasn't really looking for one.

"I never asked to be a mother anyway!" she added.

Keith cringed, judging it entirely possible her son had heard her from the parlor.

At that moment, it dawned on Keith that Patricia already knew she should be more attentive to Dennis. The fundamental problem was she resented being a mom in the first place, and guilt alone wasn't going to make her prioritize her son or the innumerable responsibilities he represented. There was no winning here. All he could do was back off, let it go.

Yet Patricia wasn't done. "And it's okay for *you* to get stoned, but not *me*?"

He kept his voice low, but had a quick response to that one: "No prob for me, man...I don't have a kid at home. Anyway, *I'm* just a social partier."

Patricia's eyes narrowed at him as she processed what he'd said and what he'd implied. Then she stood, whirled away, and raged out of the room.

CHAPTER 24

UNATTENDED

FTER GROCERY SHOPPING WITH his mother, she assigned Dennis the task of shuttling the bounty from the car trunk into the house, solo. The stockpile of frozen TV dinners and the bags of various items were easy enough, but the three cases of Genesee Cream Ale in longneck bottles were too heavy for him to lift. Same for the mix-case crate of O-So pop, but at least those were for him. He had to resort to taking half a case of the beverages on each trip, so the entire ordeal took a while. Regardless, he was not about to complain, seeing as he now had a well-stocked food supply.

"Did you put one of the beers in the freezer?" his mother asked him when she appeared in the kitchen, just as he was finishing. She had changed and refreshed her makeup while he tended to the chores.

"Yup. And eleven in the fridge. The rest are in the pantry."

"Good boy. Now pick the dinner you want, and I'll show you how to use the oven before I split."

Dennis poked his head into the freezer to examine the portfolio of new selections. "Salisbury Steak and Mashed Potatoes," he said, plucking it out. "You're leaving already?"

"Yes, and I'm running late. Keith is waiting."

It was early August, shortly after Harmon Manor's electrical work was finally finished (aside from a few open "punch list" items that would need to be completed before the last payment would be made). Having spent over ten weeks at the mansion, Keith was now working elsewhere, and Patricia became scarcer at home than ever.

After skimming over the back of the box, she hurriedly showed Dennis how to prepare the package for warming and how to set and turn off the oven. Dennis wasn't exactly certain he caught it all, but he knew not to ask her to go through it again.

She fed the foil package into the stove. "Make sure you use those oven mitts when you take it out, so you won't burn yourself."

She then grabbed the beer from the freezer, popped the cap with the bottle opener, took a swig, and with the beer in tow, scurried out of the kitchen.

"And whatever you do, *don't* forget your dinner is in the oven!" she called out over her shoulder. Then she chuckled from the hallway, adding, "Grandpa would be really pissed if you burn down his future home!"

———— ◦ ————

Dennis watched what remained of *Daniel Boone* until the appliance timer buzzed. He managed to remove the meal from the oven without burning himself, then he triple-checked to be sure the stove was turned off.

With the full palette of O-So pop colors available, he went with his favorite: orange-ish flavor. He set up to eat in front of the TV using a little folding table, watching *Bewitched* while he dined. It was a summer rerun, but one he hadn't seen.

Bewitched was over at nine o'clock, and there was nothing interesting on afterward, so he went about cleaning up the kitchen when something thudded in the front hallway.

Evening shadows were spreading like a rising tide, obscuring his view. He clicked over the light switch and stared down the hall. It took him a moment to process what he saw. He cocked his head, blinked, and looked again...same thing: a ball. A ball had bounced *up* from the cellar.

His back stiffened, and his face flushed as time ground to a halt. Holing up in the parlor became his first impulse, but he stood his ground, reminding himself that this presence didn't seem to mean him harm. After his brain cranked away, he concluded that as the man of the house, he needed to investigate.

Every muscle in his body flexed as he made his way down the hall, hands clasped together and held against his mouth. He felt like he was wading through maple syrup and couldn't help but imagine this was how the astronauts had felt when they walked on the moon.

Edging along the wall opposite the opening, he leaned forward, peeking into the stairwell. He could make out nothing through the ink that had pooled there.

After taking two more tentative steps, he stretched out, his skin prickling as he reached inside for the switch. With a swift motion, he flipped on the stairway ceiling lamps and withdrew his arm.

When nothing happened, he groaned. *Really? Add it to the punch list, Mom!*

Dennis backed away, keeping his eyes fixed on the darkness below, while picking up the motionless ball. He swallowed as he stood. Rolling the rubber ball around in his hands, he examined it. This wasn't his. In fact, he'd never seen it before.

He called into the unseen depths. "Hello? Who's there?"

He waited and listened, but the tapestry of shadows gave no reply.

On a whim, he tossed the ball into the pit. He heard only a single soft pat—no bounce.

He waited, grinding his thumb against his forefinger for a few endless seconds. Then the ball flew back out of the blackness in a high arc, and he flinched away, letting it bounce on the floor and off the opposing wall. It settled near his feet.

Compressing his legs like springs, Dennis stood charged and ready to leap away if anyone—any*thing*—came lunging out of the gloom. He straightened his shoulders as he stared at the ball before him, snatching at the fragments of thoughts shooting through his brain, trying to arrange them into some semblance of reason.

After a spell, Dennis picked up the ball and tossed it back into the cellar a second time. Again, a single pat sound, then a few seconds later, the ball flew back. This time, he caught it.

His mind raced as he considered what he was experiencing. He was playing catch with someone—or some*thing*—shrouded in the darkness of the cellar.

Dennis threw the ball back into the murk. This time, he heard no pat sound. Instead, the ball bounced on the cellar floor a few times, rolled, then clanked into something. Silence followed.

A small part of Dennis thought about going into the cellar, but he promptly dismissed the loathsome idea. He backed away from the doorway, reaching out until his fingers touched the opposite wall. Unwilling to peel his gape from the cellar, he moved away and toward the parlor, grazing the backs of his fingernails along the wall as a guide.

As he plopped onto the couch, his head rattled. *What the heck just happened?*

While the television babbled away, Dennis's gaze kept drifting back to the hallway.

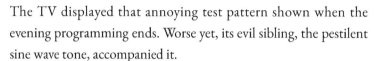

The TV displayed that annoying test pattern shown when the evening programming ends. Worse yet, its evil sibling, the pestilent sine wave tone, accompanied it.

Dennis shook the grogginess from his head and pulled himself up from the couch. When he turned off the television switch, the room went dark, aside from the residual glow gradually fading from the tube. *Weird*, he thought. *Weren't the lights on when I fell asleep*?

He edged his way to the parlor entry and snapped on the hall sconces. He looked around for signs of movement. The silence surrounding him seemed to be growing, becoming almost...*loud*.

He shuddered at the puzzling thought, then set out in the direction of the entrance hall. Passing the cellar, he moved swiftly, his shoulder brushing against the opposite wall.

When he entered the foyer, he flipped on the chandelier light switch and scrambled to the top of the well-lit stairs. He turned on the bedroom wing hall lights before turning off the chandelier, being careful to follow that sequence to avoid immersing himself in darkness for even an instant.

He made himself take the time to brush his teeth (albeit less thoroughly than usual), then hastily retreated to the relative sanctuary of his bedroom. With the room illuminated by the dim glow of his nightlights, Dennis crawled into bed.

By this point, he was wide awake. As he lay there trying to relax, he heard a muted *THUNK*. He sprung upright, eyes wide, listening, then heard it again: *THUNK*.

What is that?

THUNK.

Then it clicked. He was hearing the ball, rebounding off the cellar floor one bounce at a time, the sound reaching him through the entrance hall. *THUNK.*

Was it...like...an invitation to play catch? *THUNK.*

Should he go downstairs to check it out? *THUNK.*

But that's a silly question. There's no way. *THUNK.*

He would stay in his room and wait it out. *THUNK.*

He crept out of bed, pushed his door closed and turned on the bedroom lights, then bolted back and pulled the covers over his head. Buried under the blankets with the door closed, he didn't hear the sound again.

Gradually, his panting subsided, followed by the tension draining from his body, and after almost an hour of visualizing his impending return to Illinois—his *true* sanctuary, he drifted off to sleep.

When Dennis awoke in the morning, his bedroom light was off, and the door hung ajar.

CHAPTER 25

PROLONGMENT

Dennis realized that this cat was determined not to be petted. No matter how slowly he drew in, it would back away, always keeping between them a distance equal to the width of the creek Dennis hunted crayfish in.

This was the third time he had seen the feline behind the house, and the second time he tried to approach it.

The cat sat upright, watching Dennis, who perched on the edge of the back porch—the usual distance between them, of course.

"What are you afraid of?" he asked, quietly, so his mom and grandpa wouldn't start to wonder if he'd taken up talking to ghosts. "*I'm* supposed to be afraid of *you*." It was a black cat, a witch's companion, a bringer of bad luck, and all that. But the very end of its tail was white, so Dennis figured that rendered it practically harmless.

The cat blinked its green eyes at him, slowly twitching the white tip of its curved tail. After a minute, it lost interest altogether, and sauntered off like a drunk—probably back to whatever barn it ruled over.

"We're getting a late start on the plumbing," Grandpa said to Patricia, from inside the house. "The electrical work took a lot longer than it was supposed to."

Dennis kept his ear tuned to the open kitchen window. Grandpa had arrived the night before and had met with the plumber earlier in the day to finalize the contract.

"He's a chrome dome," Patricia had observed to Dennis when the bald plumber stepped out of his van upon his arrival, and Dennis was relieved to hear her make the disparaging remark.

Grandpa said, "What would you think about staying here longer?"

Dennis sat upright, sensing where this was heading.

"Fine by me," Patricia said. "I like it here. So does Dennis."

I do? His homesickness had not waned. Then there was the house—and more precisely, the presence that seemingly occupied it. During the daytime, when he considered the strange happenings that had occurred, feelings of wonderment outweighed his fear. But at nighttime, his curiosity faltered, and the imbalance would shift. Either way, back in Illinois, there was none of this strangeness.

Dennis pushed himself to a crouch and tiptoed under the window.

"How long are you thinking?" she asked.

"Plumbing's going to take eight weeks. That alone will put us into mid-October. But I recently learned we need to drill a new well and replace the septic system. Winter will be coming on by the time all that gets wrapped up."

"Dennis can go to school here," she said.

The boy's face ignited. Was he going to get a say in this? The idea of starting at a new school in this foreign land made him feel sick in the pit of his stomach.

"Kids adjust. Our bigger concern is you, Patricia."

"Me?"

"Your recovery."

"I'm doing great, Dad. Coming here has *helped* my recovery. I *needed* this independence."

Oh my God! Does Grandpa believe this?

Unfortunately for Dennis, the answer was yes.

Dennis studied the psychedelic poster on the kitchen counter.

Blossom music center presents:

Janis Joplin

with special guest Faces

Friday August 29

He picked up the placard. "What's this?"

His mother sat at the table, wearing sunglasses and smoking a cigarette—a new habit she'd taken up. "A concert I'm going to in a couple of weeks."

Dennis pretended to examine the flyer. "Another concert?"

"What are you, my father?"

There was no lighthearted tone in the question nor a playful look on her face.

"Mom, are you alright?" He turned to her with eyebrows raised, breath held.

Her glare bored through her shades. She took a swig from the Genesee Cream Ale bottle grasped in her hand, and after swallowing, she answered, over-enunciating each word, "Mind your own *goddamned business*."

Dennis's blank gaze returned to the poster. Clenching his teeth, he blinked away the sting of oncoming tears. He felt the need to respond, but could not find the words. A hollowness formed in his chest as he waited for her to say something else.

Patricia took a heavy pull on her cigarette, then slowly blew the smoke in his direction.

"I'm just worried about you." Immediately, regret jabbed him in his gut, but there was no way to reel his words back in. He held his breath again.

She took another puff, crushed the smoke in the ashtray, then got up and grabbed her purse and car keys off the counter.

"Nothing to worry about, Dennis," she said as she walked toward the hallway. Then she stopped, wheeled around, and reached across the table to pick up the bottle of beer she'd left behind.

Patricia stormed off, out the front door, and drove away.

CHAPTER 26

HELTER SKELTER

A s if he didn't already have enough on his mind, Dennis settled in the parlor with his country-fried chicken TV dinner and cherry-ish flavored O-So at half-past six, when there was nothing on but the news.

The anchorman wore a grim face as he delivered the top story: "Los Angeles has had another incident of multiple murders. Last night a middle-aged couple was stabbed to death in a case that has striking similarities to the mass murder Saturday of actress Sharon Tate and four friends..."

Dennis instantly turned Argus-eyed. Newsreel showed corpses in body bags being removed from a house, others shrouded in white sheets on the lawn, while the chilling report continued:

"Late last night, another bizarre murder in Los Angeles, the second in two days...

"...found in his home, his head covered by a white hood, a meat fork stuck in his chest...

"...found in the bedroom, dead, her back brutally cut by a whip...

"...on the refrigerator door, smeared in blood, were the words 'DEATH TO PIGS'...

"...police said they found no connection between the two crimes, but both murders involved the same bloody signature, the same bloody wounds...

"...tonight, the city of Los Angeles is uneasy, after two strange murders have left seven dead, and no clues as to the identity of the killers..."

The words stirred up disturbing images that swirled in Dennis's head. Who could have done such a thing? What did it mean? Could something like that happen *here*?

———————⬧◯⬧———————

Slamming car doors awakened Dennis from a troubled sleep. He looked around his room, half expecting to see DEATH TO PIGS scrawled in blood on the wall. He scooted out from under the covers and peered through the window, then his shoulders slackened when he saw his mom and Keith talking in the driveway.

Climbing back into bed, the boy felt comforted by the knowledge that his mother had returned home. Most nights, she did not.

Soon the high-pitched crank of Keith's Dodge resounded, then the van purred away. The front door opened and closed. Dennis laid back in bed, listening as his mom climbed the steps. The doorknob turned, then the hinges rasped.

He pretended to be sleeping when she peeked in, expecting she would enter and rouse him. He'd let her apologize, and they'd have a chance to talk everything out. Instead, the latch clicked shut, and she receded down the hall, her own door softly closing as she withdrew to her bedroom.

The night turned quiet again, and Dennis began to regret how he hadn't said anything when his mom looked in on him. He tried not to dwell on it, hoping they would patch things up in the morning.

His mind drifted back to what his mom had said while arguing with Keith: "I never asked to be a mother in the first place!" He had played her words back so many times in the days that followed, wishing repetition would numb away the hurt.

At least he would not be spending the entire night alone.

But as Dennis Harmon tried to fall back asleep, sickening imaginings of what before long would become known as "the Manson Family murders" crept back into his weary mind, bedeviling him with tortured thoughts and a fragile sleep.

CHAPTER 27

ABANDONMENT

MEN YELLING ABOVE THE racket of machinery woke Dennis up. Early morning sunshine bathed his room.

When he stepped into the hallway, he felt relieved his mom's door remained closed. She was home, still sleeping, so he wouldn't have to talk to her yet.

He stood at the kitchen counter eating a bowl of cornflakes, wincing at the Janis Joplin concert flyer. *Mind your own goddamned business* echoed in his head.

He made a brief, lame attempt to defend his mom's behavior, reasoning that she wasn't herself. But then the anger flared back, and he pushed the placard aside. It slid across the counter, caught on the edge of the stove, then dropped into the narrow gap between the oven and the cabinet.

A floorboard creaked above. His mother's bedroom.

Dennis toyed with the idea of running away. *Better if I choose to be alone. Except...* Who was he kidding? He had no place to go, no way to support himself. He couldn't function on his own. Not yet, at least. Maybe in a year or two, when he was older. For now, he had to ride it through, hoping his mother could straighten herself out.

As he finished his cereal, the floorboards squeaked once more. His mother might be coming down soon, but he didn't feel ready to talk. He wandered onto the back porch to watch the men, squinting his eyes against the sunlight. An excavator worked at digging a new leach field. Back some distance, further up the slope, a truck with a large auger drilled a new well.

Dennis strolled out into the yard, keeping a safe distance from the digging and drilling operations. Watching the equipment operate was a welcome distraction from the painful thoughts of his mother. After passing the worksite, he walked behind it, along the edge of a wooded area he guessed formed the rear boundary of the property.

Movement in the house caught his attention. He gulped when a shape stepped forward into an upstairs window, the empty bedroom across the hall from his mother's. The figure faced him and seized his gaze.

He looked away to clear his vision, but when he turned his eyes back, the glaring figure remained.

He squinted, studying what appeared to be a woman wearing strange clothing that immediately told him this was not his mom. The figure began gesturing, but he couldn't make out what she was communicating. He moved in for a better view.

He stopped when he reached the end of the hole that was being excavated, raised a hand against his forehead to shade the sun, and examined the lady. It was the same smiling woman who had faded away in the parlor.

Doris.

The ground shook. Dennis first thought the earth was quaking, then he decided that wasn't it, his knees were wobbling. But soon he figured out he was feeling vibrations from the digging and drilling operations. The nearby machinery roared. He continued moving past the men and their equipment, his gaze fastened on the figure in the window.

Doris was not old, but not as young as his mother. Her brown, wavy hair was cut short, just above the shoulders. Thin and attractive, she wore old-fashioned-looking clothes and hairstyle.

She motioned for him to come, and it was then he realized how frantic she appeared. Dennis pointed to himself. Doris nodded urgently.

He froze. His lips went numb while he tried to marshal his thoughts. This was a ghost, right? Dennis thought of the black cat with the white-tipped tail, and he suddenly understood why it had kept its distance.

Yet Doris didn't seem to be a threat.

Again, she gestured for him to come, her hands and arms motioning hysterically this time.

Okay. Dennis pushed aside his distrust and willed himself forward. He crossed the short stretch of lawn, then the veranda, entering the back door with a spiking pulse, leery he could be walking into some sort of supernatural trap.

He walked up the grand entrance hall stairs, pausing with each step to scan his surroundings. He gasped when he reached the top, grabbing the banister to steady himself as his knees weakened.

No longer in the empty back bedroom, Doris now stood at the end of the hall, pointing at the closed door of his mother's room. In a slightly translucent image, she appeared like she might recede from this world at any instant.

The machinery thundered outside, rattling the mansion, the workers oblivious to the astonishing encounter Dennis faced within.

Still pointing, Doris shook her hand with urgency. Dennis gritted his teeth and stepped forward into the hallway, straight toward Doris. A staticky charge bloomed in the air and grew as he approached. She slid aside, clearing his path to his mother's bedroom door, nodding at him with a grim expression as he drew in.

Grabbing the glass door handle and turning it, Dennis heard a click and felt the latch release. He pushed the door open. The sunlit room came into full view. His breathing stalled.

His mother lay on the bed, staring at the ceiling with an empty look. A needle dangled from her arm, its tip plunged into her skin.

Dennis registered what had happened, having seen a TV movie where a man overdosed after shooting up with a syringe. He'd turned off the program but was left with a sick feeling he couldn't shake. Now, Dennis suddenly felt overcome with nausea, but this time, he couldn't switch the channel.

Breaking free from his stupor, he ran to her bedside, pulled the needle out, and threw it on the floor. For a moment, a rush of anger filled his head, and he wondered how she could have done such a thing. He shook her. "Mom! Mom! Wake up!"

But she didn't wake up. She didn't even move. His mother just lay there, with her constricted pupils fixed on the ceiling.

"Mom! Please! Wake up!"

He grabbed her face and turned it, but immediately noticed it wasn't as warm as it should have been. Putting his finger under her nostrils, he waited for the draft of her breath on his skin, but felt nothing. He grabbed her wrists and desperately searched for a pulse—something his grandma had shown him how to do—but found none. She was already gone, and there was no way to deny it.

She still smelled like his mother, but he knew this meant nothing; the stench of death would soon take its place.

And with that thought, Dennis collapsed to his knees. "Mommy!" He repeated the word, saliva dribbling and mixing with the streams of tears into an expanding blot of wetness on the bedsheet.

———◇———

Patricia went peacefully, overcome with a drowsy blissfulness. When she laid back on her bed for the last time, she felt like she was floating through a whiteout snowstorm—like one of many she'd experienced in Chicago when she was just a kid—except she was lighter than the air, and everything was deliciously warm. The room around her seemed to calmly dissipate as she stopped breathing, and her body was starved of oxygen.

———◇———

Dennis stayed kneeling beside his dead mother for some time. He squeezed her palm, his cries gradually dissipating into hitching sniffles. The racket behind the house persisted, although it had flagged into little more than vague background noise.

Dennis eventually stood, still holding his mom's cold fingers. The electrostatic charge rose in the air, and his hair lifted from his head. When he turned to see Doris had stepped up beside him, he felt too numb to be startled. She glimmered, tiny sparkles flittering over her image. Through this bleary depiction, he saw sincere grief on her face.

"I'm so sorry, Dennis." Her words sounded muted, yet sharp, as if she had whispered them directly into his ear.

He took a deep quivering breath, wiping the tears from his cheek. He studied her and her old-fashioned dress. She was pleasing to look at, and nice. She was...motherly.

She held out both hands, her soft voice coaxing him toward her. "You can live with me now."

Dennis's mind spun in a paralyzing dullness. His entire future—his very existence—seemed to totter before him. As alone as he'd felt recently, irreversible abandonment had just sunk its claws into him. He stared at Doris, watching as she reached out, beckoning him forward.

"Dennis..." Her chalky voice grated in his ear. "Live with me, Dennis...Denny." The tone repulsed him, yet her words mesmerized him.

He bit his lower lip and fought back another wave of tears. He nodded, dried his cheeks with his palms, and held his breath as he reached out to take Doris's hands.

Static discharged with a sudden snap when they touched, and Dennis Harmon's world flashed purple and silent.

CHAPTER 28

MANHUNT

Sheriff Roger Miller allowed himself to finish his Lucky Strike, hoping it might help him face the task. He leaned back to draw in one last drag, which he inhaled extra deeply. He exhaled the smoke while stubbing out the cigarette in the overflowing ashtray on his desk.

The manilla folder sitting in front of him lay open, a county coroner report on top:

PATRICIA HARMON
FEMALE – 25 YEARS
Accidental death from general hypoxia
due to unintentional heroin toxicity

Meeting with the victim's family was the hardest part of the job. He closed the folder and stood. On his way, he stopped at the coffee station for a refill.

"Mr. Harmon," he said when he entered the witness interview room, reaching out in greeting.

Fred Harmon turned to face him. "Sheriff."

The handshake was grim, as they usually were in this room.

"Can we get you another coffee?" the sheriff asked, although he'd already noticed Mr. Harmon hadn't touched the cup they had given him. "Or warm that one up?"

Fred Harmon shook his head. "Any progress on the case?"

Sheriff Miller motioned to the tiny table and the pair of chairs. "It's our top priority, Mr. Harmon."

The men sat across from one another.

"You can imagine it's hard for us to be patient, Sheriff."

The sheriff nodded. "We conducted another manhunt."

Mr. Harmon said nothing.

"We'll continue to search, but..." The sheriff cut himself off, unwilling to admit he had already lost hope. There had been eight ground searches in four weeks, and all came up empty. Dennis Harmon had vanished without a trace.

"What about that boyfriend of hers?"

"We've got nothing on Keith Richardson." That much was true. The hippy electrician had a solid alibi—he was working with his father when the Harmon girl overdosed, between eight and ten in the morning, according to the coroner's report. He had appeared just as distraught about his girlfriend's death as her family, and he was forthcoming from the onset about their drug usage. "But I draw the line at heroin," Keith had explained. He was the one who had found Patricia's body the evening of her death, and he'd promptly called the sheriff's office.

"We know that bastard caused it," Mr. Harmon said.

"I understand how you feel," the sheriff said. "But we have to look at the facts. No facts point to Richardson."

Fred Harmon studied him, waiting for more.

"We arrested the drug dealer who sold Patricia the heroin."

Harmon narrowed his eyes.

"The dealer's just a dumb kid. He's pleading guilty, talking openly. According to him, Keith even tried to stop Patricia from buying the heroin."

The room fell silent as Harmon processed this. "But he still might have had something to do with my grandson's disappearance."

"We're not ruling anything out, Mr. Harmon." But the sheriff didn't think Keith had anything to do with the boy's disappearance, either. Two of the workers were the last ones to see him when he wandered from the backyard into the house. The sheriff had thoroughly interrogated each of the men as well as Keith, but found no evidence of foul play.

The case of the missing boy was unprecedented in the quiet rural community of Homer County. Hundreds of citizens attended each manhunt, helping the police scour the countryside. But they'd uncovered no clue of his whereabouts or his fate.

Meanwhile, speculation and rumors were spreading about what had transpired at Harmon Manor. With the recent happenings compounding the legacy of the home's more distant but equally dark past, the house of horrors was now being referred to as "Misery Mansion."

"We're canceling the rest of the renovation work," Fred Harmon said. "We won't be moving in."

The sheriff could only nod, stigma and reminders being what they are.

"Will you be searching the house again before we have it boarded back up?"

An odd, fleeting thought popped into Sheriff Roger Miller's head when he pictured Misery Mansion being boarded up: *To keep people out? Or to keep something in?*

PART FIVE

PHANTOM REALM

CHAPTER 29

RESETTLEMENT

T HE BOY STOOD UP from the parlor couch and walked toward the hallway. He hesitated for a moment at the entranceway, turned, and said, "Again, I'm really sorry."

Jessica Putnam could only shake her head.

He gave an awkward smile before adding, "I'll be in the foyer...if you need me," then disappeared from the room.

Jessica's mind reeled. She felt as though fuses were popping inside her head in rapid succession—like a strip of firecrackers.

Keep it together, her mind's voice repeated into her mind's ear. She focused on breathing, steadily pulling air into her lungs, then pushing it out, concentrating on the lulling effect of the rhythm. *In, out, in, out.*

Eventually, Jessica allowed her thoughts to drift back to the boy's explanations. It was a vexing puzzle comprised of pieces that would not—could not—fit together.

She had just spoken with a ten-year-old named Dennis Harmon, a boy who had vanished in 1969. Now, thirty-four years later...he's still ten! *He disappeared—and now I'm with him!*

According to legend, the missing boy had been killed by his mother before she took her own life. Now Jessica knew that was completely wrong...yet the real story was even more inconceivable.

"We're in Doris's realm," he'd informed Jessica, although he clearly didn't understand everything about his circumstances. He had recounted the life of Doris, but most of his information came from Doris herself, who purposely left holes in her stories, such as what happened to her son Danny. Doris had told Dennis she felt partly responsible for the fate of her son, but she hadn't elaborated, and Dennis had never pushed the issue. Doris had confessed that it was the loss of her beloved son that ultimately drove her to suicide.

More than once during their conversation, Jessica bit her tongue. It was ironic: with her knowledge of Harmon Manor's folklore, she knew more about Doris's family history than the child who'd been living—if that's even the right word—with Doris for decades. It was common knowledge in Homer County that Albert Harmon had been murdered by his son, who was subsequently committed to an insane asylum, but she saw no point in telling this to Dennis if Doris herself had chosen not to.

Dennis had told Jessica his own story. He'd tried to keep a brave face as he related how his mother had spiraled into drug abuse, but he cringed repeatedly, having to live through it once again. He had described how Doris had called him to the house, gesturing from the window.

Back in the moment, Jessica stared at the ceiling, thinking about how Halloween Ghost Lady had been gesturing from the window. *Only...why would Doris have been gesturing to* me*? She'd been trying to warn Dennis about his mother overdosing. Was she trying to warn* me *about something? It just doesn't make any sense.*

Jessica shook her head and pried her gaze from the barrel-vaulting above her, then went back to reflecting on other things Dennis had told her.

Doris had invited him to live with her, and without understanding what that meant, he had accepted. He would soon discover he was bound to the house, a permanent captive to this other realm where Doris's soul lingered.

"I call it the 'phantom realm'," Dennis had said. "It's a lot like the Phantom Zone in my Superman comic books—that's where they send prisoners to live like ghosts. The convicts can observe the regular world, but they can't interact with it. Just like us." He'd explained how the simple act of grasping Doris's hands had carried him into her phantom realm, with no way to depart.

"Everyone worries about ghosts coming into our world, but I never heard anyone talk about us going into *their* world," Dennis said. "Or how that's even possible without dying first, I guess."

Jessica pondered his insight, recognizing the wisdom in it. Yet Dennis had crossed over...alive, right? And now, so had she.

"2003," she had answered when he asked what year she came from. Then she'd considered that he was from 1969. "Does that mean you've been here for thirty-four years?"

He'd shrugged and said he had no idea how long it had been. "Time doesn't apply here. I know that sounds odd, but you'll understand what I mean soon enough."

Dennis had explained how the home's interior never changes, remaining perpetually fixed in the same state as in Doris's memories during her happiest days.

Jessica looked around at the décor of the room, and it seemed clear he was right. The style of all the furniture and decorations was from a different era. It was an eclectic mix of heavy Victorian and newer, lighter art nouveau and art deco styles. But there was nothing even remotely modern in sight. A Victrola sat nearby, ready to be played—undoubtedly the same phonograph Jessica had heard playing, first as a teenager, and later, during her first night sleeping in the mansion.

The boy had described how, outside the house, time *does* change. He referred to it as the "outside world," and the people on the outside were "outsiders."

But then he had explained how when you view the outside from within the phantom realm, time doesn't progress steadily. Rather, it shifts randomly, jumping back and forth through years, seasons, and time of day. "It's like the house is playing back its memories of its surroundings. It might be nighttime in the winter at one point, then it's daytime in the summer. You might see an old car on the narrow road, then a modern one on a wider road."

As if on cue, the sunlight had blinked out from the windows, and darkness took its place.

"See?" Dennis had said, pointing at the window. Then he motioned to the illuminated floor lamp across the room. "This is why she leaves the lights on."

He went on to describe how they were bound to the house. "You can't interact with physical things. Your hand passes right through them. Like...you can't pick up a book, or open a door. You sort of float on the surface of the floor and the chairs you sit on. Like this couch...see how you're not really making contact with it?"

As she had nodded, a thought had popped into her head, and she reached out and touched Dennis's forearm. She'd made normal contact and could feel his life through the warmth of his skin. He'd held his hand out and grasped hers. They'd smiled at each other,

sharing an unspoken comfort so starkly different from the lifeless-
ness surrounding them.

"Are you sure we're not dead?" Jessica had asked.

"No, we're not dead," Dennis had answered without hesitation.
"I would know it if I had died, wouldn't you?"

Jessica had shrugged. "Sometimes they say ghosts don't know
they're dead."

"Okay, but when I touch Doris, she's cold. You're not. I hear her
footsteps, but not ours. We can't touch things here, but she can."

Jessica had sighed and leaned back onto the couch, rubbing her
temples.

Dennis had eventually continued, "We can't leave the house.
Something holds us back."

Jessica had thought about how she had tried to walk through the
door but was unable, like something pulled on her from behind.

The discussion had then reverted to Doris, and Dennis explained
how he'd developed a strange closeness to her, with Doris even asking Dennis to call her "Mother." A sullen look had washed over his
face, and he lowered his eyes like he was trying to keep a picture from
forming in his head. "She's a better mom to me than my own mom
was."

He'd described how they read books together, and his cheeks
flushed red when he admitted she had taught him how to swing
dance.

From the beginning, Doris called him "Denny," he'd recounted. He went along with it willingly, although "nobody ever called
me Denny before. I was always just plain old 'Dennis'. Except my
uncles…" he had added with a grin. "…they called me 'Dennis the
Menace'."

The similarity between "Denny" and "Danny" hadn't been lost on Jessica, and she wondered if when Doris was alive, her son might have addressed her as "Mother." She'd kept these thoughts to herself.

"I feel bad for Mother—Doris, I mean," he'd said, and paused as thoughts worked in his head. "She's lonely."

"A lost soul," Jessica said.

Dennis had nodded. "That's a good way to put it."

She'd waited for him to go on.

"I appreciate her taking care of me and all that, but I don't want to stay here." He'd stared at the floor as if collecting his words, then added, "I belong in the normal realm. I want to feel *alive* again."

Jessica had choked up when she heard his haunting words, but she cleared her throat to chase the sensation away. "Where's Doris now?"

The boy had shrugged. "Sometimes she's here, but usually she's not. She comes and goes—just sort of appears, then she's gone."

"Gone?"

"Yeah, like she's slipped out of the realm, off to some other dimension or something. I've asked her, and she doesn't know why—she doesn't even have any memory of it."

Jessica had rubbed the back of her neck while she considered this. "Does Doris understand what's happened to you? How you're locked up here forever?"

He'd shaken his head. "Doris isn't a complete person. It's like only part of her is here—"

"The part searching for the happiness she lost," Jessica had finished. "Having you here fulfills her."

"Mm-hmm," Dennis had said, before losing himself in thought.

They fell silent for a spell. Jessica had briefly contemplated what demons had driven this boy to crave maternal attention so much that he would tolerate such an existence, but she'd chased away the pitiful thought with an arduous swallow. "Will Doris know I'm here?"

Dennis had pondered her question for a moment. "I don't know. I guess we'll just have to wait and see."

"What about you? Can you see people when they come in the house?"

"Yeah, but the weird thing is, they can't see or hear me. I'm not a ghost. But it's like I'm a ghost to them—like a *quasi-ghost*." His eyebrows had risen when he spoke the emphasized word, as if he was proud of himself for the concoction. "I've noticed people can only see me if they are outside, looking in."

Jessica had pictured the figure she'd seen in the window of the front door and asked if that had been him.

"Sorry, I didn't mean to scare you. But man, your dog was really bookin'!" He'd chuckled.

An ache had formed in Jessica's chest at the mere mention of Arik. She'd mustered a hollow smile, then asked, "And the Amish teenager saw you in the kitchen?"

"Yes." Dennis had squinted like he was glimpsing into the past. "I couldn't stop looking up into the bedroom through the hole in the ceiling. I haven't been…in that room…since… That's where my mom died." His voice had weakened, then croaked out, and his face grew long with distress.

Jessica had felt bad for the boy. But while she didn't want to push on a topic that made him uncomfortable, there was something she didn't understand, so she'd gently asked a follow-up question: "But if the house always appears as it was when Doris lived here, why were you able to see through that hole in the ceiling?"

"Yeah, that's a good question," he said. "It seems like the construction work damages her realm, but it's temporary. The realm restores itself."

Jessica had turned and looked at the nearby wall, the one she'd removed in the renovation. She had swung the sledgehammer at it herself, but here it was, after all. "But wait...have you ever seen *yourself*? I mean—"

"—the outsider version of me," Dennis said, and he'd nodded. "Twice. But the slices of time aren't predictable—"

"—so, there's no way to know when it will happen," she'd finished.

"Exactly. But it's a real trip watching yourself! Both times, it was something I remembered happening."

Contemplating the notion, Jessica had blown out a breath through pursed lips. "But the house has been mostly empty since Doris died, so you probably don't see people often, right?"

"Right. You'll rarely see anyone." He had told her how he'd taken to touching the occasional visitors who come inside the house, because he could actually feel them, unlike anything else in the house. "When I touch an outsider, even for just a second, it makes me feel sort of normal again. I can feel their...*life*."

A dull, empty ache had formed in Jessica's gut. She'd thought about how she'd felt a hand on her back, twice. "I felt you touch me," she had said, being careful not to convey how frightened it had made her.

"Yeah," Dennis had wrinkled his brow. "...and that's why you ended up here." He'd explained how, by a stroke of pure bad luck, he'd been touching her when lightning struck the house, and somehow the energy surge catapulted Jessica into the phantom realm.

"Now we're both stuck here. I didn't mean for that to happen! I'm *so* sorry."

Jessica had no longer been able to hold back her emotions when she heard this. Tears burst forth and ran down her cheeks, and she'd reached out to grasp the boy's hands, attempting to reassure him, and herself as well.

But now, alone in this dead world, whatever reassurance she'd conjured had dwindled away.

———•◦•———

Pacing the parlor, Jessica could feel her agitation continue to swell as the conversation with Dennis sunk in.

She decided a diversion might quell her manic thoughts through a tour of Harmon Manor as it had appeared in Doris's age. An examination might even yield a clue about a way to escape.

She wandered from room to room, viewing an alternative manifestation of the house she already loved, admiring the period furnishings and décor within. Every little detail was its own welcome distraction, and before long, she truly did feel calmer.

Jessica stopped at the doorway to the dining room and peered in. She had to count the chairs around the vast mahogany table: *Twelve!* A carved walnut sideboard buffet sat at the end of the room, adorned with griffins on either side, supporting an upper-level shelf. At the opposite end of the room, the built-ins displayed fine chinaware and crystal glassware. She wondered how long after Doris's death these antiques had been removed, and where they'd ended up.

She moved on toward the front of the house.

Dennis stood sentry in the entrance hall, looking out a small pane positioned precisely at his eye level in the front door's leaded glasswork. Jessica recognized this was his station when she had seen him from outside.

The boy turned and smiled when she entered the foyer.

"Watching the outside world?" she asked.

"Not much else to do here," he said with a wink, then turned back around to continue gazing.

Jessica wandered into the library. Volumes of bound books filled the shelves. Rich upholstered furniture centered the library, including a tête-à-tête style loveseat. Beyond the fireplace, an office area made up the other half of the L-shaped room, featuring a leather-top partner desk. A very cool bronze inkwell, cast as the macabre figure of a sneering devil imp, sat on the desk.

She returned to the entry hall, passed the statue that was Dennis, and ascended the staircase.

On the wall at the end of the bedroom wing hung a silver crucifix, fine, but garishly sculpted, with a brass figure of Jesus hanging from the cross. It gave Jessica the shivers, although she didn't linger long enough to put a finger on why.

Beautiful furniture and fine linens and bedcovers were appointed to each of the bedrooms. She studied the configuration of the master bedroom, with a sitting room on one side and a dressing area on the other. When she crossed the open floor space, movement across the room caught her eye, and she flinched. But she was relieved to discover it was just her reflection in a full-length pier mirror.

Jessica approached the wall-mounted mirror, wondering how she, in her current form, would reflect within it. But the sight of her reproduced image was nothing out of the ordinary. Examining her reflection, she could easily discern the strain she suffered, plainly shown on her face and in her posture. She sighed and reminded herself to relax. Oh, if only it could be so simple.

A dressing table stood beside the pier mirror, with a framed black-and-white photograph on display. Momentarily forgetting her limitations here, Jessica reached to pick it up, but her hand passed through it. She blew a raspberry and instead leaned over to examine the picture.

Doris with Danny, she presumed. Elegantly dressed, they'd posed beside the parlor fireplace. Danny looked to be about ten years old in the photo. Doris's brown hair was cut short, styled in neat waves. Both wore cheery natural smiles, as if they could never have envisioned what a tragic turn their lives would take.

Jessica backed away and resumed looking around. Surveying the master bedroom, she considered how the teenaged Amish cabinet installer had observed Dennis gazing up into this room, where his mother had died—and which he'd vowed to never enter again. She shook her head, shoving the pitiful notion aside, then left the bedroom.

Next, she climbed the stairs to the attic, inhabited by mostly unidentifiable items covered with sheets. In some way, the attic harbored a deeper loneliness to it, so she didn't stay there long.

Jessica continued to ascend, following the last remaining stairway to the belvedere. As her head cleared the floor, she noticed there were no window coverings. She felt thrilled by this revelation because all the other windows in the house had curtains or sheers over them, making it impossible to see outside with an unobstructed view.

A single item occupied the room: an ancient and well-worn deacon's bench, perhaps banished there on account of its aged appearance. It sat in the middle of the room, tucked aside the balustrade lining the entrance opening.

Jessica had been at the top level during the day a few times before. But each time was brief, and she had never taken a good look outside.

She approached the middle window on the front side and looked out toward the street.

Early springtime in the outside world, daffodils flowered in patches along the driveway. Trees had begun to bud, lightly misted with their first hints of color, and the grass shone with a vibrant emerald shade.

The mansion's driveway was gravel, while red brick paved the roadway, barely wide enough for one vehicle, winding along the creek beyond. Designed in the same Victorian Italianate style as the mansion, the carriage house stood about halfway between the home and the road. Jessica recalled how Dennis described the scene outside varying through random slices of time and understood she was viewing a bygone era. *A memory from the house.*

On the other side of the creek lay an endless stretch of forest, continuing as far as she could see in either direction. She was observing the native woods populating the fertile valley floor before someone had cleared the area for farmland.

The windows facing rearward provided an expansive view of the formal gardens. Laid out in geometric shapes matching the blueprints she'd been given, the landscape design featured flower borders, a rose garden, stone terraced walls, and meticulously groomed evergreen privet hedges. Along the back of the property stood a cluster of hawthorn trees, their showy pink flowers just starting to bloom.

In the adjacent side window, a grassy mound rose above the surrounding ridges, and she recognized it as Kassel's Hill, the tallest point in the county. Even then, it had already been cleared for livestock pasturing.

As she crossed the room, she again glimpsed out the back windows at the amazing gardens, but in a snap, they disappeared. Time shifted, flipping to summer, the trees covered in leaves. Light rain trickled from the clouds that filled the sky. But there was no trace of the manicured gardens. Just like that, the property behind the mansion became a vast stretch of unkempt grass, much like it had appeared when Jessica bought the house.

She approached the final side and looked out to see the garden access drive beyond the stretch of trees, where, as sixteen-year-olds, she and Erin had parked under the full moon of Halloween. She nodded with familiarity as her eyes followed the subtle trough in the treetops, tracing the path they'd each taken through the woods to reach Harmon Manor.

Thinking back to that frightful experience of seeing Halloween Ghost Lady, it occurred to Jessica she was standing in the very same window the apparition had appeared in.

And just as this thought flitted across her mind, it hit her, so unexpectedly and with such force it was as though she had been sucker-punched in the face. Her hand jerked up to stifle a cry. Her mind ricocheted, questioning if it could be true. A powerful wave of faintness passed over her, and she fought to not permit her legs to buckle underneath her.

She moved her hand from her mouth to her hair, draped over her shoulder. Running her fingers through it, she followed the length of her locks down her upper arm to her elbow, where it ended. "I have long hair," she said aloud to herself, as though she wasn't already aware. "Blonde hair. Straight hair."

Her heart fired into a hammering frenzy, and she struggled to keep her quickening breaths steady enough to avoid hyperventilating.

She thought back to the photograph she'd just seen. "Doris has brown hair. Wavy hair. Short-cut hair."

An image formed in her mind of Halloween Ghost Lady. Long, straight hair, light enough for the moonlight to reflect off it. The phantom's hair was not at all like Doris's; rather, the phantom's hair was like her own.

It wasn't the spirit of Doris in the window...

And now, all these years later, Jessica Putnam finally understood why that figure was so frantically pleading for help.

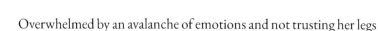

Overwhelmed by an avalanche of emotions and not trusting her legs to keep her upright, Jessica sat on the bench.

She struggled to believe what had happened to her. If only she were merely dreaming, she could wake up and forget this nightmare. But she knew with cruel certainty it was all too real.

What if she had somehow recognized herself as Halloween Ghost Lady? Instead of running away—*like a coward*, could she have done something to avert the predicament she now found herself in?

The maddening absurdity of her captivity sparked anger. The reality about what she would be missing was becoming brutally clear. Was life as she knew it over? What about all the things she had never yet had a chance to do? Was all of that gone now? Would she ever see those she loved again? What hell were they going through since her disappearance?

But the real source of her growing rage was knowing she'd provoked her own plight. A normal person would have never bought the mansion in the first place, but she had *chosen* it. It wasn't merely that the house was *reputed* to be haunted—she practically *knew* it was. Yet she had convinced herself it was all harmless. She'd received the warnings and ignored them, thinking supernatural stuff was cool, messing with things she couldn't possibly understand.

Jessica howled with fury until her throat felt raw. When crushing tiredness began to beat out the anger, she crumpled to the floor, sobbing.

That's when she spotted Dennis looking up at her from the bottom of the stairway, his cheeks glistening with tears.

When Jessica's eyes met his, he stepped back and away, leaving her alone, as if recognizing how helpless he was to assist her in coming to grips with her new existence.

———◦———

When Jessica managed to gather herself enough to venture downstairs, she found Dennis back in the entry hall.

He looked up at her and gave a silent nod.

"I'm sorry," she said with a hoarse voice from the gallery above him.

His head turned downward. "*I'm* the one who should be sorry."

"Please don't say that." Jessica moved to the stairs and began to descend.

When she arrived at the landing, she paused. "I'm usually stronger than that."

"I know you are."

"I had a good cry, though, so I feel better now." She really did—at least her mind felt numb. "Doris isn't here?"

He shook his head. "But she can appear at any moment."

Jessica continued down the last flight, crossed the foyer, and settled on the bench of the hall tree. "This is beautiful," she said, summoning him over.

The seat was wide enough, so Dennis joined her.

"It's kind of creepy looking." He grinned. "But I like that sort of thing."

"Me too...although my tastes might change if I ever get out of here."

He laughed heartily, perhaps relieved she was up for joking.

"Were you scared when you moved into the house?" she asked.

"Not so much."

She couldn't tell if he was telling the truth or trying not to be viewed as a chicken.

He clarified, "I thought it was cool because it looks like the Addams Family's house."

Jessica chuckled. "My friend Erin used to say that."

Dennis paused while his eyes went hazy, and when they cleared, he continued, "I didn't even really mind much when Doris started showing up. She wasn't a scary ghost. She was like a cartoon ghost from when I was little—"

"Oh, I know about Casper," Jessica said with a smile. "The Friendly Ghost."

His face lit up. "So, what's TV like in 2003?"

She told him about the current programs, and when *CSI* piqued his interest, she wondered if he might make the perfect viewing partner. It flabbergasted him when she described the modern high-def thin-screen TV, and how many channels were available, but he wrinkled his brow when she explained how the signal came through a cable wire.

Jessica changed the subject. "I saw what you mean about time shifting. It's so weird how the outside transforms without warning."

"When we lived in Chicago, my grandpa always said 'If you don't like the weather, wait a minute'."

Jessica gave a silent chuckle. "I think they say that everywhere, but it takes on a whole new meaning here. So, the time slices are random?"

He nodded. "There's no pattern to the changes, or when they occur."

Jessica rubbed her chin as she thought this out, then said, "You can kind of figure out the era based on what you see."

"Exactly. Except there's one thing that never changes, though. Can you guess?"

Jessica puckered her lips to one side as she considered this, then shrugged. "I give up."

"The Amish!" He giggled. "No matter what year the outside is in, they're wearing the same duds and driving the same old buggies."

She joined him in his laughter, recalling how her mother joked that the phrase "Amish fashion trend" was an oxymoron.

"No offense, but your car's really square," Dennis said, on a playful roll. "'60s cars are a lot cooler."

She smiled. "True. But newer cars are a lot more reliable. Safer too."

This time it was Dennis who rubbed his chin, as though it was the first time he'd ever considered the importance of these factors in an automobile.

Jessica steered the conversation back to her plight. "Do we...sleep here?"

"No, I never even feel tired. I don't eat or drink either. Or use the bathroom." His gaze wandered awkwardly around the room. When he quit fidgeting and turned back to her, he flashed a wide grin. "Close your mouth—we are not codfish."

Jessica realized her mouth had indeed been hanging open. She snapped her jaw closed and tightened her lips. "Codfish?" She raised her eyebrows at him.

"My grandma used to say that to me. She got it from Mary Poppins."

She laughed, pleased the boy had such a good sense of humor.

"Of course, I don't get any older either. It's like we're in a state of 'suspended animation'," he said with a serious expression.

Jessica held a straight face, despite being amused by his manner, and gave him the quizzical look he was expecting.

"They had that on *Star Trek*," he explained, "and on *Lost in Space* too."

She nodded in a businesslike way, trying not to chuckle at his attempt to account for paranormal phenomena with sci-fi television concepts. But in truth, it was as good of an explanation as any. "I'm breathing though." It was a question as much as a statement.

"Yeah, we breathe, but that's the only normal thing here." A mischievous smile formed on his face, and he warned her, "I hope you like your clothes."

She looked down and thought *not especially*, but laughed at his wisecrack anyway, remembering something her father always said: "Sometimes you just have to laugh, because if you don't, you might cry."

Something rustled upstairs, followed by the sound of footsteps. Jessica and Dennis exchanged the same apprehensive look before he stood and scampered soundlessly back to the front door. She rose to her feet and took one step forward, but realized she had no idea what to do or where to go. She clenched her hands into fists and stayed right there.

The footsteps grew in volume, and Dennis shot Jessica a glance, like his eyes were pantomiming "now we'll find out, won't we?"

A lean, pretty woman emerged from the hallway above and walked along the gallery balustrade toward the stairs. Jessica's breath caught when she recognized Doris from the photograph.

"Hello, Denny," Doris called down from the gallery above.

"Hello, Mother," Dennis responded, looking up with a smile.

Something about their exchange made Jessica's hair stand on end.

Doris didn't acknowledge—or even seem to notice—Jessica. *Is she ignoring me?* If so, she put on a good show.

Wearing an old-fashioned skirt with a belt around the waist, Doris appeared to be in her mid- to late thirties. She began to descend. After making the turn at the landing, she proceeded down the last flight. Jessica stood perfectly still, waiting to see what would happen, but Doris didn't seem to even perceive Jessica's presence. *It's like she can't see me.*

When Doris stepped onto the marble floor, Jessica shuffled backward, attempting to give way so Doris could pass. But Doris took a wide turn, and Jessica, standing near the hall tree, had little room to yield. Doris walked directly where Jessica stood, coursing *through* her.

A potent surge cut through Jessica's body, a searing sensation chirring so deep she seemed to feel it inside her bones. Her vision blinked out, and in its place, she saw purple. Her hearing toggled off; utter silence took its place. Then the purple screen cleared, like a roller blind had been released, and her hearing returned as if the audio switch had been toggled back on.

When her senses returned, Jessica found herself debilitated—unable to even breathe, like the wind had been knocked out of her.

Yet Doris, completely unperturbed, walked on by.

Taking the first gulp of air was the hardest, but after that, the spasms in Jessica's lungs started to subside, and each breath grew steadier. By the time Doris reached Dennis, Jessica could wiggle her fingers and toes, having regained some feeling and control of her extremities.

Doris led Dennis toward the back of the house. The boy looked back at Jessica with a concerned expression, but she faked a reassuring smile that seemed to satisfy him.

When Jessica had recovered enough from the nearly crippling sensation to mount the steps, she retreated to the belvedere, giving Doris and her surrogate son their space.

CHAPTER 30

———◆◇◆———

GLIMPSES IN TIME

MONITORING THE OUTSIDE WORLD through the views of the belvedere became an obsession for Jessica. Wandering from side to side, she watched for any activity as the outside scenes fluctuated haphazardly through time.

She seldom saw people, on account of the house being so isolated and vacant for much of its existence. Wildlife was more common, yet still unusual enough that a sighting provided Jessica with a welcome rush of excitement. Most often, it was squirrels, which were practically ubiquitous. Turkey vultures, hawks, and eagles soared in the sky above. Deer, groundhogs, and raccoons roamed on the ground below. From time to time, an elusive mink would appear, moving in its distinctive bounding gait along the creek across the road. In a couple of rare instances, a black bear ambled by, but only when the outside world was in an older era before the last of the breed had been extirpated from the region.

At one point, a pair of owls nested where the decorative wrought-iron railing was mounted in a corner of the attic roof. Jessica wished she could reach out and touch them, stroke their luxuriant feathers and feel their life. It wasn't a suitable spot for a nest, though. A heavy rain could wash it away—and perhaps that was their fate, because after time shifted, she never saw the nesting owls again.

From her lookout, Jessica observed the abrupt switch between seasons and time of day, while the landscape hopped aimlessly from one era to another. *The house is playing back its memories of its surroundings*, Dennis had surmised. It was as good of a theory as any she could come up with.

The occasional passing vehicle provided an indication of what period she was observing, ranging from early cars and trucks to modern versions, or the occasional farm equipment moving over the road, varying in size and complexity as agricultural technology advanced.

But Jessica noticed she didn't observe anything more futuristic than what she knew of. *No Jetsons in their flying cars*, she noted. It was only the passing Amish buggies that never seemed to vary in design or style. Jessica concocted "modern buggy" as a new oxymoron. This made her think of her mother, whom she worried about and missed dearly.

When time shifted, it happened in the quickest instant imaginable, so fast Jessica figured if she blinked, she would miss it.

———◆○◆———

"Knock, knock," Dennis called up from the bottom of the stairway.

"Who's there?" Jessica answered over her shoulder.

"Me again," he said.

"Come on in, Meghan."

They both laughed for at least the tenth time. What a shame that between them, they only remembered five knock-knock jokes.

"I think we should just call this 'Jessie's room'," Dennis declared as he reached the top of the steps.

Jessica appreciated Dennis calling her "Jessie." He had started using this nickname on his own, unaware that Richard had done the same. As she got to know Dennis better, her fondness for him continued to grow.

"There's two Amish girls on bikes coming this way," Jessica said, and she leaned forward until the counteracting backward pull took hold, just before she touched the glass.

Dennis stepped up on the deacon's bench to see.

The girls were peddling along the road, nearing the driveway apron. One of them suddenly stopped and pointed up at Jessica, illuminated by the late afternoon sunshine streaming into the window.

"She sees you," Dennis said.

Jessica nodded. "Just me though. You're too far back from the window."

The other girl braked to discover what the first girl pointed at, and their eyes grew wide in unison as they debated what they were witnessing. They simultaneously turned around and rode away in a frenzy, back in the direction from which they had come.

"I'm the ghost of Misery Mansion," Jessica bellowed in a dramatic voice.

Dennis giggled. "Quasi-ghost," he corrected, as he hopped down from the bench and walked over to Jessica.

"I've been thinking about it," Jessica said. "I'd bet every ghost sighting through the years—not just Halloween Ghost Lady, but all of them—was me."

She had already been spotted by at least a dozen outsiders. A few, like these Amish girls, were passersby, catching a glimpse of Jessica during daylight hours. But most of them had been teenagers on a nighttime adventure, seeking a fright. Jessica felt a sense of pride knowing she had given them what they were looking for.

"You're probably right, seeing as Mo—*Doris* never comes up here," Dennis said.

"Never?"

"I've never seen her leave the first two levels," he said.

Everything she needs is there, Jessica thought. *Including a proxy for her son.*

"Besides," Dennis added, "she avoids this part of the mansion. This is where she died."

"In that case, it must be me outsiders see. The top of the house is where people would always claim to see a ghost."

"What about me?" Dennis asked.

"Most outsiders can't see you. Remember, for most of the home's history after Doris died, the front door was boarded over."

"But I can see out."

"Because from the phantom realm, the house is in the state it was in when Doris died: not boarded up."

Dennis pursed his lips and nodded as it registered.

"It's sort of like a one-way mirror," Jessica explained. "You can see out, but from where you stand, most outsiders can't see in."

"Too bad the front door is the only uncovered window I'm tall enough to see out."

Sunlight cut out and nighttime took its place, yet Jessica only noticed in a vague, subconscious way. A gibbous moon hung in the sky, casting ample moonlight into the room through the wide stretch of windows.

She stepped over to the shadow she knew to be the bench and sat. "Can I ask you something?"

"Sure." Dennis followed her back to the middle of the room. He stood beside her, awaiting the question.

"Have you ever sensed your mom here? I mean...your real mother?" she clarified, then wished she hadn't.

He let it go, but immediately shook his head. "Never." He took a deep breath and sat on the other end of the bench.

Jessica opened her mouth, froze for a moment, then closed it.

Dennis studied her in the dusk. "Are you wondering...about your husband?"

Jessica sighed. The boy was wise beyond his years. "Yeah. Richard." Saying his name made him feel a shade closer.

"You'd think being here would give us some connection with the dead, right?" He spoke in a small voice, his stare drifting across the room, settling on nothing. Then he blinked his thoughts away and turned back to face Jessica. "Except it doesn't work that way. Not even my mom, and she lived—and died—in this house. It's only Doris here. It's *her* phantom realm."

"Hmmm..." Jessica expressed despondence; her throat was too tight to voice any words. She missed so many people in her life. She often thought of her mother, whom she hoped was doing okay after the last of her chemotherapy treatments, her father, who worked too hard for someone his age, and Erin, with her new baby. If she could ever find a way out, how much time would have passed? Would her parents even still be around?

But more than anyone, she thought of Richard, who was more distant than ever. That was another life. Another time. Another realm.

Dennis reached out and took her hand. "That would have been nice though, wouldn't it?"

She nodded solemnly and wrapped her fingers around his hand, pressing them into his palm.

He glanced her way. Despite the dim light, she saw a twinkle in his eyes, and she knew he found the same comfort in their touch.

After a while, Dennis turned his head to face the stairwell. "I'd better get back to my post." He gave one last squeeze before letting go and pushing himself up. "I don't want to miss anything outside."

Jessica smiled at him, but her stomach tightened, knowing Dennis felt obligated to be available when Doris appeared.

The scratchy Victrola music echoed through the house, channeling its way up to the top level where Jessica dwelled. This was the trumpet piece. Most likely Louis Armstrong, this song seemed to be Doris's favorite, on account of how often she played it. Jessica knew all seven tunes by heart. As much as she tried to not let the scant playlist drive her crazy—after all, records would have been quite expensive in those days—it was becoming increasingly difficult.

The trumpet's lilt finished and Doris's footsteps clacking across the marble foyer floor soon took its place.

Jessica usually kept clear when Doris was around. This time, curiosity took over, and she made the spontaneous decision to venture downstairs. When she arrived at the bedroom level, she heard the hushed tone of conversation between Dennis and Doris below, in the library.

Jessica continued down to the foyer, where she looked in on them. They were sitting on opposite sides of the tête-à-tête seat. Doris held a book up, so both could see it, and she read, "All this time Dorothy and her companions had been walking through the thick woods. The road was still paved with yellow brick..."

The Wonderful Wizard of Oz, Jessica thought.

There's no place like home, her mind recited, just as Dorothy had in the famous movie she'd watched so many times as a child.

Dennis turned his eyes toward her while Doris read, and he gave her the most subtle of head dips.

Jessica, finding the scene strangely charming, smiled in return.

"...With one blow of his paw, he sent the Scarecrow and the Tin Woodman spinning over to the edge of the road." Doris stopped and turned the page.

Dennis read next. "Little Toto, now that he had an enemy to face, ran barking toward the Lion..."

Doris turned her head and lifted her eyes upward, toward the foyer. Her brow furrowed.

Jessica almost flinched away but caught herself. *She doesn't see me.* All the same, Jessica froze.

Doris scanned across the entry. Did the sweep of her eyes drag for a moment as they passed over the spot where Jessica stood?

Jessica held still and didn't breathe.

Doris tilted her head and skimmed back the opposite way. Once again, the arc of her glance seemed to hitch as it crossed Jessica's position.

Doris hesitated, gave a slight shake of her head as if to clear it, then turned back to Oz.

Dennis read on, "I know it, said the Lion, wiping a tear from his eye with the tip of his tail. It is my great sorrow. Whenever there is danger, my heart begins to beat fast." When he finished the page, he peeled his gaze from the book. Without moving his head, he looked Jessica's way, narrowing his eyes.

Jessica understood the look he'd given her: *Don't push it.* While Doris might not be able to see her, perhaps she can *sense* her...and Jessica did not belong here.

With a fluttering heart, she withdrew from the entrance and headed back to the stairway.

There's no place like home, she thought wistfully as she ascended the stairs. Indeed, *there's no place like home.*

CHAPTER 31

PURGATORY

SITTING JUST OFF THE north side of Clarkton's town square, St. Patrick's was the only Catholic church in all of Homer County. Jessica attended PSR—short for Parish School of Religion—at St. Patrick's through her Confirmation, when she was fifteen years old. Looking back, it would've been a slog without Erin Watson. Together, they made their shared Catholic indoctrination bearable, and, at times, even fun.

Mrs. Weber, the PSR teacher, once lectured about purgatory, which, as Jessica recalled, was some state of post-death suffering where one waits for an indeterminate period to find out whether they'd be admitted to heaven, or damned to hell.

Jessica couldn't help but compare her liminal existence to purgatory.

But being stuck here permanently, that's worse than purgatory, which isn't eternal. Here, no one's going to show up and decide her fate. Or is there? And in purgatory, you might end up going to heaven when you eventually make it out. Was there any chance of a reward after all this?

Like purgatory, but worse.

The phantom realm was like a different embodiment of the same place—a space confined within Harmon Manor, but in a different time. Or perhaps more precisely, hidden beneath in a lifeless layer, where the notion of time makes no sense.

Time doesn't apply here, Dennis had explained when she first got trapped. How true!

"Geez," Jessica said out loud to no one, as she sucked in a deep breath. "I miss time." *It's the linear nature of time that provides order, predictability, and a sense of progress—yet there's none of that here.*

Doesn't time also form the cycle of life? Everything withers away. The words unexpectedly popped into Jessica's head, and she recalled thinking this while feeling weepy during her first visit as the new owner of Harmon Manor.

Except here, there's *no mortality*. Mortality itself is such a key element of the human experience. Can you really be alive if you can't die?

And without death, there was no prospect of being reunited with Richard—or anyone else she'd loved.

Everything withers away...but not here. In the phantom realm, *nothing* withers away, because time does not pass...and that's *so* much worse.

A different layer. A lifeless layer.

Here the veil between the living and the dead is so thin Doris could pull Dennis into her side. Jessica followed. Entombed on the dead's side, interned within the spectral home of Doris, nothing but a construct of the dead woman's memories.

A veil as thin as tissue paper.

Do the phantom realm and the normal realm intersect? If so, how?

Intersections are the key to escaping.

Jessica watched as a white pickup truck pulled into the driveway. It looked familiar, but she could not immediately place it.

"Ah..." she said, recognition clicking when a man with a mullet slid out of the passenger side, followed by the red-bearded driver. Her father's crew...but so far, no sign of Dad.

She hustled down to the entrance hall. Dennis, standing by, greeted her with a grin.

When the door swung open, the sound of a text alert double dinged. While Beard-man went about extracting his phone from his pants pocket, Jessica lunged at the open doorway. But before breaking the plane of the doorjamb, the counteracting force grabbed her and halted her momentum. She yanked against it and the force strengthened.

"I've tried that," Dennis said. "Even if the door's open, you can't get out."

Jessica went slack and shrugged. "I didn't really think it would be that easy, but I had to try."

The boy smiled.

Oblivious to the nearby commotion, Beard-man busily pushed buttons on his phone. "Marty sent a message: 'Doing an estimate. ETA 9'."

Dennis looked at Jessica. "Marty's your dad, right?"

She nodded, feeling dispirited. What would she give to see her father?

"And where's Jessie?" he asked.

The memory came back to Jessica. "It was a chemo day."

Mullet walked over to the side of the veranda and hocked, spitting it into the grass.

"You're disgusting," Beard-man said, and stepped inside.

"You can say that again," Jessica said.

Mullet said nothing in his own defense as he followed Beard-man in, and the men headed down the hall. Dennis tailed them, with Jessica falling in behind.

"That SMS thing's cool," Mullet said. "You need to show me how to do it."

"We'll go outside during lunch. It's a dead zone inside the house."

Dennis's head whipped around, and his jaw dropped open.

"You can say that again too," Jessica said.

They both laughed, but suddenly fell silent when they reached the back of the house.

The hallway walls were gone, and the kitchen was in shambles.

"Hope you're not too hung over to swing that sledgehammer," Beard-man said.

"Nah, I'm always up for that."

Beardman went to work shoveling plaster and lathe scraps into the bin by the back door. Mullet picked up his tool of choice and started smashing away at what was left of the wall enclosing the pantry. A plaster dust cloud began spreading through the area.

Dennis stepped up behind Mullet and said, "Watch this, Jessie."

Jessica covered her mouth with her hand and cringed underneath.

Between swings, Dennis placed his hand on Mullet's back.

The man froze, then turned to look behind him. His gaze swept across the area multiple times, as he searched in vain for whatever he'd felt touch him. He said nothing, but gave his head a quick shake and went on with the demolition.

Dennis backed away and grinned. "He'll just try to ignore it. Want a whirl?"

Jessica dropped her hand to expose her grimace and shook her head. Never mind the risk of pulling Mullet into the phantom realm; having experienced her own fright in this way, she wasn't about to pile on. "I don't think you should mess around like that. That's how I ended up here."

"But that was with lightning." Dennis looked over at the window, as if verifying it wasn't storming.

Jessica bobbed her head from side to side as she considered this. "But we don't *really* know how it works. Maybe we shouldn't…"

Suddenly, the scene changed. The men and the dust vanished. The kitchen restored to Doris's era.

———◇———

Jessica sat on the bench in the dark when time shifted, and the room filled with sunlight.

She rose and approached the front window. The sky was solid blue, and hints of early fall colors dappled the foliage. Then she gasped, blinking her eyes twice. A smile formed on her lips.

Lying in the grass, a greyhound was enjoying the early autumn sunshine, his leash staked in the middle of the turnaround circle of the driveway.

"Arik!" she yelled.

She didn't expect he'd be able to hear her, yet he lifted his head off the grass and looked around.

"Arik!" she yelled again, as loud as she could, and this time, Arik looked directly at her.

A quiet dog by nature, Jessica knew how to rile him up when she decided to. She waved with both hands, and the greyhound jumped up and ran toward her. The short leash promptly snapped against his collar. He wagged his tail and barked to acknowledge her.

"Good boy!" She began jumping up and down, which sent him into a barking frenzy, tugging in her direction against the leash.

Then Jessica saw herself—the outsider version, about two months before she became ensnared in the phantom realm—walking from the front porch toward Arik.

"Jessica!" she yelled at the top of her lungs. It felt strange, yelling to herself, calling her own name. "Jessica, it's me!"

But the outsider Jessica didn't seem to hear her. She continued toward the dog. "Hush, Arik!" outsider Jessica yelled.

But he continued barking, all the while fixed on the top of the house.

"Look up here, Jessica!" she yelled to the outsider, and through her glare, she implored the outsider to turn around and look up. The scene tarnished into a purple tint. The outsider froze, then her head began to rotate toward the house.

Suddenly, they were gone. In a split second, the color and light snuffed out, displaced by nighttime, and big fluffy snowflakes fell peacefully from the sky. The carriage house had materialized beyond the driveway, a blanket of snow glimmering on its roof.

"No!" Jessica yelled at the time hop. She dropped to her knees in despair. "No! No! No!"

With the outsiders nowhere in sight, as if they'd never been there in the first place, Jessica's heart went hollow with anguish.

"Jessie!"

Dennis's call snapped Jessica back from her plunge into hopelessness. She stood and hurriedly composed herself, wiping tears from her face.

"Jessie!" he yelled again, now closer, on his way up.

"I'm coming," she called down, starting her descent. She almost reached the attic floor when they met.

"Did you see that?" he asked excitedly from the foot of the belvedere's stairway.

"Yeah," she said, her voice feeling frail. She sat on the steps.

"Time shifted, and all of a sudden, *you* were at the front door. I watched you come in, then Arik started barking, and you walked out."

Jessica nodded. "I saw it too. I called to them...to me. And Arik. But they disappeared before—"

"Denny?"

They both flinched at the sound of Doris's voice. She was nearing the top of the steps, almost at the attic.

Jessica rose to her feet and froze, knowing there wasn't enough time to retreat upstairs. Dennis spun and hopped a step away, just before Doris turned the corner.

"What are you doing, honey?"

His eyes grew larger, and he stammered, "N...nothing."

Jessica stiffened, holding her breath.

Doris drew toward him but didn't look over to the stairway. She reached out and put her hand on Dennis's shoulder. "There's nothing up there." She still didn't look in the direction of the steps, as though she couldn't bring herself to face that way.

"I know." His gaze turned down to the floor.

"When I didn't see you at the front door, I became frightened. Why are you here?"

He shrugged. "Just...looking around."

Doris finally swept her head upward, tracing her line of sight from the bottom to the top of the stairs, but passing straight through Jessica's position. Then she promptly looked away, back at Dennis. "Did you hear something?"

"No." He responded a bit too quickly, shaking his head as if to reinforce the answer, his stare still glued to the floor.

"Sometimes I think I hear things," she said slowly, glancing up the steps one more time.

"I didn't hear anything," he said. Then he looked up and asked, "Do you want to read?"

She smiled and nodded, slipping her arm across his shoulder while she steered him away. As they strode across the attic floor, Doris cast a backward glance up the stairway.

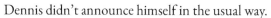

Dennis didn't announce himself in the usual way.

"Jessie, we need to talk," he said as he hurried up the stairs.

When Jessica met him in the middle of the room, he was breathing beyond his exertion.

"This sounds serious," she said with a smile, attempting to lighten his mood.

"It is," he said, not following her lead. "She knows."

"She knows…" Jessica narrowed her eyes and cocked her head. "*Doris* knows?"

"Yes. Well, she suspects."

"She suspects…what?"

"Doris told me she thinks there's someone else in the house." The words were spilling out of his mouth.

"Relax. Let's sit." She led the way to the deacon's bench and sat. "What did you say?"

"I acted surprised." He sat, turned his head away, then back. "But I'm not a good liar, so I'm not sure she believed my innocent act. I think she feels threatened."

Jessica swallowed, having half expected to eventually hear this. "Threatened?"

"This is *her* realm, Jessie. She only invited me into it." He frowned and shook his head. "She doesn't want anyone else here. If she knew we were talking right now…"

He didn't finish, and the room fell silent.

"I see," Jessica eventually said, but it sounded like a croak. She cleared her throat. "What do you think she'd do if she knew? I mean…like, what can she do to me?"

Dennis hesitated in a way that told her he didn't want to say. His stare fastened on the floor.

His inability to answer caught and halted Jessica's breath. *Stay calm,* she urged herself, and she waited for his response.

Eventually, he answered softly, "Doris said she'll eradicate the intruder." He looked back at Jessica and asked, "What's that mean?"

She felt lightheaded. Unable to speak, Jessica just shrugged.

Eradicate.

But indeed, that was the question: what's that mean? After a spell, she regained her voice. "Eradicate means to erase."

Dennis nodded slowly as he turned his head away. "I had a bad feeling about it."

Her brain wrestled with the question of exactly what eradication from the phantom realm might signify, but she couldn't convince herself it would be anything good. Being wiped out of existence would mean no hope of ever returning to the normal realm.

"I've thought about telling her," Dennis said. "It was all just an accident. You're a friend. She'd like you too. Except...Doris the person would have understood—"

"—But Doris the ghost would not," Jessica finished.

"No." Dennis shook his head, still looking away.

Neither of them spoke for a while.

When Dennis turned back to Jessica, a tear rolled down his cheek. "I feel so bad I got you stuck here, Jessie. At least I have a mother here...sort of. But there's *nothing* here for *you*. I'm so sorry."

Jessica reached out and took his hand. "But if you hadn't, I would never have met you."

Dennis squeezed her hand and gave a feeble nod.

"Besides, I'm not going to be here forever," she said.

He nodded again, but said nothing, which Jessica took to mean he had his doubts.

After a stretch of silence, he let go of her hand and stood, preparing to leave.

"And I'm bringing you with me," she added.

Dennis looked down, and with his eyes on hers, gave Jessica a hearty smile.

To avoid stoking Doris's suspicions, Jessica seldom left the belvedere.

Alone for eternity with little more than her thoughts, she had so many questions she had no way to answer, but an endless stretch to wonder upon.

Jessica figured and probed until her head ached and she could ponder no more, yet continued because she couldn't turn it off.

She contemplated existential questions: *Is there a purpose to life outside just living it? Is there an afterlife?*

Scientific questions: *How vast is the universe? How did it all begin? How did life form? Is there life elsewhere in the universe?*

Religious questions: *Do you need religion to know right from wrong? Is there a God? Is there a heaven and a hell?*

Philosophical questions: *What makes a person happy? What is love? What is consciousness?*

Questions about the souls in the house, the house itself, one's identity, and morality. Life and death, good and evil, love and hate.

She considered the nature of time and space, the relationship between them, and how the bardo-like phantom realm warped what she thought she had understood about their properties.

She reminisced about the people in her life, both consequential and insignificant. She played back recollections of everyone and anyone who lingered within the depths of her memories: those she loved, those she avoided, and those she knew only fleetingly. She considered the makeup of her relationships, what formed them, what they meant to her, and how and why their influence helped shape her into who she was.

Without the satisfaction of answers or the mercy of peace, Jessica felt as though her mind was consuming itself, and she was teetering on the brink of madness.

CHAPTER 32

ACROSS THE VEIL

A T LONG LAST, IT finally came to pass.

A car coasted by. Jessica shifted her eyes upward. The Milky Way glistened, and a full moon shone through a cloudless sky. She nodded, but reminded herself clear skies with a full moon were not uncommon over a long span of time.

Leaning forward, she scanned the colorless nightscape. It was autumn. Could this be what she'd been keeping an eye out for? The vehicle followed its headlights into the garden access drive, and her heart began to race when she spotted spoked hubcaps. But she knew her father's Buick wasn't the only car with those kinds of wheel coverings.

The vehicle pulled beyond the band of overgrowth along the roadway's edge, and the headlights blinked off.

Tension coursed through Jessica's body as she watched someone emerge from the passenger side and jog onto the trail toward the house. *But lots of teenagers did the same dare through the years,* Jessica reasoned. The trees were mostly barren of leaves, so she could follow the figure's progress.

Jessica jumped with elation when young Erin emerged from the woods. Moonlight glinted off the shiny metal crucifix in her hand.

Running onto the lawn toward the house, Erin disappeared from Jessica's line of sight, since the room at the top of the mansion sat back some distance from the edge of the mansard roofline.

Jessica balled both hands and pressed them against her mouth. "Please don't let time shift," she whispered into her fists. She looked back at the car and saw the faint glow of the lighter being raised to the cigarette she had smoked while sitting alone in the darkness.

Erin reemerged into view from the front side of the house, running toward the trail. Before long she arrived at the car as Rocky Balboa, and Jessica laughed aloud, having forgotten this detail. The driver's car door swung open, and the interior lights briefly lit up the windows.

The girls crowded beside the car for a moment before Erin circled around to the passenger side. Young Jessica set off on her own venture toward the house.

At the end of the path, the teenaged Jessica stopped, then stepped back into the trees. *What's she doing?* Jessica thought, a stab of panic rising in her gut. Then something caught her eye out the front window: an Amish buggy passing through—another detail she had forgotten. Relief flared through her mind.

After the buggy receded in the distance, the teenager stepped out from the tree line and proceeded on her way onto the lawn. Jessica began waving her arms, seeking to catch the girl's attention. The teen stopped and looked up, but after a brief pause, she lowered her head and continued toward the mansion. She headed toward the back porch and moved out of view.

Jessica crossed both fingers, praying that time wouldn't shift.

The Victrola started to play. The music echoed through the mansion, carrying up through the open stairwell from below.

Jessica's head felt like a balloon being over-inflated. She raised her hands to her face, pressing her palms against her upper cheeks, and squeezed her fingers against her throbbing temples.

The girl reemerged into view from the front corner of the house, running like a rabbit toward the path. When she stopped to turn around, Jessica leaned forward hard against the restraining pull from behind. She glared with all her might, straining to catch—and hold—the girl's attention.

The teenager looked up, and her eyes grew wide.

Jessica bored through the space between them, reaching out to the girl, connecting with her. Everything went purple and silent while Jessica clutched their linkage. Yet her brain was telling her this had not worked the first time, so she had to concentrate harder to get the message through.

Then the purple silence cleared. Jessica started yelling and waving, hoping fiercely that the younger version of herself would heed her pleas and do *something* to rescue her.

The girl gazed up in astonishment while slowly stepping backward. The connection frayed, then snapped, and the teen turned and ran. She vanished briefly in the copse of trees before reappearing near the car at the opposite end of the trail.

The girl pulled open the driver's side door and jumped in. An instant later, the headlamps turned on and the reverse lights lit up. The Buick backed out into the road, then sped away, its taillights blinking out beyond the road bend.

PART SIX

JESSICA - 1990

CHAPTER 33

REPRISAL

GRIPPING THE STEERING WHEEL, Jessica's knuckles glimmered under the moonlight. She leaned forward, knowing she was driving too fast.

"Tell me! What *happened*?" Erin threw her hands, palms upturned, with each word.

Jessica took a deep breath as she barreled past the familiar red barn with CHEW MAIL POUCH TOBACCO painted on the side. She considered how she'd probably put two miles between them and the mansion by now and eased her foot off the gas pedal. "It was freaking awful."

"*What* was?"

Jessica leaned back and pressed an open hand against her own chest, hoping to restrain her ricocheting heart. "I *saw* the ghost-lady!"

"No way!"

"Way!" Jessica shot back the response out of habit, just as Wayne would have said to Garth. "She was in the window at the top of the house...I just about crapped my pants!"

Erin narrowed her eyes.

"I'm dead serious, Erin! She was waving to me!"

"Waving? Like saying hi?"

"Like she wanted me to come. She was frantic."

"What, like she needed *help*?"

Jessica huffed and dropped her head back against the seat's head restraint. "Maybe?" She pursed her lips and gritted her teeth, coming to the realization there was no *maybe* about it. She now grasped with cold certainty the ghost wasn't gesturing in a threatening way; the ghost was pleading for help. "I was so scared I didn't even think about that. As soon as I could break free, I ran."

"Break free?"

"It's hard to describe…" Goose pimples crawled along Jessica's flesh as she thought about what she had seen—what she'd *felt*. "…she *connected* with me."

"Connected?"

"Yes. Her eyes…they paralyzed me. My brain locked up, and all I saw was purple color. After it cleared, I ran."

"Purple?" Erin slowly turned away to ponder this facing the passenger window.

"Yeah…purple." Jessica rubbed the side of her head.

Erin stared out at the blackened countryside for an extended moment before adding, "And why would this ghost-lady need help?"

Jessica continued rubbing her head. "Good question."

Erin turned back to Jessica. "Are you okay? Want me to drive?"

"I'll be fine. I just want to go home."

CHAPTER 34

———◆◇◆———

TIPPING POINT

B Y THE TIME THE Buick rolled back into Clarkton, the official trick-or-treat hours had ended and the streets were empty.

When Jessica pulled into Erin's driveway, the car's headlights swept across the house before settling like a spotlight blazing through the kitchen window. She toggled them off, not needing to give Erin's mom another reason to complain about her. Mrs. Watson tended to blame Erin's teenage rebellion forays on Jessica's bad influence. Both girls knew this was only half true. The other half of the story was Erin's bad influence on Jessica. It was a true team effort.

"Try not to think about it tonight, Jess," Erin said as she drew a tube of scented lotion out of her purse. "We'll talk about it more in the morning, okay?"

Jessica nodded weakly.

Erin squirted a creamy bead into her palm, then held up the tube to Jessica. "New flavor: Candy Apple."

"Mmmm," Jessica said, opening her hand for a dollop. The administration of scented lotion was usually the concluding ritual of their evenings together, which they figured would cover up the cigarette odor. She held her hands near her face as she smeared the moisturizer over her skin, taking in a long sniff. "Smells delicious."

"It's like diet comfort food," Erin said. "You've got my cross?"

Jessica dredged the wooden crucifix out of her pocket and pressed it into Erin's glistening palm. "You *did* leave them upside-down, right?"

Erin pulled her lips into a cringe. "Mrs. Weber says it's not satanic. It means Christian humility, right?" She scrunched up her nose and turned to gauge Jessica's reaction. "Sorry?"

Jessica scoffed, relieved to know some other force hadn't inverted them.

Erin switched back to her cross and stared at it for a moment. "I still can't believe this was the big gift my holy roller aunt and uncle gave me for my First Communion." She huffed, feigning indignation at the injustice of it all. "My brother got a *turtle* from *his* godparents."

Jessica chuckled through her nose, even though she'd been hearing Erin's grievances on the matter all the way back to second grade. Nonetheless, she did appreciate her friend's lame attempt to lighten the mood.

"I'll be up until eleven, so call if you need to." Erin slipped the crucifix into her own pocket and leaned over to give Jessica a hug. She climbed out and stooped, looking Jessica in the eye. "Adios, mi amiga."

"Buenos nachos," Jessica said, and forced her lips into a smile.

Erin paused and sighed before stepping clear of the door and swinging it closed.

A short time later, Jessica parked in her own garage. As usual, Birdieboi waited for her in the mudroom, and he greeted her with affectionate head nuzzles. She lingered, relishing the therapeutic effect of his purring.

The cat followed her into the family room.

Jessica's parents were planted in their usual spots: Dad stretched out in his recliner, Mom on the couch, twisted up under a blanket like a chocolate-covered pretzel.

"Hi," she said, in as cheery of a tone as she could summon. Her parents merely waved, engrossed in *Doogie Howser, M.D.*

"Well, good night," Jessica said, and blew a kiss.

"Good night, Honey," they said in almost perfect unison, but their attention immediately turned back to Doogie and Vinnie, who were making a chainsaw slasher movie.

Jessica was glad to have returned home at the start of their favorite show, which suppressed the "how was your evening?" questions. On the way to her bedroom, she detoured into the living room to replace the silver crucifix on the wall. It seemed her mother hadn't noticed it had gone missing.

After her shower, pajama-clad Jessica slipped into her bedroom, with the cat darting in just before the door closed. He sat upright beside the bed, waiting for her to climb in so he could nestle nearby. Jessica leaned on the edge of the bed and looked at him.

"I don't want to think about Misery Mansion, Birdieboi," she whispered.

He blinked slowly.

"I don't want to think about the ghost lady."

He blinked again, like he grasped what she meant.

But the memory of the frantic woman flashed inside Jessica's head, like a wretched picture cast onto a tiny internal screen. She shuddered. Squeezing her eyes shut, she shook the image clear, like a child might erase a drawing on an Etch A Sketch.

She pulled down the blankets and climbed into bed. The cat leaped up and padded around as Jessica burrowed in.

"I'm going to read, so I won't think about it," she told him, but when she reached for the book on her nightstand, she cringed and withdrew her hand. The evil-looking cat on the cover of Stephen King's *Pet Sematary* bared its teeth at her. Birdieboi turned and gave her a diametrically harmless look.

Jessica shivered, thinking back on where she'd left off in the story: the family cat had returned from the grave with an irremediable noxious aroma and a wicked demeanor. She pushed the horror novel aside and picked up the paperback beneath it: *The Grapes of Wrath*, by John Steinbeck, which she was reading for a school assignment.

Rolling onto her side, she propped the book against her forearm, and found her place. While concentrating on the words helped block other thoughts, her mind felt weary, and soon the prose blurred together into a meaningless jumble. Her eyelids became heavy, and her head melted into her pillow.

In her next stretch of awareness, Jessica was back at Misery Mansion, standing at the edge of the lawn. The specter appeared in the window and began gesturing, before everything turned purple and silent.

For a fleeting instant, Jessica's perspective shifted, and she discovered herself peering out from the belvedere, as though *she* were the apparition. Moonlight glistened on the gnarled branches of the tree stand below, appearing like skeletal fingers clawing at the sky. A rift in the woods formed the path, and Jessica saw herself anchored at the trailhead, her terrified face tilted upward.

In that brief but powerful flash of time, Jessica felt overcome with empathy for the woman, and she understood without doubt the magnitude of her desperation.

The moment passed, purple returned, then cleared, and she was back outside, watching the frenzied apparition in the window above her.

Unlike earlier in the evening, Jessica could now clearly hear the woman. Or perhaps she didn't so much *hear* the words—perhaps she simply *knew* what the woman said, because somehow the words were *inside* her head:

"Help! Jessica...I *need* your help! Please...save me!"

Jessica awakened with a jolt and soon realized she was in her bed. The nightstand lamp burned brightly.

Birdieboi lifted his head, looked at her, and yawned. He had been tucked up beside her legs in his usual Superman position.

She found herself panting, her mouth dry, while sweat drenched her pillow and forehead. Peeling her tongue from the roof of her mouth, she patted her covers. A lump turned out to be her book, which she returned to the nightstand.

It was a dream, she told herself. *No,* she countered. *A vision.*

She wiped the moisture off her face with her pillowcase, then rolled the pillow over before dropping back on its dry side. Her temples throbbed. Taking a series of deep breaths, Jessica kneaded each temple with a thumb, holding her eyelids closed. Her mind drifted back to the dream—*vision*, and the words clanked and resonated inside her head: *Help! Jessica...I* need *your help! Please...save me!*

Jessica sat up. Still sensing the lingering connection she'd made with the ghost lady, she developed a sudden compulsion to help her. Certain the apparition was not a threat, Jessica realized how deeply she would regret it if she didn't.

This instant was the tipping point, and it could have gone either way. She could either try like hell to forget what she'd seen—and what she'd dreamed—and go on with her life, or she could take action.

That's when Jessica Putnam resolved to help. Though she had no idea what she was about to face, she could not simply look the other way and let the poor soul suffer.

Jessica slipped out from under the covers and tiptoed to her bookshelf, then tucked the book she sought into her backpack and returned to bed.

The next morning, Erin arrived on time for a change. When the Fuglymobile pulled into the driveway, Jessica picked up her bookbag and headed for the front door. "Bye, Mom."

"Have a good day, Honey," her mother called out from the kitchen.

Jessica flung her backpack onto the back seat of the 1983 Ford Escort, which they had befittingly nicknamed Fuglymobile. Erin's brother had recently left for college, so it belonged to her now. *Lucky girl.*

"Hola," Erin said. "Feeling better?"

"Si, señorita." Jessica unzipped the bag and fished the book out to keep it with her.

Erin shifted into reverse while she waited for Jessica to settle in the front seat.

Immediately after closing the door, Jessica asked, "Are you free after school?"

Erin scanned her mirrors and began backing out of the drive. "Well, it's Thursday... I guess so, if I don't get some big-ass home-work assignment today."

Jessica drew in a deep breath and held it for a moment. "Let's go back to Misery Mansion."

Erin came to a stop in the road and held up there. She turned to Jessica and studied her. "What for?"

"I had this..." Jessica's voice tapered off. She shook her head before starting over. "I need to see if the ghost lady's there."

Erin sighed, turned back to face the windshield, and shifted into drive. "I mean, if you need to."

"I do." Jessica held up *Ohio Ghostly Road Trip.* "Remember this?"

Erin nodded. "I know it well."

The spine had creased at the Homer County pages, so Jessica easily located the Harmon Manor entry, and began to read it aloud:

"Popularly referred to as 'Misery Mansion'...blah, blah, blah.

"The macabre history of this unoccupied home began during the Great Depression, with the execution-style killing of the man of the house, a prominent banker, at the hands of his teenage son, who was subsequently condemned to an insane asylum. The deranged, murderous teen's commitment prompted his mother to hang herself in the tower atop the mansion.

"Decades later, an heir of the only family who has ever owned the estate died of a drug overdose in the house, and her young son simultaneously disappeared, never to be found again. Blah, blah, blah.

"It is said that the ghost of a woman can sometimes be seen looking out the windows atop the imposing and fearsome-looking house of horrors.

"Beware of Misery Mansion!"

Jessica closed the book. "This doesn't tell us a whole lot, does it?"

Erin shrugged like she was mostly wondering where Jessica was going with this.

"According to this," Jessica said, tapping her finger on the book, "there are two women who could be the ghost."

"Yeah, so who did you see?"

"Right. But could the ghost be someone else?" Jessica stared out her window as they passed Clarkton's town square, unable to shake the creepy feeling she had some connection with the apparition. "And why does she need help?"

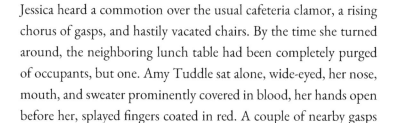

Jessica heard a commotion over the usual cafeteria clamor, a rising chorus of gasps, and hastily vacated chairs. By the time she turned around, the neighboring lunch table had been completely purged of occupants, but one. Amy Tuddle sat alone, wide-eyed, her nose, mouth, and sweater prominently covered in blood, her hands open before her, splayed fingers coated in red. A couple of nearby gasps became shrieks, and the surrounding tables began evacuating as well.

As the other students cleared away like scurrying ants, Jessica calmly collected several unused napkins from her table and walked over to the bleeding cheerleader spectacle.

"It's just a nosebleed," she said to Amy, but loud enough for others to hear too, and held out the bundle of napkins. "Take one and pinch your nose with it."

The normally snooty Amy appeared to relax only slightly, perhaps now more worried about embarrassment fallout than the health crisis itself. "But I've never had a nosebleed," she pleaded, as if this might mean she was immune to them and would make it all just go away.

"It's no big deal," Jessica reassured her, having had them herself a couple of times in the past—fortunately, always at home. *Although this one's a real gusher*, she thought, knowing how the scene would provide the student body with a lasting memory.

The crowd seemed to decompress when Jessica sat down next to Amy and began wiping the blood off her face. "C'mon, I'll walk you down to the nurse's station."

"Ugh," Amy said. "Thanks. It's Jessica, right?"

CHAPTER 35

SCOUTING

AFTER SCHOOL ENDED, JESSICA headed to the parking lot to meet Erin for their trek out to Misery Mansion.

"Dude, I heard all about sixth-period lunch," Erin said as she approached. "And *you* were the hero."

Jessica waved it off, although her role in the incident had surprised even herself.

The day was warmer, but drizzling lightly, just enough that the wipers couldn't be left off. Throughout their drive, the wiper blades chattered noisily with each intermittent sweep.

The girl's conversation dwindled as they made their journey east, and they were barely speaking by the time they passed the CHEW MAIL POUCH TOBACCO barn. They stared silently at Harmon Manor when it came into view.

Erin flinched when the wipers dragged. "God, I hate that sound."

Jessica just leered at the mansion.

Erin turned into the garden access drive. She looked in the rearview mirror, then at the side mirrors. "People will see my car."

Jessica turned around and examined the terrain. "Pull up a little further."

Erin propelled the Fuglymobile forward, weeds scraping the underside, until a branch caught and started dragging. "That's as far as I'm going."

"It'll have to do," Jessica said, pulling her hood over her head.

"I wish I'd changed shoes," Erin said before stepping on the soggy ground, gingerly, like she was holding onto a sliver of hope she might be able to keep her L.A. Gears clean.

Jessica ignored her comment and set off, trudging toward the trail. "It's not so bad coming here during daylight."

Erin, a few steps behind, hunched under her hood without responding.

A truck trundled by on the roadway, causing them to pause, although the trees were too bare of leaves to provide much cover. The truck rumbled on, receding around the bend. Jessica resumed her march, and Erin followed.

As she closed in on the end of the path, Jessica slowed her pace, then froze where it opened onto the lawn. Feeling like her nerves were stretched so tight they might snap, she reminded herself she was here during the daytime, and she wasn't alone.

She turned her gaze upward and studied each window of the belvedere. "This is where I was when I saw her."

Erin sidled beside Jessica, so close their shoulders almost touched. She pointed at the top level of the mansion and whispered, "And that's where she was?"

Jessica nodded. She went on scanning each of the windows of the attic, then the second level. All were empty. Boarding covered the windows of the first level. She tilted her ear toward the house and listened for that creepy, old-timey music.

"There's nothing there," Erin said. "Let's go."

Jessica shook her head. "Let's see if we can get inside."

Erin gasped. "*Hell* no. Are you insane?"

Jessica couldn't blame Erin for her reaction—she hadn't seen the frantic woman, nor endured the vivid dream with the phantom pleading. But Jessica had, and she knew she would regret it if she simply ignored what she'd experienced.

The roar of another engine arose in the distance. They withdrew behind the tree line and held still as a speeding pickup passed the property, while Jessica examined each of the mansion's windows once again.

"We need to get out of here, Jess. Someone's going to see us." Erin pulled Jessica's arm, and when she didn't budge, Erin tugged harder. "C'mon!"

Jessica sighed, took one last look at the uppermost windows, then turned away to follow Erin back to the Fuglymobile.

CHAPTER 36

———◆◇◆———

DIGGINGPAST FOLKLORE

THE NEXT DAY WAS Friday. After school, Jessica had Erin drop her off at the county library. She couldn't possibly hold off until Saturday morning to see what she could learn from the newspaper archives; even waiting this long had driven her mad. She called home from the lobby payphone and told her mother she was doing research for a school project and would walk home in time for dinner.

Jessica settled at the microfiche reader in the library's basement. She laid out the stack of envelopes the reference librarian had helped her collect from storage.

She fumbled around with the switches and dials despite the tutorial she had just received on the complicated machine. It took her a while, but she would feel like a master by the time her visit ended.

Carefully loading each fiche into the system, Jessica scanned the projected images from The Homer Reporter articles she had found:

BANKER HARMON EXECUTED AT HOME
Son is Suspect; Held in Custody

SON OF BANKER NOT GUILTY IN FATHER'S MURDER
Committed to Asylum for Schizophrenia

BANKER'S WIDOW FOUND DEAD AT HOME
Suspected Suicide by Hanging

HEIRESS DEAD AT HARMON MANOR
Overdose Likely; Son Goes Missing

HARMON AUTOPSY CONFIRMS HEROIN OVERDOSE
Search for Missing Boy Continues

HARMON MANOR MYSTERY: WHERE IS THE BOY?
Suspicion Toward Dead Mother Grows

"Attention patrons…"

Jessica jumped at the PA announcement.

"…The library will close in fifteen minutes. Please check out any materials you'd like to take home or turn them back in. The library will reopen Saturday at nine a.m. Thank you."

Jessica leaned back in the chair and stretched the tension out of her neck. She had read each article twice, giving her a clearer understanding of the true history of the mansion. She considered what her *Ohio Ghostly Road Trip* book had said about Harmon Manor. The newspaper articles had provided more historical detail than the book's brief summary, but made no mention of certain folklore sensationalized in the book.

People had been claiming to see a ghost at Harmon Manor long before the hippie woman died in 1969. Jessica's parents had told her people had talked of seeing an apparition since before they were growing up in the 1950s. Considering the history of the home and the tragic circumstances of her life and death, it seemed logical that the apparition she had seen was Doris Harmon.

But the articles didn't yield any clues about why Doris might need help, especially from Jessica, who couldn't detach herself from the bizarre bond she still felt lingering inside her. She puzzled over this, but she'd begun to understand the only way she might find answers would be to get inside the mansion. The very thought terrified her, and she imagined the only things that could make the undertaking worse would be either going in alone or entering at night.

As it would turn out, she would end up doing both.

After a quick dinner and a change of clothes, Jessica took the Buick to pick up Erin for the Friday night football game. As soon as they left the Watson's neighborhood, the girls each lit a cigarette, and Jessica gave Erin a rundown on the archived newspaper articles.

"Seems like Halloween Ghost Lady is Doris Harmon," Erin said. "But what does she need?"

Jessica blew her smoke out of the cracked-open window. "I think there's only one way to find out."

Erin whipped her head toward Jessica and studied her. "Not by going in there."

"We *need* to, Erin."

Erin squinted and tilted her head, as if she was confused about what she'd heard. "We?"

"I don't know what else to do."

"How about just *forgetting* about it?"

Jessica took another drag on her smoke. She knew this would be a tough sell.

"No way, Jess—I'm not going in there. And you can't either!" Erin shook her head and turned toward her window. "You're taking this too far."

Jessica chewed on her lower lip.

"Let's say you *did* see what you think you saw."

Jessica felt her face twitch. "Okay, let's say I did," she said sarcastically.

"Did it ever occur to you that it might be a trap?"

"It's not a trap," Jessica said, recalling the sincerity of the ghost's pleas during the encounter and in the dream/vision that followed.

Erin threw her hands up in exasperation. "Will you please just let it go?"

Jessica brought the cigarette back to her lips and took a hit, but didn't answer.

"I need you to promise me."

Jessica exhaled with a sigh.

"Promise me!"

"Okay, Erin. I'll let it go."

"Promise?"

Jessica had found just enough room inside her L.A. Gears to cross her toes. "Promise."

Chapter 37

———◆◇◆———

Intrusion

J ESSICA NOTICED HER HANDS were sweating when she passed the moonlit CHEW MAIL POUCH TOBACCO barn. She placed her smoke in the ashtray, and one at a time, set about wiping her palms dry on her jeans. A minute or two later, when the silhouette of Harmon Manor emerged into view, she eased off on the gas pedal but kept her eyes defiantly trained on the road.

She rolled to a near stop at the gardening entrance, then turned in and pulled forward until the weeds rasped against the undercarriage disconcertingly. After toggling off the headlights, she sat in the darkness with the engine idling, psyching herself up for her mission.

Jessica had tried almightily to convince herself she did not have to come at night. But the more she thought about it, the more she reached the loathsome conclusion she had to do this after sunset, when the risk of her or the car being seen dropped to virtually zero. And there was no debating this had to be the night, partly because Jessica was so anxious to uncover the truth, but mostly because she somehow felt the sooner she helped this poor soul, the better.

Mulling over what to do with the keys, she decided to simply leave them inserted, figuring there was nobody around to mess with the vehicle, but wanting them there at the ready in case she had to make a quick getaway.

She hadn't touched her cigarette since the MAIL POUCH barn, but she'd had enough. She took one last heavy drag, snuffed it out in the ashtray, then rolled up the window, turned off the ignition, and swung open the door. The usual nicotine head rush hit her when she climbed out, so she leaned against the car to regain her poise.

Jessica retrieved the flashlight, the pry bar, and the Coleman camp lantern from the floor of the back seat. The lamp was a gas model her dad had owned since childhood. While her father was away (luckily, this was one of his working Saturdays), she'd dug it out from the camping gear storage shelf in the garage and located the gallon jug of fuel under the workbench. The steel can was so old it had rusted. She had to pry the lid off with channel-locks before she could fill the lantern's reservoir.

She slid the flashlight into her coat pocket, grasped the pry bar in one hand and the lantern in the other, then bumped the door closed with her hip.

After nodding encouragement to herself, Jessica headed forth. *Ready or not, here I come*, she announced under her breath, using a blasé tone—although she felt anything but lighthearted.

It was a chilly evening, much like her last nighttime visit, although colder yet. The day had been clear with a bright sun, but cool, and after sunset, the temperatures had plummeted below freezing. Once again, the sky was cloudless, only the nightscape appeared a few shades darker, with the moon having waned to a gibbous.

Though well past the peak of fall, that distinctive crisp smell of autumn still lingered in the air. Her breath formed huge vapor plumes, and a light coating of frost had crystalized on the grass, which crunched underfoot.

The gloom deepened around her as she entered the thicket. Struggling to see in the darkness, Jessica slowed her pace, although she stayed determined to avoid using the flashlight, which would not only ruin her night vision, but it would also give her away if anyone passed the property.

As she progressed along the path, her eyes adjusted, and the bordering tree branches and understory started to take shape. With the benefit of this murky eyesight, she quickened her pace.

Jessica had lied outright to her parents, telling them she was going to Erin's house for the evening. If they called the Watson's home looking for her, she would be dead meat. But that wasn't the only risk. She'd told Erin she and her parents were visiting relatives this evening. At some point, Erin might call her house, asking for her. *Risks all around*, Jessica thought at the very moment Harmon Manor first came into view through the trees.

She took ten more steps and stopped to stare at the twilit house looming before her. She examined it, searching for movement in each of the windows that wasn't boarded over—especially those in the uppermost level.

Holding her breath, she listened for the Victrola. But she heard only the natural murmurs of the night.

Jessica realized she was procrastinating and forced herself to proceed with the plan. She blinked her eyes tightly closed before opening them wide and stepping forward onto the lawn. With a renewed sense of determination, she pushed onward toward the rear entrance of the mansion.

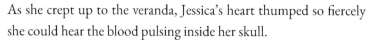

As she crept up to the veranda, Jessica's heart thumped so fiercely she could hear the blood pulsing inside her skull.

She placed the lantern on the steps leading up to the back porch and took one last look around. All was still. When she pressed the Maglite button with her thumb, the bright light momentarily blinded her. She laid it down, spotlighting the lantern, and set aside the pry bar.

Jessica's eyes soon adjusted, and she studied the apparatus. Through the years, her dad had given her demonstrations on how to operate this lamp, and he always reminded her: *Be careful! These things can become firebombs if you don't watch out.*

Conjuring her father's voice inside her head, Jessica followed along as he talked her through the procedure: *Make sure the main light valve is off. Cover the hole in the center of the pump knob with your thumb. Turn it counterclockwise to open the air check valve. Pump it twenty times, but no more than twenty. Turn the knob clockwise to close the check valve. Switch the main light valve to the START position.*

The lantern hissed as the pressurized gas vapor began to flow into the burners. She rifled into her pants pocket to retrieve the Bic lighter.

Now light it, but don't delay, or too much fuel will accumulate.

Jessica tried to hurry. She flicked the lighter three times before it lit, then guided the flame under the lighting hole. The gas ignited with a sudden *POOF*, and the globe filled with an orange ball of fire.

Having cleared the most hair-raising step without burning herself, Jessica blew out through her lips and pocketed the lighter. She turned the valve to the ON position. The orange flame gradually faded away as the mantles started glowing, shifting in color from orange to yellow, then to a brilliant white, all while accompanied by the steady soft whistle of the flowing fuel.

Jessica turned off the flashlight and slid it back into her coat pocket, then slipped the pry bar into the other side's pocket. She moved the lantern to the edge of the porch deck, opposite the rear entry door, and mounted the steps. The lamp produced a ghastly white glow that danced in a slight rhythmic waver. When she padded her way toward the entrance, the guttering light behind her cast a giant shadow of herself hovering on the brickwork above.

She cracked her knuckles while searching for the heads of the nails attaching the boarding over the door. When she found the first two, she slid the pry bar's claw between them, working the chisel end between the plywood and the doorframe.

The fasteners creaked as she pried them out. Each pull made a piercingly loud sound, but Jessica could do nothing about that other than work fast. *And pray*, she casually suggested to herself, although she just as quickly ignored the proposition.

Removing the plywood from the door was turning out to be an arduous task. The board was tightly fitted against the door frame, secured with more than a dozen nails. She fretted about being caught breaking in, but stayed focused, alternating between the chisel tip and the claw end, patiently removing one nail at a time. As she worked, the chore became easier, because she could use the loosened boarding as a lever to pry out the remaining fasteners.

By the time she had the last nail removed, Jessica had worked up a sweat, despite the chilly temperature. She slid the plywood aside and set about opening the locked door, which she had little choice but to use brute force to break open.

She wedged the tip of the pry bar between the door and the frame, closed her eyes, and pulled with all her might. The wood splintered as the hardware tore through the jamb. When the door swung partway open, the hinges creaked in a discordant chorus which resonated into the rear entrance hall and beyond.

The lantern cast gloomy beams of light into the near corner of the hallway, illuminating the barren interior of the house for the first time in ages. A thick layer of dust coated the floor. Utter darkness concealed the hallway beyond the reach of the lantern's light.

Jessica propped the tool against the brickwork and went back to retrieve the lantern.

The momentary distraction of the board removal task had held fear at bay. But now, as she stood in the doorway, Jessica's breath petered out, and her hands began to tremble. *Why are you doing this?* her mind asked, but she refused to debate it. She took a long, quavering breath before stepping over the threshold and into the house.

Once inside the doorway, the air grew thick with a musty odor. Jessica gulped. She felt her entire upper body shudder. The lantern rattled, fluttering its luminescence.

"Hello?" Her voice felt feeble. She swallowed. Louder, she called, "Do you need help?"

She paused to listen above the hiss of the gas, her jaw clenched, and her muscles tensed. Pushing the door open further, the corroded hinges wailed, shattering the silence of her surroundings.

As the echo dampened, Jessica felt the sensation of a hand on her back. She flinched and choked on the scream that formed in her throat.

Chapter 38

Disentanglement

Jessica sat on the deacon's bench when the prying sound first resonated through the mansion's structure. She cocked her head. When she heard it again, she rose and hastened to the steps. As she descended the darkened stairways, the sounds increased in volume. Near the bedroom level, she met Dennis, who had already been on his way up to summon her.

"Someone's trying to get in the back door," he said, turning around and waving her toward the entry hall.

"I didn't see anyone outside," she said.

"Me neither. I would have seen anyone out front."

"Actually, I might have just missed it." Jessica sighed. "I wasn't even paying attention."

Dennis laughed. "Remind me not to hire you as a watch guard."

The volume of the piercing sounds rose as they approached the back of the house. When they reached the interior end of the rear entrance hall, they held up.

The prying ceased, and there was a rumble as the plywood slid aside. After a moment of silence, the door rattled, groaned, then suddenly splintered, tearing loose from the jamb. As it swung part-way open, its hinges wailed resoundingly.

Beyond the opening sat a lit camping lantern. A figure moved toward it, casting a shadow into the doorway. The anonymous form picked up the lamp and turned toward the house, holding it at waist height. *Lift it higher!* Jessica thought, as she strained to make out the outsider's features. The lantern's ventilator blocked the light from shining upward, so the figure's upper body appeared as a mere shadow.

The silhouetted form approached the entrance, paused, then stepped over the threshold.

"Hello?"

It was a young female's voice.

She called louder, "Do you need help?"

After a moment, she pushed the door open further, inducing another creak from its stiffened hinges. The outsider stood quivering just inside the open doorway.

Dennis moved down the hall while Jessica watched the scene play out from the opposite end. The girl raised the lantern above her shoulder, and luminescence spilled over her face. Jessica studied her features, distorted by shadows shifting with the moving light source. All at once, a sense of understanding clicked in Jessica's mind, and she identified the intruder. *It's me—as a teen!* Eons had passed since she had seen her circle the house on Halloween night, but *she came!*

Just as this realization formed in her mind, Dennis reached out and placed his hand on the teenager's back. It happened so fast Jessica did not have a chance to stop him. She stepped forward, hastening toward the pair.

Teenaged Jessica flinched at Dennis's touch, and her jostling caused one end of the wire lantern bail to dislodge from the frame.

The lamp dangled for a moment from the other end of the bail, but as it wobbled, it slid off that side too, and the lantern detached from its handle and fell, crashing on the hallway floor. The globe shattered, and the fabric mantles jarred apart from the burners. A ball of flames erupted from the exposed jets with a hideous *WOOSH*, lighting up the entire length of the entry hall.

The teen jumped clear of the flames and backed away, moving deeper into the hallway. The fire filled the width of the entranceway, fueled by the pressurized gas now flowing freely into the open air, blocking her exit through the rear door. She hesitated, staring at the fire. All at once, the seriousness of the matter seemed to hit her, and she bolted toward the interior end of the hall.

Half-way down the corridor, the older embodiment of Jessica stopped in her tracks, and the scurrying teen swept through the unseen adult version of herself.

Jessica felt an electric sizzle pass through her body, so powerful it almost toppled her. Everything went solid purple, like someone had ignited a brilliant violet fireball, and her surroundings fell silent. As the sensation subsided, she felt a rapid succession of jolts inside her head. Then the purple cleared, and her senses sparked back, fully restored.

Momentarily crippled, Jessica leaned against the wall to steady herself. Then it struck her: she was able to feel the wall! She curled her hand into a fist and rapped against the plaster. Knocking sounds rang out. *But why* wouldn't *I be able to touch the wall?* she wondered. She examined her arm, recognizing the jacket she'd donned to stay warm on this chilly night. *The teenager's jacket.*

She turned to face a boy standing nearby, staring at her with eyes wide and mouth ajar.

A spark of recognition triggered from some fresh cache of memories in her brain, like a feeling of déjà vu. "Dennis…" Jessica managed, although she couldn't say how the name came to her.

He stared blankly at her, then his eyes narrowed, like his mind was slowly processing what he'd witnessed. "Jessie?"

Jessica nodded as a broadened sense of self-awareness blossomed inside her head. The two versions of herself had melded into the physical embodiment of teenaged Jessica, yet she'd also assimilated an extra layer of consciousness from her older self.

His eyes shot back open, expanding to the size of silver dollars, and he nodded rapidly as it sank in. "You're a teenager!"

She grinned.

"Is my Jessie in there too?"

Jessica poked her sternum with her thumb. "I'm here too."

His eyes drifted upward and to the side, and he rubbed the back of his neck while he took this in. "Wow! Wait…you mean *I* could have done that?"

Jessica shrugged. "Who knew?"

Something in the fire popped, launching embers their way. Jessica grabbed Dennis's forearm and pulled him away from the fiery end of the hall.

As they retreated into the mansion's back corridor, music began to play. Jessica pivoted to peer around the corner into the parlor and stopped dead. An apparition—Doris—stood facing the Victrola, its record wobbling as it spun on the turntable, a trumpet crooning from the gramophone's horn. It was the second time Jessica heard this—no, it was the thousandth time. The figure turned her head and looked straight at Jessica. A questioning expression passed over her face. She squinted, then glared at Jessica, who recoiled. This time it was Dennis tugging on Jessica's forearm, pulling her away from the parlor.

Passing the rear entryway, Jessica paused to assess the fire. Flames crawled along the wood flooring and up the walls on either side, halfway to the ceiling, where a layer of smoke accumulated. Absorbing this, Jessica became aware of the danger of the situation. The fire voraciously consumed the old house, a virtual tinder box.

Suddenly, a gasket inside the lantern burst, spewing a large reserve of fuel onto the fire. The blaze flared toward them. Even at the end of the hall, the surge of the heat scorched the exposed skin of Jessica's face and hands, and she jumped away.

She pushed Dennis onward toward the front hallway. As they scrambled past the kitchen, Jessica noticed hearing only one set of footsteps: her own.

Upon turning into the front hall, she held up and cast a backward glance. Doris stepped out from the parlor and stopped to study the fire. A confused look formed on her face, as though she was uncertain what was happening, or perhaps more specifically, what it meant.

Jessica led the way down the front hall, past the cellar and dining room, into the foyer. She grabbed the front door handle, turned it and pulled, but it did not budge.

"It's deadbolted," she said, and turned to the hall tree to see if any keys hung on it.

"The key's in the parlor," Dennis said.

Of course it is, Jessica thought. She assessed the adjacent tall window, judging whether it would be wide enough to squeeze through. It would be no problem for Dennis, but tight for her.

She reached up and tore the sheer curtains from the top rod, ripping the fasteners from the window trim. The orange glow from the fire at the end of the hallway reflected off the inside surface of the otherwise darkened glass.

Pulling the Maglite from her coat pocket, Jessica remembered her father explaining how police officers use a slightly larger model as a baton. "Stand back," she told Dennis.

"Pfft." He grinned and raised his palms upright. "You can't hurt me!"

She needed a second for this to sink in. "Hah! I forgot that you're almost invincible."

He flexed both arms, but stepped away nonetheless.

Jessica raised the Maglite over her head, grasping the handle tightly, and with her eyes closed, she smacked the head of the light into the window. A resounding *BANG* was all her timid strike yielded.

She swung harder on the second try. The window cracked, but the flashlight head rebounded back, and Jessica lost her handhold. The Maglite spun to the marble floor, took a hard bounce, and skittered into the library. She scrambled after it and when she lined up for another strike, made sure to tighten her grip.

With the third hit, her strongest yet, the glass finally shattered. But the head immediately hit something solid with a dull *THUD*, and a shock reverberated through her arm. The instant after impact, it clicked in Jessica's mind: plywood covered the window on the outside. *All* the windows and doors on the lower level would be boarded over. She cursed herself for having lost track of this reality.

She reached to her pocket for the pry bar, and a sick feeling welled up in her stomach. She had left it on the back porch, which was now engulfed in flames.

"Denny?" the faint voice called out from behind. Jessica and Dennis both spun around. The specter of Doris emerged from around the corner, near the end of the hallway. She came forth, a layer of smoke tracking above her.

"Quick!" Jessica pulled Dennis along as she leaped to the foot of the stairway.

They stumbled up the steps. By the time they reached the top, the smoke had rolled down the front hallway and began pouring into the foyer. Jessica took in a lungful and choked. When she glanced at Dennis through watering eyes, he seemed unaffected.

As they crossed the gallery balustrade, a wave of heat rose from below. Jessica led them into the bedroom wing hallway, when an idea took root. "In here!" They turned into the front bedroom. She switched on the Maglite, half expecting it would not light after the drop. But the beam shone through the darkness, and they followed it across the room.

At the corner window, she pushed the curtains aside and pressed the head of the flashlight against the glass, illuminating the roof of the front veranda. "We can get out this way." Jessica pocketed the Maglite and yanked the curtains down. She steered Dennis several steps away from the window before pulling the flashlight back out.

Raising the Maglite over her head, she gripped it hard and closed her eyes. This time, the glass shattered on her first swing. When she shot Dennis a jubilant smile, he nodded his approval with a grin.

Jessica used the head of the flashlight to clear window fragments from the frame, then placed it on the nearby dresser, pointing the beam out of the exit hole. She draped the curtain over the bottom edge of the opening.

The song playing on the Victrola ended, making the cracking and popping sounds of the fire even more threatening.

"Denny? Honey?"

Jessica stifled a groan. Doris had reached the top of the stairs, and as she neared, smoke started rolling into the bedroom.

Jessica remembered "Fireman John" visiting her classroom when she was in elementary school. He had explained how most people who are killed in a fire actually die from smoke inhalation. Having already experiencing a taste of that, Jessica crouched down as Fireman John had showed the class, and climbed out the window frame, being careful not to touch either side, where shards of glass remained. Acrid fumes tainted the last breath she took before poking her head outside.

A cold breeze washed over her as she stepped onto the soldered sheets of oxidized copper atop the porch. She coughed out the toxic breath she'd taken and replaced it with a deep inhale of fresh air. Turning around, she motioned for Dennis, still standing beyond arm's reach from the window amidst the thickening smoke, to step forward. "Let's go!"

But Dennis did not move. "I can't leave, Jessie."

The apparition of Doris appeared in the doorway behind the boy, smoke swirling all around her.

Jessica reached through the window frame and beckoned him toward her with her fingers. "Yes, you can! Take my hands!"

Dennis hesitated for a moment, then drew forward and grasped her hands. She pulled him firmly toward her, and as he passed through the plane of the window frame, he gasped. Fragments of shattered glass crunched under his feet as he situated himself next to her, coughing.

Dennis's eyelids fluttered. "Purple." He spit out the solitary word, then lifted his chin and stood tall, while the dazed look in his eyes cleared.

"Yes. Purple," Jessica answered, understanding exactly what he had experienced at the intersection between realms.

She suddenly noticed strands of her hair lifting with static charge.

"Denny?" Doris called from the bedroom, her voice cracking with angst.

Dennis turned to face Doris, and Jessica noticed his hair rising too. She pulled him away from the window. The static lessened.

At the end of the veranda's roof, Jessica looked back. Doris peered out the gaping hole that had been the window, tiny sparks sizzling across her image, while smoke rolled through her. She squinted as though she couldn't discern what lay beyond the walls of her realm. Jessica felt goosebumps slide down her arms at the sight. She felt no fear of Doris, only pity for this soul who was on the verge of losing everything she held dear.

When Jessica turned to Dennis, he was looking down. She wrapped her arms around him, and he returned the embrace, quivering in her hug.

She pulled away and pointed to the tall conical evergreen growing next to the house. "We're going to jump into this tree." The arborvitae. Or as her father would have called it, *the Devil bush*. Jessica led the boy toward the corner of the roof, the closest spot to the tree. "It's our best way down, but inside, the branches will be sharp. We're going to get scratched up."

Dennis nodded slowly, then began to pivot in the direction of the window.

Jessica steered him over to the edge of the roof. "Jump into the tree and grab the branches, so you don't crash to the ground. Then lower yourself down."

"You first," he said. "I'll watch how you do it."

She nodded and stepped over the wrought-iron railing. She shuffled her feet, feeling for the solid corner of the roof structure. "Wish me luck!"

"Good luck, Jessie!" Dennis raised both hands while crossing his fingers.

Jessica took in a big gulp of air and leaped into the devil bush. A flurry of boughs assaulted her, poking and scraping her body and face.

As she dropped through the branches, she flailed with both hands, groaning, seeking a solid limb to hold on to. For a moment, she feared she might plunge straight to the ground, but as she started to brace for the impact, her body landed squarely on a thick bough. It bent, then cracked under her weight. She dropped slightly, but solid lower branches caught some of her mass, and she settled, heavily scraped up, but dangling securely in the tree.

"Let me get down before you jump," she yelled through the foliage, unable to see Dennis. She shifted from side to side, working her way down, trying to ignore the lashings she took, to avoid causing Dennis to hesitate in following her.

Soon she spotted the ground. She positioned herself between two solid branches, then lowered her legs and let go. When her feet met the solid earth, Jessica knew she was truly free. Although she wanted to drop to her knees and kiss the ground, she resisted the temptation. Dennis still hadn't escaped, and the fire—and Doris—were that much closer now. She brushed debris from her hair and stumbled out from under the tree. "I made it!"

But when she looked up, her heart sank.

"Dennis?!" She stepped further back from the porch to see beyond the edge of its roofline.

Then she saw him. Dennis, a mere shadow, stood *inside* the window. He looked down at her, plumes of smoke coursing all around him, and with the ghostly hands of Doris on his shoulders.

"Thank you, Jessie," Dennis called down. "Thank you for everything!" He held up a hand, turned, and stepped away from the window, disappearing into the smoke, with Doris at his side.

"Dennis!"

The empty window gave no response.

Jessica staggered backward in stunned dismay, trying to process it all. At the tree line, she circled toward the side of the house. "Dennis!"

Orange light glowed from behind the house and sparks rose into the sky, glimmering in the reflection off the upper-level windows. Smoke poured from the back of the mansion as the fire's intensity grew, and the burning reek tainted the night air.

Knowing it was merely a matter of time before someone saw the fire, Jessica slowly backed away, moving in the direction of the pathway to her car. But the tether from the vision pulled taut; she couldn't depart just yet.

Stopping at the entrance to the trail, she felt a swell of warmth from the propagating flames, even at this distance. Hellfire gushed from the back portion of the house, emitting a cacophony of pops and crackles. Embers rose in the vortex of heat pouring from the inferno, swirling into the sky until they blinked out amongst the thick plume of smoke that continued into the darkness of the night.

A faint orange glow flared up in the lower periphery of the belvedere's windows. As seconds ticked by, the glow bloomed, illuminating the interior. Surveilling the room, Jessica watched for movement, searching for a figure, while flames licked up within the frames of the windows. When the blaze swallowed the structure, she grew certain there was no longer any presence dwelling within.

The tears she had been holding back burst forth, releasing a bittersweet blend of emotions. The sudden loss of her dear friend Dennis diminished the exuberance for her own liberation. A piece of herself had been left behind, gone forever.

Jessica wiped the tears and clasped her hands into knots, then shoved them into her jacket pockets before turning away from Harmon Manor. She set off on her trek along the trail—toward her car, toward her life. She knew the path and understood she should resist the temptation to veer from its course. Yet Misery Mansion—which would soon be reduced to a smoldering mound of cinders and ash—had provided her with an unimaginable gift. So even in that moment Jessica was already charting potential detours, rare deviations she just might permit herself to take, despite the risk of ripple effects.

Unbound at long last from her nightmare, having at least saved herself, Jessica Putnam walked onward to meet her future.

EPILOGUE

JESSICA - 2005

C LINKING SOUNDS WOKE JESSICA up. She lifted her head off the neck pillow and followed them to the antique silver spoon-handle keychain, which dangled from the ignition, pinging against the steering column as the car leaned into a turn. After wiping her face with both hands to clear out the sleep, she looked outside, and it registered that the minivan was exiting the interstate onto State Route 880.

She rubbed her eyes. "We're here already?"

"Yup. Both of you were dead to the world," Richard said, grinning.

The baby stirred in the car seat, making a sound that was a mix of a yawn and a squeak. Jessica twisted back, smiled, and waved into the seat mirror. "Did you have a good nap?"

Arik lifted his head and wagged his tail, slapping it on the door panel beside him, seeking his fair share of attention. She reached back and patted the dog's head. "Sit tight a little longer, Arik. We'll be at Grandma and Grandpa's house soon."

"Speaking of that..." Jessica turned back, found her Blackberry, and typed "ETA 1 hour" before pressing the SEND arrow. Her mother had assured her this time she'd keep her cell phone in her pocket.

When they rounded the bend in the road, Harmon Manor's property came into view. Richard slowed down as they passed the remnants of the old gardener's driveway.

A hollow feeling took hold in Jessica's chest when the minivan turned into the crumbling remnants of the main driveway. Neither of them spoke as the vehicle crept up the gentle slope, broken-up chunks of old gray asphalt crunching under the tires.

Richard rolled to a stop at the end of the drive and put the gear shifter in park. "Take your time, Jessie. Arik and I will stretch our legs out by the road."

Arik crawled forward toward Richard, tail wagging.

Jessica nodded and gave her husband a nervous smile. She took a deep breath, pushed open the door, and stepped outside.

After sliding the back door open, her spirits rose at the sight of her baby's face. She had waited until birth to find out the baby's gender and was thrilled to discover she'd had a son. Now, in the uncharted part of her life, she cherished every surprise, and this was as big as they come.

She blew a raspberry as she unbuckled him from the car seat. He gave her a big toothless grin and voiced a soft coo in response. Lifting him out, she gently laid the baby over her shoulder and wrapped her arms around him.

Jessica's heartbeat quickened as she followed the walkway that remained, ending where the sandstones had once met the front porch steps.

The meadow in front of her covered a subtle mound, so inconspicuous an out-of-town passerby would never have even noticed it.

But Jessica saw the slightly raised hump of earth clearly and knew what lay buried beneath.

The grass and weeds grew thick and tall—almost up to her thighs. Jessica had planned accordingly, putting on long pants with knee-length socks that morning when they left Boston, to help keep ticks off her legs. She waded through the vegetation and stopped in the middle of the mound.

It was close to sunset, the shadows from the western stand of trees reaching toward her. She tightened her arms around the baby, took a deep breath, closed her eyes, and waited.

Bullfrogs were just beginning their evening chorus of croaks from the creek behind her, and birds chirped their early summer songs in every direction. A pleasant breeze blew through her hair.

It didn't take long. It never did.

Jessica responded with an audible sigh and her eyes welled up with tears when she felt the small, familiar hand touch her back.

She lifted the baby off her shoulder and leaned him back on her outstretched forearms. He looked up at his mother's eyes, blinked, and smiled.

Jessica's throat cinched, but with a hard swallow, she managed to whisper the words, "I named him Dennis."

Afterword

T HERE'S A VERY COOL old house not far from where we live that my wife Mary and I have long admired, called the "Farnham Manor." Many years ago, when it went up for sale, we decided to request a showing.

Just as we arrived at the house, a hellacious thunderstorm struck, and inside, as we began looking around, I became convinced the power would go out at any moment. I desperately hoped this wouldn't happen when we were in the cellar, inspecting the bones of the house.

We believed the house to be unoccupied, as it had been undergoing renovations. Imagine our shock when we walked into one of the upstairs bedrooms and discovered a boy sitting at a desk. Stranger yet, he never even acknowledged us.

A fleeting thought passed over my mind: perhaps the boy was really a phantom, and we had encroached into his world. This idea fascinated me—sort of the opposite of a ghost story, where a living person finds herself in a phantom's world, rather than the other way around.

In Cleveland's Ohio City neighborhood, there's another far more infamous house, known as the Franklin Castle. This amazing Queen Ann Victorian stone mansion is regularly mentioned as one of the most haunted houses in Ohio. One of the enduring tales about the Franklin Castle is you can see the ghost of a woman peering out the upper windows of the circular tower at night.

It just so happens we also had a showing of the Franklin Castle when it was listed for sale in the 1990s, prior to seeing the Farnham Manor. It saddens me to report we experienced nothing odd during our tour of the mansion (aside from meeting a man we would later learn was Mickey Deans, Judy Garland's last husband—it seems he owned and resided in the Franklin Castle at that time). But I recall looking out through those upper windows of the circular tower, and wondering whether someone on the outside might see us in the window and believe us to be ghosts.

Well, it turned out we passed on both houses to purchase, but each of them provided a seed of inspiration for this story.

Although I attempted to portray actual historical events in the story accurately, I own any mistakes. I apologize to the psychology profession for bending the timeline of the leucotomy practice to suit my storyline. Those versed in the field will know leucotomies were performed a few years later than depicted here. In my defense, this *is* a work of fiction, after all.

Speaking of, Clarkton and Homer County, Ohio are also fictional renderings but are fashioned in my imagination from areas of Coshocton, Holmes, and Tuscarawas Counties I regularly venture to. Harmon Manor itself was inspired by an amazing Victorian Italianate house I happened upon, sitting all by its lonesome in this region.

I feel drawn to this beautiful region in the Ohio countryside, although I also wonder: am I alone in feeling it conceals a lonesome and haunting presence?

ACKNOWLEDGMENTS

Having had little formal education in writing, when I started *Phantom Realm*, I was oblivious to the fact that there are best practices for fiction writing. My high school creative writing teacher, Mrs. Yucas (who happened to be one of the nicest teachers I remember growing up) encouraged me to write, yet I somehow forgot whatever I'd learned in her class. I suppose forty years has that effect.

During the more than two years I worked on this story, I leaned on many people to help me mold it into its ultimate form. Emily Votaw patiently helped me when the draft was in its rawest form. Early readers included my friends John McCloskey, Scott Haluska, and John Henry, my daughter Kerry Bryan, my sister Diane Sater-Wee, and, of course, my wife Mary. Each of them provided me with helpful observations and needed encouragement.

It was Diane who described the narrative as "sort of dry." Leave it to your big sister, right? But she was polite about it, and while she wasn't able to articulate exactly what needed work, I couldn't deny something did. Author Amanda Uhl had the guts to (diplomatically) confirm this, and provided guidance on how to go about improving my storytelling skills. More revisions followed.

288 NEIL SATER

Several fellow horror writers dedicated many hours marking up the manuscript, teaching me along the way. I'm grateful to the Horror Writers Association for matchmaking me with a mentor, Bill Halpin. Bill did the heaviest lifting, followed by Sean Seebach, a close second. After these two gentlemen prodded another overhaul out of me, Kelly Griffith helped apply some polish to the finished product.

Author D.M. Guay generously shared her knowledge and experience with indie publishing, making me comfortable in taking the leap. Greg Chapman with Dark Designs did a wonderful job creating the book cover and put up with me as I obsessed over it. AK Forde, my official proofreader, caught plenty of errors in my manuscript after I had judged it to be error free.

Back to my wife Mary, who never once questioned my decision to spend untold hours on this novel, and never once complained about it. Not many spouses would have done so. She's one-of-a-kind, and I can't say enough about how much I've benefited from her love and support in this effort, and in so many other ways since we started dating over 41 years ago.

I'd like to acknowledge the many horror writers who have entertained me and provided inspiration for me to develop my own horror writing craft, including my two modern-day favorites: Stephen King (the first horror novel I remember being victimized by was *'Salem's Lot*) and Stephen Graham Jones (I consider SGJ's *Mapping the Interior* to be one of my all-time favorite horror stories, alongside King's *Pet Sematary*).

And finally, I'd like to thank YOU for taking the time to read *Phantom Realm*. I hope you liked it, and if so, I'll share the credit with the many who have contributed to what you've read. It takes a village, right?

Thank you, every one of you.

ABOUT THE AUTHOR

A FANATIC OF ALL things dark and creepy, Neil Sater lives with his wife, Mary, in the Cleveland, Ohio area. They have two grown children and two grandchildren. Having spent his career doing other things, Neil is happy to be now finding time for writing. His debut novel, *Phantom Realm: The Haunting of Misery Mansion*, earned the #1 New Release rating in Young Adult Ghost Stories. His latest book, *Mercy Killing: The Haunting of Ghoul House,* was released in May 2024. A member of the Horror Writers Association, he's currently working on *Atrocity*, a horror novel also based in Homer County, Ohio.

Sign up for Neil Sater's newsletter through his website:
https://authorsater.com/

Printed in Great Britain
by Amazon